WAY OF THE GUN

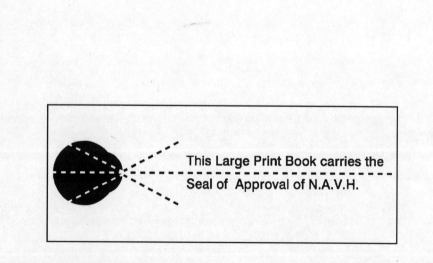

This Large Print Book carries the
Seal of Approval of N.A.V.H.

WAY OF THE GUN

CHARLES G. WEST

THORNDIKE PRESS
A part of Gale, Cengage Learning

GALE
CENGAGE Learning®

Detroit • New York • San Francisco • New Haven, Conn • Waterville, Maine • London

GALE
CENGAGE Learning·

Copyright © Charles G. West 2013.
Thorndike Press, a part of Gale, Cengage Learning.

Thorndike Press® Large Print Western.
The text of this Large Print edition is unabridged.
Other aspects of the book may vary from the original edition.
Set in 16 pt. Plantin.

LIBRARY OF CONGRESS CATALOGING-IN-PUBLICATION DATA

West, Charles.
 Way of the Gun / by Charles G. West. — Large Print edition.
  pages cm. — (Thorndike Press Large Print Western.)
  ISBN 978-1-4104-6163-6 (hardcover) — ISBN 1-4104-6163-7 (hardcover) 1.
Large type books. I. Title.
PS3623.E84W39 2013
813'.6—dc23   2013017293

Published in 2013 by arrangement with NAL Signet, a member of Penguin Group (USA) Inc.

Printed in the United States of America
1 2 3 4 5 6 7 17 16 15 14 13

For Ronda

CHAPTER 1

Looks like I might have company, young Carson Ryan thought as he watched the two riders approaching the North Platte River. Always one to exercise caution, he remained in the cover of the cottonwoods on the north bank until he could see what they were about. *Cowpunchers from the look of them,* he thought, no packhorses that would indicate it was just the two of them on their way somewhere — maybe scouts for a wagon train of some kind. As he watched, the two separated to inspect the banks up and down the river, almost to the point of Carson's camp. It was obvious to him then that they were selecting a crossing. Unable to contain his curiosity any longer, he led his horse over beside a tall cottonwood and pulled off his boots. Then he stood on the buckskin's back to reach a stout limb. Climbing up in the tree, he looked back to the south and soon got the answer to his

7

question. A faint cloud of brown dust in the distance announced the approach of a cattle herd. He remained up in the tree until he saw the first steers. With no further concern for caution, he descended from the tree to drop down on the ground. When the two point men rode back to meet the herd, he sat down and pulled his boots back on.

It was getting a little late in the day to cross the river, he thought. They'd most likely hold them on the other side tonight and cross them over in the morning. He knew from experience that cows weren't fond of river crossings. Although only seventeen years of age, he had worked with cattle for most of those years, so he guessed it would always be in his blood. He was hoping to catch on with a herd heading for Montana where there were already some big outfits grazing their cattle on the vast open bunchgrass prairies. He had come up from Texas with a herd of twenty-five hundred head belonging to Mr. Bob Patterson. Starting on the Western Trail at Doan's Crossing near Vernon, Texas, they went only as far as Ogallala. Mr. Patterson tried to persuade him to return to Texas with him to pick up another herd, but Carson wanted to see Montana. Patterson wished him well, and Carson set out for Fort Laramie, thinking it a possibility to catch a herd stopping there for supplies. It was a long shot, but at seventeen, a boy can wait out the winter and hope for something in the spring.

Carson was thinking now that he must have luck riding with him, because he had decided to make camp earlier than usual — and along comes a herd right where he camped. Maybe they could use another hand. One thing for sure, they weren't looking to buy any supplies at Fort Laramie, because if they were, they missed the fort by a good forty miles. "We'll just sit right here and see what kinda outfit they are," he told the buckskin gelding. On second thought, he decided it would be better to cross over to the south side, since that was more likely to be where the herd would be bedded down for the night. While he waited, he decided he would inspect the river to find the place he would pick to cross a herd.

"Well, now, who the hell is that?" Duke Slayton asked when he sighted the lone rider waiting by the river.

Johnny Briggs turned in the saddle and looked where Duke pointed. "Damned if I know," he replied. "He weren't there when me and Marvin scouted the banks."

"Well, he's sure as hell there now," Duke

came back. "You and Marvin go on up ahead and make sure he ain't got no friends lyin' below that riverbank, waitin' to pop up, too."

Johnny wheeled his horse around a couple of times, straining to get a better look at the man before he complied with Duke's order. He had his suspicions the same as Duke, and he wasn't anxious to become the sacrificial lamb in the event that there might be a welcoming party waiting to gain a herd of cattle. "He don't look to be much more'n a kid," he finally decided. "He might just be a stray, lookin' for a job," he said. "And we're damn sure short of men," he added.

"Or lookin' for a meal," Duke said, although he noticed that the young man was riding a stout-looking buckskin and was leading a packhorse. "You goin' or not?"

"I'm goin'," Johnny replied, and wheeled his horse once again. "Come on, Marvin." The two of them were off at a fast lope while Duke turned back to meet Rufus Jones, who was riding forward to meet him.

"I'm thinkin' 'bout beddin' 'em down in the mouth of this shallow valley, where they can get to the water and there's plenty of good grass," Rufus called out as he pulled his horse to a stop. "That all right with you?"

"Yeah, hell, I don't see why not. I ain't wantin' to try to push 'em across tonight, and that's a fact," Duke replied. They were driving close to two thousand head of cattle, and by the time the boys riding drag caught up, it would most likely be approaching dusk. The herd had been strung out for about two miles since the noontime rest.

Up ahead, Johnny and Marvin slowed their horses to a walk while both men scanned the brush and trees behind the lone stranger, alert to anything that didn't look right. With nothing to suggest foul play afoot, they walked their horses up to the rider awaiting them. Johnny was the first to speak. "Well, young feller, what are you doin' out here all by your lonesome?"

"I was campin' down the river a ways," Carson replied, "and I saw you ride up. So I thought I'd say howdy — maybe visit awhile if you're fixin' to bed that herd down here."

Johnny studied the young man carefully. He was young right enough, but he was a husky fellow, and fairly tall, judging by the length of his stirrups. He could see no deceit in the deep blue eyes that gazed out at him. "Why, sure," Johnny responded. "Right, Marvin?" He didn't wait for Marvin's answer. "We're always glad to share

11

our campfire with strangers. Where you headed, anyway?"

"Well, I was thinkin' about ridin' up to Fort Laramie and maybe catchin' on with a herd movin' on through to Montana Territory."

"Is that a fact?" Marvin asked. "Maybe you should talk to the boss." He nodded toward Duke Slayton, who was riding up behind them now. " 'Cause that's where we're pushin' this herd — up Montana way."

Maybe Lady Luck *was* following Luke, Carson thought, as a sturdy-looking man with a full face of gray whiskers rode up to join them. Like the two before him, he cast a sharp eye back and forth along the line of the bank behind Carson. Figuring that if there was any funny business planned, it would already have been happening, he nodded to the young man. "Howdy, young feller," he remarked. "Where are you headed?"

Marvin answered before Carson had a chance. "He's on his way to Fort Laramie, lookin' to catch on with a herd goin' to Montana."

That brought a look of interest to Duke's face. "Well, now, is that so? You ever work cattle before?"

"Yes, sir. I just came up from Texas with a herd that belonged to Mr. Bob Patterson, but he only took 'em as far as Ogallala."

"How come you wanna go to Montana?" Duke asked.

" 'Cause I ain't ever been there," Carson replied.

Duke grinned. "I reckon that's reason enough. Reminds me of myself when I was about your age." He paused to think about it a moment longer before deciding. "We are short a man." He glanced at Johnny and shrugged. "Hell, we could use about two more men than we've got, but one more would make a heap of difference. Wouldn't it, Johnny?"

Johnny responded with a grin of his own, "I reckon that's the truth, all right."

"I guess we could give you a try," Duke went on. "This feller, Patterson, I reckon he was payin' you about twenty dollars a month. Right?"

"No, sir," Carson replied. "He was payin' me thirty dollars."

"That's the goin' rate for an experienced cowhand," Duke came back. "And right now you're a pig in a poke." Carson shrugged indifferently, and Duke continued. "I'll tell you what I'll do. I'll give you a try at twenty until you show me you can cowboy with the rest of us. Whaddaya say?" Carson started to reply, but Duke interrupted when a thought occurred. "You ain't wanted by the law, are you?"

"No, sir," Carson answered. "I ain't." He hesitated for a moment, then said, "I reckon I'll go to Montana with you." He knew he was worth more than the twenty dollars offered, but he didn't blame the man. Besides, he figured, he was bound for Montana one way or another, so he might as well go with this outfit. It might be a better bet than looking for one passing near Fort Laramie this late in the summer. He didn't know where in Montana they were taking the cattle, but if he had to guess, he'd say they had over three hundred miles to go. So they were cutting it close as far as the weather was concerned. It was going to get pretty cold in a month or so.

"Fine," Duke said. "My name's Duke Slayton. This is Johnny Briggs and Marvin Snead. What's your name?"

"Carson Ryan."

"All right, Carson, you can meet the rest of the boys at supper. Might as well just wait around till the drags come in and we settle the herd in this valley. You can dump your bedroll and other stuff in the chuck wagon and talk to Skinny Willis — he's the

14

wrangler — about a string of horses." He turned to Johnny then. "You and Marvin pick the best place to cross in the mornin'?"

"Right here where we're settin' is about as good as any, I reckon," Johnny said. "There ain't much bank to climb on the other side."

Duke turned to Carson then in a spirit to playfully test the new man. "What do you say, Carson? This look like a good place to push 'em across?"

"No, sir," Carson replied stoically. "If it was me, I'd try it upstream a couple hundred feet, maybe on the other side of that tallest cottonwood." He pointed to the tree.

All three men looked genuinely surprised to hear his reply. "Is that so?" Duke responded. "And why would you do that? The banks are good and low on both sides right here."

"Quicksand," Carson answered, matter-of-factly.

"Quicksand?" Johnny exclaimed. "How do you know that?"

Carson shrugged. "Well, I don't know for sure, but I noticed a couple of places toward the other side where the water looked like it was makin' little whirlpools. And it wasn't flowin' around any tree roots or rocks or anything, and that's what the water looks like when there's quicksand under it."

Duke couldn't contain the laugh. He threw his head back and roared. "Whaddaya think, Johnny? Maybe we oughta go ahead and give him the thirty dollars."

"I'm just sayin' that's what the water looked like when we got into some quicksand on a drive two years ago crossin' the Red River," Carson quickly offered, afraid he might have made an enemy of Johnny. "Might not be quicksand here at all."

"Ain't worth takin' the chance," Johnny said, apparently not offended. "That stuff can cause a lot of trouble that I'd just as soon be without."

"All right, we'll cross 'em up above the big cottonwood," Duke said cheerfully. "And if we get into any quicksand, we'll hang Carson in the damn tree. Does that suit everybody?" Everyone grunted in approval, including the new hire. "Now, let's get them cows watered. Come on, Carson, I'll take you to see Bad Eye — he's the cook."

Supper that night consisted of sourdough biscuits, white gravy, and sowbelly, washed down with black coffee. Bad Eye, so named because he had only one eye, wore a patch over the empty socket where his right eye had once resided. The loss of his eye had

16

evidently occurred quite a few years back, because the rawhide cord holding the patch in place had worn a permanent furrow around the sides of his head. A heavy man, he perspired a great deal while he was fixing the vittles, causing Carson to wonder how much of his sweat had dropped into the gravy. It didn't seem to affect the taste of the food, however, other than perhaps adding a little more salt. The appearance of the cook seemed to have no adverse effect on the appetites of those lined up to fill their plates, and this included Carson. It seemed to him that the cook on every cattle drive he had ridden with was the last man to take a bath whenever there was an opportunity to do so.

The rest of the crew were naturally surprised to see a stranger at the cook fire when they had all gathered to eat supper, but all seemed friendly enough after Duke informed them that Carson was a new hire who was on his way to Montana. It was a rough-looking crew of men, but most drovers were, so Carson felt right at home. When Marvin sat down beside him with a plate of food, Carson asked, "Is Duke the owner of the herd, or is he just the trail boss?"

"Duke's the trail boss," Marvin replied after a gulp of black coffee. "There ain't no owner. What I mean is, we're all kinda partners in the herd. We own it."

"Oh," Carson said, "so I reckon I'm workin' for all of you."

"That's right," Marvin said, then chuckled. "Kinda makes you feel like the low man on the totem pole, don't it?"

"Well, it ain't like I never been there before."

Marvin laughed again. "You'll do all right as long as you pull your share of the load."

Their conversation was interrupted then when a tall heavyset man, who had been introduced as Jack Varner, knelt down to speak. "Duke says you know how to run cattle. Maybe you'll be ridin' swing with me," he said facetiously. "We've been short a man, but Duke might want you to ride drag instead, and put one of the other boys with me."

"Makes no difference to me," Carson said. "I'll do whatever job you fellers think best."

Jack winked at Marvin and chuckled. "That's the spirit, boy. Whaddaya think, Marvin? The new man always rides nighthawk, don't he?"

"Maybe so," Marvin replied. He gave a nod of his head toward the sky. "I don't know, though. The way them clouds look, we might come us up a thunderstorm later tonight."

"Nighthawk's fine with me," Carson quickly interjected. He didn't express it, but he had always enjoyed riding nighthawk.

"Good," Marvin remarked, " 'cause it was supposed to be my turn." He yelled over to Duke on the other side of the fire, "Hey, Duke, Carson says he'll ride nighthawk with me tonight."

"Is that so?" Duke called back. "He'll most likely do a better job than you. Maybe he'll stay awake." He yelled to Carson then, "You're still a pig in a poke, so there better not be any of our cows missin' come mornin'."

"I've rode night herd before," Carson responded.

"All right, then, you've got the job tonight," Duke said.

Jack got up to leave then, but made one more comment to the new man. "You'd best listen to what Duke told you. If there's any cows missin' in the mornin', he'll probably shoot you." Then he laughed when he recalled Duke's comment. "Pig in a poke, that's a good name for you — Pig, that sounds better'n Carson." He walked away then, laughing at the joke he had made.

"Don't pay no attention to that big blowhard," Marvin said. "He just farts outta the wrong end." He leaned over closer to Carson then as if what he was going to say next was confidential. "If you get hungry ridin' the herd tonight, sometimes you can sneak a cold biscuit outta that big drawer on this side of the chuck wagon. That's where Bad Eye keeps 'em when there's leftovers. He don't want nobody to get 'em, 'cause he mixes 'em up in the gravy in the mornin'. He sleeps right under that side of the tailgate, so make sure that eye patch is over his left eye. That's his good eye. He shifts the patch over it when he goes to bed." He snickered then. "Hell, if you're quiet enough, you can sneak a hot biscuit when he's fixin' supper if you sneak up on his blind side. But you'll likely get a thump on the head with an iron skillet if he catches you."

It turned out to be Carson's lot to be tested on his first night with the herd. He and Marvin rode in opposite directions around the herd, so as to pass each other frequently. The cattle were quiet enough in the small valley created by two low lines of hills. But low clouds had begun rolling over the hills on the east side of the valley not long after the camp had settled in for the night, causing Carson to unroll his rain slicker. He had seen enough thunderstorms over the prairie to know that one was coming. *They may have stuck me on nighthawk as a joke,* he thought, *but I ain't the only one who won't get any sleep tonight.* As if confirming the thought, a long, silent fork of lightning streaked through the distant clouds, and the breeze kicked up a notch. It did not go unnoticed by the cattle, and some of those on the outer edges of the herd began to get uneasy. Carson circled around the flanks, talking to them in a soothing voice, a little singsong tone that he had comforted cattle with before.

His and Marvin's efforts seemed to settle the more restless steers for a while, but it was not to last. Suddenly the wind kicked up again, this time stronger than a breeze, and the dark clouds that had drifted directly above the valley were suddenly split by a sudden flash of lightning and a sharp crack of thunder. It was repeated almost immediately, and was cause enough to terrify the cattle. Those on the lower end of the herd bolted in panic toward the divide through which they had been driven to the river earlier. The rest of the herd bolted after them in crazed abandon.

Carson sprang into action, knowing he had no time to wait for help from Marvin, who was on the opposite end of the herd. Behind him, the sleeping camp was awakened by that most dreaded alarm. "Stampede!" someone shouted, and the camp was in an immediate state of panic as every man rushed to get to his horse. Racing after the mob on his buckskin, Carson caught up with the leaders and, with the help of his six-gun, managed to turn them to the right. The rest of the frenzied herd followed as he continued to swing the leaders in a wide circle. Marvin soon caught up with him, and before long, some of the other men began to catch up, and seeing the direction Carson was turning them, they worked to keep the mass of bodies following the leaders. Gradually Carson turned the leaders in a smaller and smaller circle until they eventually wound up in a tight, slow-moving mass, milling restlessly but contained in the mouth of the valley. Soon the swiftly moving storm crossed over, and the men were able to quiet the cattle down again.

"Damn good job!" Duke exclaimed as he rode up beside Carson. "I reckon I'll pay you the thirty dollars."

Duke was not alone in paying Carson compliments on his quick action to keep the herd contained. Almost to a man, they thanked him for keeping the cattle from scattering all across the prairie, the one exception being Jack Varner. For some reason that Carson had not figured out, Varner seemed to resent the attention being paid the new hand. "Yeah, Pig," Jack commented, "you done the right thing, same as anybody else with a grain of sense woulda. You were lucky you had Marvin to back you up."

Carson responded with a knowing smile, accustomed to seeing hazing in many forms on a cattle drive. It seemed likely that Varner was set on testing him, and the use of Pig as a nickname was meant to measure the young man's grit. He didn't like the nickname, but he decided not to respond to the big man's taunts. This was only his first day with the crew, and maybe Varner would forget about it in a day or two. "I expect you're right," he said in answer to Varner's comment.

"Hell," Marvin saw fit to comment, "he didn't get much help from me. By the time I got there, he already had the herd turned."

"Huh," Varner grunted scornfully, and walked away.

CHAPTER 2

Ordinarily they would have started out at three or four o'clock in the morning, but Duke chose not to make a river crossing in the dark, thinking it difficult enough in the light of day with the small number of men he had. So at first light, Rufus Jones led the first cattle into the river at the spot Carson had suggested. The crossing went well, with no real trouble, aside from the usual reluctance of the animals to take to the water. It was well up into the morning before the last of the disinclined steers were forced into the water and the drive got under way again. Duke Slayton rode out ahead of them to scout out the trail for water and good grass. Near the head of the herd, and a little to the upwind side to avoid the dust, Bad Eye drove the chuck wagon. Rufus and Johnny rode point, Varner and Marvin rode swing, with Shifty and Carson behind them on the flanks. The major complaint came from

Lute Wilson. He had been riding drag, so he naturally thought he should be relieved of that post since Carson had just joined them. Lute looked to be as old as Duke, or maybe older, and he was quick to inform the trail boss that he didn't see why he should be bringing up the rear and eating all the dust behind the herd. Duke was just as quick to remind him that he wasn't an experienced drover in the first place, and Carson obviously was. A man who never seemed to complain about anything, Skinny Willis would have been the logical one to complain, since he brought up the rear of the entire procession with the remuda. This job was ordinarily given to a new man, or one with little experience as a drover. But he was happy with his job as wrangler, and seemed to accept the fact that he didn't know much about driving cattle.

Carson was glad it worked out the way it did. He didn't want to drive the spare horses, or to be saddled with the job of riding drag. Shifty welcomed him as a partner on the swing positions. All the stations on a herd were normally worked in pairs of two men, and Shifty had been riding one-sided at swing before Carson came along. In Carson's opinion, however, they were still undermanned for a herd that size. He felt especially sorry for the old man riding drag. He needed help trying to keep the stragglers and ornery strays up with the main herd, and Duke was right, Lute was ill-suited for the job. When he thought about it, he had to believe that the whole crew was perhaps the worst he had seen when it came to driving cattle, but he wasn't planning on staying with them for long, anyway. When they got to Montana, he would most likely be heading his separate way.

A little past noon, Bad Eye drove the chuck wagon on ahead of the herd, expecting to find Duke waiting for them, since it was nearing the time to stop for the noon meal and let the cattle drink and graze. About a mile farther on, they drove the herd through a grassy draw and found Duke and Bad Eye waiting on the bank of a creek. Rufus signaled where he wanted to settle the herd, and the men drove them in that direction. As the rear of the herd caught up, Rufus rode back along the line. When he came to Carson, he pulled up and said, "I thought we could let 'em graze here. Whaddaya think?"

Surprised that he asked his opinion, Carson replied, "Looks like as good a place as any." Then he turned to look behind him where there were still a lot of cattle strung out. "Maybe I'll go back and give Lute a hand," he suggested.

"Yeah," Rufus said, "that'd be a good idea. Help the old man out. Ain't no tellin' how many head we've lost."

Riding a bay gelding from his string of horses, Carson rode back to find Lute trying to drive a group of about a dozen cows back to the herd. Circling around to head the reluctant steers off, Carson turned them back toward Lute and together they moved them toward the creek to join the others. Carson sighted a few more mavericks trailing off toward the line of hills to the west, so he told Lute that he would go after them and catch up with him.

Once the herd was bunched and settled, Duke picked the men who would eat first while the others rode the perimeter to keep the cows contained. By the time Carson returned, the second shift of drovers was eating, so he joined them. Carrying his plate of beans and bacon and his cup of hot coffee, he settled himself down beside Lute to eat. "There were four of 'em headin' up in the hills," he told the old man. "I didn't see any more."

"Much obliged," Lute said. He knew full well that they would have been four lost head were it not for Carson's help. "I 'pre-ciate it, young feller. I had my hands full."

"Weren't no trouble," Carson replied.

Sitting cross-legged several yards away, Jack Varner was becoming more irritated with each compliment he heard paid to Carson. Rufus and Johnny were the point men, but it seemed to Jack that they ran everything by him for his opinion. "Yeah, Pig," he blurted, "you and ol' Lute make up about one good man between you. I wonder how many head we really lost."

"Maybe Duke oughta put you to ridin' drag, Varner, so we wouldn't lose no more," Lute came back. "You're such a top cowpuncher."

"It don't take much to beat you and ol' Pig there," Varner said.

"Why don't you two knock it off?" Marvin complained. He nodded toward Carson then. "You done a good job, Carson."

"Yeah, you done a good job, Pig," Varner commented sarcastically.

"I expect you're about done with that." The calm statement, without emotion, interrupted the banter. "My name's Carson Ryan. I'll answer to either Carson or Ryan. That ought not be too hard for a body to remember, even you."

Suddenly a dead silence fell over the circle

of cowpunchers. It lasted for only a few moments, however, before Varner replied, "What the hell did you say?"

Marvin, tickled by the young man's show of backbone, answered for him. "You heard what he said, Varner. I know I heard him." He turned to Rufus sitting close by. "Didn't you hear what he said, Rufus?" He turned back to Varner then. "He said you better not call him Pig no more."

"Is that so?" Varner responded angrily, incensed that Marvin appeared to be taking Carson's side of it. "Well, Pig might as well learn that I'll call him anythin' I damn well please." He pointed his finger at Carson and demanded, "What the hell are you gonna do about it? We can settle it quick enough — fists, knives, guns, any way you want it."

"Ah, hell," Marvin said, "why don't you back off? You're twice his size. It won't be no fair fight."

A belligerent smile crossed Varner's face. "Well, he don't have to fight if he ain't man enough to back up his mouth. But he's gonna have to apologize to me and tell me he likes being called Pig."

Still baffled by Varner's apparent irritation with him, Carson realized that, whatever the reason, it was going to have to be settled, and the sooner the better. "I don't know what I did that stuck in your craw, but it looks like you ain't gonna be satisfied till we go at it. Since you're givin' me a choice of weapons, I'll pick tree limbs."

His selection took everyone by surprise. "What the hell are you talkin' about?" Varner demanded. "Tree limbs?"

"Tree limbs," Carson repeated.

"I ain't never heard of such a thing," Varner snorted. "You're just tryin' to wriggle out of a good ass kickin'."

"You know, Varner, you're a dumb son of a bitch, but you oughta be able to figure this out." Carson glanced over at the trees on the creek bank. "We'll both get us a limb offa one of those trees." When Varner started to question again, Carson cut him off. "Any size limb you think you can handle," he said. "Then we just beat the hell outta each other with 'em till one of us has had enough. Is that simple enough?"

That brought a grin to Varner's face. "Fair enough," he said. "Let's get at it." With the size and strength advantage he knew he held over the younger man, he felt sure he could make short work of it. "If that's the way you wanna get your ass busted, hell, fine by me."

By this time, the whole crew was aware of the confrontation building up between the camp strongman and the new hand, so they followed the two adversaries to the trees on the bank. Even those watching the herd were staying close to the creek, hoping not to miss what promised to be a short and brutal beating. Rufus brought a hand ax with him for each man to use to cut his weapon, and Varner eagerly grabbed it and went to work on a cottonwood limb about the size of his upper arm. When it crashed to the ground, he chopped it off to a length of about five feet. Satisfied with his choice, he tossed the ax over to land at Carson's feet, then hefted the sturdy section of limb confidently.

"Damn, Varner," Marvin remarked facetiously. "You reckon that's big enough? You coulda saved yourself some trouble and picked up that log lyin' over yonder."

Marvin's remark pleased the gloating bully. "I reckon I coulda handled it, but I didn't need it for this little job." He turned to Carson then and goaded, "Hurry up, Pig. I ain't got all day."

Ignoring Varner's taunting, Carson picked up the ax and fashioned his weapon from the same limb. Moving out toward the smaller end, he chopped off a section that was about the thickness of a broom handle at the butt end and tapered off to the size of a pencil after a length of around eight feet. He trimmed off the smaller branches, then tested the feel of it. Satisfied, he said he was ready to start.

Varner laughed at the size of Carson's weapon and asked, "You sure you can lift that?"

"What about the rules?" Rufus asked. "I ain't never heard of a tree limb fight."

"Rules?" Varner roared. "We don't need no rules. When he can't get up no more, then it's over. That's all the rules we need."

"That all right with you, Carson?" Rufus asked.

"I reckon," he replied. "Just stand back a little and give us room." The few men standing around them backed up a little. Carson knew he needed room to move. Varner was big and powerful, but Carson was sure he was quicker than the lumbering bully, and he knew that was his best defense against him. He had counted on Varner to pick a sizable length of timber, and the big man had not disappointed him. His plan was to wear him down to the point where the heavy limb became too cumbersome to wield with any degree of effectiveness.

"Go to it," Rufus signaled.

As Carson expected, Varner immediately charged like an angry bull, the heavy limb raised in both hands over his head. Carson held his ground until Varner was almost upon him, and then he easily sidestepped him and popped him across his cheek with his cottonwood whip, leaving a stinging welt. Varner yelped in surprise, almost dropping his cumbersome weapon when he grabbed his cheek with one of his hands. He yelped again when seconds later Carson popped him several times around his head and neck while he was groping to regain a position to attack again. Like a man fighting a grizzly, Carson backed slowly in the face of Varner's advance. With his longer whip-like weapon, he was able to deliver a steady series of stinging blows while moving quickly enough to frustrate Varner's efforts to get in close enough to use his bludgeon. Varner tried to grab the stinging whip, but he found that he could not effectively hold up his heavy weapon whenever he took one hand off. And even though out of range, he continued to try to swing his limb, hoping Carson would slip and he would land a blow. He figured that one solid strike with the heavy limb would be enough to stop Carson in his tracks. The rest would be easy. So he swung away, wincing with each blow that Carson landed.

To those watching the contest, Carson's seemed a hopeless defense, serving only to delay the certain outcome when Varner would eventually land one of his blows and likely crush the young man's skull. Fiercely determined to end the swarm of painful welts that were accumulating all over his face and neck, Varner swung his heavy club again and again, only to have his target shifting out of the way from side to side, and darting in to administer a sharp rap with the butt of his whip. On one such attack, the bully recoiled when he felt a blow across the bridge of his nose and heard the crack that told him it was broken.

Consumed by a blind fury then, Varner lunged after a slowly retreating adversary, swinging the huge limb as hard and as fast as he could until, exhausted, he was forced to pause to catch his breath and regain his strength. Each time he did so, he paid a painful price as Carson would close in and deliver a series of sharp raps with the butt of the cottonwood limb. Finally Varner's arms became so weary he could barely raise his club to strike, now resembling a buffalo beset upon by a pack of wolves. Unsteady because of the constant rain of blows about his head coupled with his fatigue, he staggered drunkenly while trying to protect himself from more abuse. The obvious fact that Carson, although wet with perspiration, was as quick and in control as in the beginning caused further despair.

It was clear to the spectators then that the fight was over, although Varner was doggedly lumbering after the quicker man, still absorbing blow after blow, each one more telling now as Carson could afford to be less concerned for retaliation. It was Rufus who finally spoke. "Hell, Varner, he's done whipped you. Call it off before he beats you to death."

Carson stepped back to allow Varner's response. The beaten man, bloodied and bruised, stood unresponsive for a long moment, his brain scrambled by the blows he had taken. Then without a word, he suddenly dropped to his knees and remained there for a few more seconds before falling face forward in the sand of the creek bank. Nobody said anything for a moment or two, stunned by the outcome of a fight in which they expected to see the young man destroyed by the overbearing bully. Marvin uttered the words that summed up the altercation. "I reckon he don't wanna be called Pig."

The cattle drive continued north for the next two days, causing Carson to question Duke's line of travel, if indeed he was still

35

planning to go to Montana. He was not that familiar with the country north of the Platte, but his reasoning told him that it would make more sense to head in a more northwest direction. If they continued on in the direction they were now heading, they would wind up in Dakota Territory. He didn't express his opinion to anyone, satisfied to continue on to Dakota if they didn't change course in the next few days. As far as Varner was concerned, there had been nothing more from the beaten man. Carson became wary of the sullen man, however. He didn't seem the kind to consider the incident ended. There wasn't much Carson could do to prevent a vengeful attack if that's what Varner had in mind, so he slept with his rifle and handgun close to him. Varner never called him Pig again. In fact, he never spoke to him at all. But sometimes Carson would turn to find Varner looking at him, then quickly turning away rather than meeting Carson's gaze. What Carson didn't understand was, like a big dog that's had his tail cut off, Varner was humiliated by the loss of his bluster. When it came to the rest of the crew, Carson was treated fairly enough, but he still felt like an outsider. It was almost as if they shared Varner's humiliation. Maybe, he thought, it was because they had started out on the cattle drive together. So Varner was one of their own, and he was not. After all, he allowed, Duke said they all owned shares in the herd, so he wasn't really one of them. The one exception was Marvin Snead. He seemed to have taken a liking to Carson. Carson appreciated that, but he had already made up his mind that he was saying good-bye to them when he got to Montana, so he didn't spend much time worrying about his place with the crew.

They pushed on for two more days before Duke ordered a change of course and headed them in a more northwestern direction. Carson commented to Marvin that it might have made more sense to have followed the North Platte to Fort Laramie and then head up through the Powder River Valley. Marvin replied that Duke had just as soon avoid the army and their restrictions on herds traveling up that way. "It might be handy to be close to the fort if we get hit with an early winter," Carson said, "but it ain't my say."

Marvin chuckled. "Duke's got some funny ways of doin' things, but we usually make out all right."

Another day found them at the Niobrara River. They arrived early enough to cross that afternoon, and while Rufus and Johnny led the leading steers into the water, Carson went back to help Lute bring up the strays. He found the old man over two miles behind, trying to drive twenty cows up the trail left by the main herd. He was obviously having a difficult time of it, so he gave Carson a wave of appreciation when the young man appeared. Carson circled around behind him and chased a couple of ornery strays back with the others. Then with Lute riding the other side, they got the cows headed in the right direction. Things were well in hand until they heard the sound of gunshots in the distance.

"What the hell?" Lute yelled. "That don't sound good." He looked across at Carson, who was standing in his stirrups listening. "Injuns?" Lute wondered aloud when the shots continued as if the herd might be under attack.

"Damned if I know," Carson yelled back. "Don't seem likely to be Injuns this close to Fort Laramie. Sounds like there's a lot of 'em. I expect we'd better come back for these cows later and go see if our boys need help."

"Right," Lute replied, but he didn't seem too eager to ride. "I expect that's what we oughta do."

Sensing the old man's reluctance to hurry to what might be a full-scale Indian attack on the herd, Carson told him, "I'll go on ahead. Why don't you bring these strays along?"

"Right," Lute replied.

Not wanting to push an already tired horse too hard, Carson pressed the sorrel he was riding to a steady lope. He didn't want to ride blindly into something, but he knew he had to help if his gun was needed. He could see the herd now, split into two bunches. Half of them had crossed over to the other side of the river, and half were still milling around on the near side. Something was definitely wrong. There were men riding around on both sides of the river, but they were soldiers. He could see none of the drovers. The chuck wagon was on the other bank, but Bad Eye was nowhere to be seen. As he rode closer, he was startled to see several bodies on the ground. Right away he figured the herd must have been hit by a large party of Indians and the soldiers had arrived too late to help the drovers.

He saw a group of soldiers standing by a man sitting on the ground, and they turned to watch him as he approached. When he pulled the sorrel up before them, he realized that the man on the ground was Varner, and it appeared he had been shot, because there was blood soaking the left shoulder of his shirt. He dismounted and asked one of the soldiers, a lieutenant, what had happened. Varner looked up at him, but said nothing.

"You riding with this bunch?" Lieutenant Fred Vickers asked.

"Yes, sir," Carson answered. "I was roundin' up some strays. What happened?" He looked a few yards beyond them to discover a body sprawled awkwardly across a clump of bushes where it had evidently landed when knocked out of the saddle. It was Marvin. "Damn," he exhaled softly. Marvin Snead was the only one of the crew who had openly befriended him.

"I'll tell you what happened," the lieutenant said. "These men you see lying on the ground decided to fight instead of surrendering. They paid for their mistake. You made a wise decision." He motioned toward a soldier who had moved to stand behind Carson. "Take his weapon, Sergeant."

"What the hell?" Carson exclaimed when he felt his .44 lifted from his holster. He immediately turned to resist, and received a rifle butt in the back of his head for his efforts. The force of the blow was enough to knock him to his knees and send his brain reeling. The soldier who had hit him drew back to hit him again, but was stopped by the officer.

"That'll do, Private. I don't think he's going to cause any more trouble. Tie his hands behind his back." Addressing Carson then, Vickers said, "You and your friends made a helluva mistake driving those cattle up through here."

His head splitting with pain, Carson was thoroughly confused. None of this made sense. He had heard that the army sometimes refused to permit cattle drives to proceed up the Powder River Valley, but that was several years ago, before the Sioux were defeated. This was crazy. When his head cleared a little more, he insisted, "What right has the army got to stop a herd of cattle from goin' to Montana?"

Vickers looked at him as if amused by the question. "A little more right than a gang of cattle rustlers," he answered, "especially a gang that killed the owner of the herd and most of the drovers."

The lieutenant's words struck Carson with the force of a sledgehammer. Already dazed by the blow to his head, he attempted to get to his feet again, but was held where he knelt by two soldiers standing behind him. Thoughts and images flashed across his mind of incidents during the drive that had caused him to think that Duke Slayton's men were a poor crew of drovers. And now this curly-haired lieutenant with the neatly cropped beard was telling him he had ridden with a gang of thieves — and murderers! The impact caused his brain to clear right away. "Whoa!" he blurted. "Wait a minute! I'm no damn thief, and sure as hell not a murderer. I don't know anythin' about any rustlin'. I just had a job drivin' cattle."

His desperate claim brought a knowing smile to the officer's face. "Is that a fact? Well, I'm sure when you tell that to the judge, he'll let you go."

Varner, who was still sitting as if in a stupor a few feet away, spoke for the first time since Carson rode in. "He's tellin' you the truth, Lieutenant. He just joined up with us back at the Platte. We never told him where we got the cattle."

"Are you two trying to see who can tell the biggest lie?" Lieutenant Vickers replied, looking at Carson. "You expect me to believe you just hired on to help drive this herd, and nobody told you anything about where they came from, or how they got them?"

"That's the truth of it, Lieutenant," Carson insisted. "I never stole anythin', and I

42

never killed anybody. I was just workin' my way to Montana." The expression on the officer's face and the grins of amusement on the faces of the soldiers standing around told him that he was wasting his breath. "What are you aimin' to do with me?" he asked, realizing the serious situation in which he found himself.

"We oughta hang you and your friend right here, but we'll let you tell your story to an army judge back at Fort Laramie," Vickers replied. He felt certain the wounded man was trying to save the young man from serving a prison sentence, but it wasn't going to do him any good. The lieutenant wasn't about to fall for it.

"Whaddaya wanna do with 'em, Lieutenant?" the sergeant asked.

Vickers paused for a moment to decide. "It's a little late in the day to start back. It's a good forty miles to Laramie from here, a good day's ride. But it'll take three or four days to drive these cows back, so we'll just make camp here and start back in the morning. Take these two and tie them to the wheels of that chuck wagon. I want two guards posted to watch them the whole time, day and night. Some of the bastards got away, but I want to make sure these two get tried for the murders of those Texas cowpunchers."

Carson and Varner, now on his feet, stood under heavy guard while Bad Eye's team was unhitched from the wagon. Then they were seated and tied, one to a front wheel and one to a back wheel. Still somewhat dazed, Carson sat there while Sergeant Wheeler made up a guard detail to watch them around the clock. There was nothing he could do but wait it out and hope he could convince a judge of his innocence. He watched in despair as a group of soldiers rounded up the remuda, which had evidently scattered when the shooting started, for he saw his buckskin among them, as well as his packhorse. It was as low as he had ever felt since his father's death, and he feared his helplessness would drive him crazy. Gone also was the Henry rifle that had belonged to his father, his .44 Colt, and everything else he owned.

As he sat there despairing, he remembered Lute, and realized that he had never shown up with the twenty strays. It made him wonder if Lute had feared something like this might be happening, and he had gone in the opposite direction as soon as Carson left. *That old son of a bitch,* he thought, *he could have given me some kind of warning.*

44

Now that he had time to think about it, it occurred to him that Varner had spoken on his behalf, something that he would never have expected to happen. This prompted him to reach out to the man who would have crushed his skull with a tree limb. "Varner," he called. "I 'preciate what you did back there. I wanna thank you for tryin' to tell that lieutenant the right of it."

Varner didn't turn to look at him, staring straight ahead as if still in a daze. After a moment's hesitation, he replied, "I ain't completely rotten. We shoulda told you right off, but we needed the help, and we was afraid that if you knew them cows was stole, you mighta took off and brought the law down on us. I didn't have no business ridin' you so hard. I'm sorry for that."

The big man's astonishing apology left Carson at a loss for words for a long moment. He could only assume that the belligerent bully was suffering genuine regret, thinking that he might be nearing a meeting with his maker. "Well, that's over and done with," Carson said. "Looks like we're both in a helluva fix now, though." Then remembering, he asked, "How bad are you hurt?"

"I don't know. I caught a bullet in my left shoulder, and I think it mighta broke a bone or somethin', 'cause I can't move it without it hurtin' like hell."

"I reckon they'll let the doctor look at it when they take us back to Fort Laramie," Carson said. "What about the rest of the boys? Did anybody get away?"

"Yeah, Duke and Johnny hightailed it across the river — and Bad Eye, I reckon. Leastways, he's not here, but I didn't see him ride off. Skinny was settin' right next to me in the middle of the river when they hit us. He got shot right through the neck. I made it out of the water before I got hit — knocked me outta the saddle. I don't think anybody else made it. They're all lyin' around here somewhere. The soldiers caught us in the middle of tryin' to push the herd across. We never knew they was anywhere about." He paused to think for a few moments, and then continued. "It wasn't all one-sided, though. Two of their soldiers was hit. I think one of 'em's dead. I don't know who done it. It wasn't me. I never got my gun outta the holster, and by the time I made it out of the river, they got me."

"Damn," Carson muttered. That was not good news. There was little hope for leniency with two troopers shot.

"Just so you'll know," Varner went on, "I never shot nobody when we took the herd from them fellers. Rufus and Johnny was the ones doin' all the killin'. I ain't got no reason to lie about it."

"Maybe they'll take that under consideration," Carson said, while thinking it very unlikely. He was seeing a side of Jack Varner that he had never seen before — afraid and repentant — and he wanted to offer encouragement if he could. Although he had hope that Varner's statement to the lieutenant might be enough to substantiate his innocence, his better sense told him that it, too, was unlikely. More likely, a judge would see him no differently than any other member of the gang. He resolved to let the military court have a chance to find him innocent and set him free. But if that didn't happen, he was determined to escape somehow, or die trying. He had committed no crime, and he had no intention of spending his life in prison.

CHAPTER 3

Though it was still late in the summer, it was a chilly day when Lieutenant Fred Vickers rode into Fort Laramie at the head of a fifteen-man detachment escorting two prisoners. The rest of the lieutenant's original thirty-man patrol were serving as drovers, bringing the stolen cattle along behind. Carson Ryan was astride a bay gelding that had belonged to Skinny Willis, his buckskin having been denied him. Varner was on one of the horses in his string. A red roan, it had been found standing not far from the wounded man where he had lain on the ground. He sat slumped in the saddle as the detachment led the prisoners across the parade ground to the guardhouse. Since their hands were tied behind them, they were helped to dismount, although Carson could have accomplished it without assistance. Varner, however, cried out in pain when he was roughly pulled from the saddle.

Being a man of some compassion, Vickers instructed two of his detail to escort Varner to the hospital. Carson was led into a common cell room, where he was greeted with the curious stares of a handful of military prisoners, most of whom were incarcerated for less serious offenses — drunkenness, asleep on guard duty, insubordination, petty theft, things of that nature. One man was locked up for desertion. Carson and Varner would be the only serious offenders.

"When can I talk to a judge or somebody to straighten this mess out?" Carson asked the sergeant as the cell door was locked behind him.

Sergeant Michael Devers favored him with an indifferent grin. "What's the hurry, young fellow? You got an appointment somewhere?"

"I'll tell you what's the hurry," Carson replied. "They arrested me by mistake. They got my horses and my weapons, and all my possibles, and I need to get outta here before somethin' happens to 'em."

His plea caused a low murmur of snickers from the other prisoners. "Son," Devers replied patiently, "you might as well sit down and make yourself comfortable. It'll be a while before they schedule you for trial."

"But, damn it, Sergeant, I ain't done nothin' to get locked up here in the first place!"

Still with no show of impatience with the prisoner's complaint, Devers said, "Most likely the provost marshal will be by here to talk to you. Tell him that. Maybe he'll let you go." This brought an outright laugh from the other prisoners.

Confinement went against the very soul of Carson Ryan. Since he was a youngster, he had never known boundaries that were closer than the horizon in all directions. It was a full week before he was escorted to the provost marshal's office, and during that time, he paced the width and length of the cell room constantly, like a leopard in a cage. The other inmates nicknamed him "Walkin' Ryan." The name did not bother him, but the confinement was more than he thought he could bear for very long.

On the third day after his incarceration, the soldiers brought Varner back to the jail. He looked in bad shape, but he claimed his wound was getting better. A lieutenant named Shufeldt was the post surgeon, but Varner said a civilian doctor was the one who treated him. The doctor told him that his collarbone was broken, and they bound him up with bandages that pinned his arm to his chest. "I ain't gettin' along too good as a one-armed man," he told Carson. He looked so down that it was hard not to feel sorry for him. "He said I might not get full use of my arm again. I don't reckon it matters much, since they'll most likely hang me before long."

"Did anybody say when they might have our trial?" Carson wondered aloud.

"They got a bunch of officers that meet once or twice a month to act like judges, and accordin' to what Dr. Grimes told me, it'll most likely be next Monday." He gazed at Carson apologetically. "I'm hopin' I can get away with a prison sentence, if I can convince 'em I never shot nobody. Hell, I did help steal them cows, but, Carson, I swear I'll tell 'em you never had no idea we rustled that herd."

"I 'preciate it, Varner." He couldn't help asking the big man about his change of heart. "I'm gonna tell you the truth, I never thought you'd speak up for me, I mean, after the little tussle we had. Hell, I was sleepin' with my pistol cocked, expectin' you to come after me."

Varner chuckled. "I ain't gonna lie. I thought about it. But I got my ass whipped fair and square, and it was me that started the whole thing, so I deserved what I got."

When the day came to be taken to the provost marshal's office, Carson and Varner were placed in chains and marched out of the cell room. It seemed to Carson a hell of a lot of caution considering that the provost marshal was awaiting them on the second floor of the same building. The officer, a captain named Goodridge, wasted little time interviewing the prisoners. "So, you two are all we've got left from your murderous run from Oklahoma Territory. You'll go on trial day after tomorrow. We don't house serious criminals here on the post, so you'll most likely be shipped to the territorial prison in Laramie, where your sentences will be carried out, whether that's imprisonment or hanging. Any questions?"

"Hold on a minute," Carson protested. "Don't you even wanna hear if we're guilty or not?"

Goodridge shook his head indifferently. "That's not my responsibility. We'll find out at your trial if you're guilty or not."

"Hell, I know now that I'm not guilty of a damn thing," Carson came back. "If somebody would just listen to my side of it. I never had any idea those cows were stolen. I only signed on at the North Platte. I wasn't even with 'em in Oklahoma. I came up from Texas with another herd."

Goodridge was not impressed. "Young fellow, you're wasting your time with me. Why don't you do like your friend here and just bide your time till the trial?"

"He's tellin' you the truth," Varner said. They were the only words he spoke during the interview.

Goodridge didn't bother to respond. Instead, he ordered the prisoners to be returned to the cell room. He did, however, comment to Carson as he was led out, "Son, you've made some bad choices in your life. You'll do better if you just accept your punishment and don't cause trouble."

Back in the guardhouse, Carson was already thinking about escape. He had a sinking feeling now that there was no way a judge, or jury, or whatever they were going to have, would simply take his word as truth — or Varner's, either, for that matter. He wasted a few minutes lamenting his misfortune, but finally decided that there was no use in crying over spilled milk. His thoughts now must be directed on how to get himself out of the situation.

As he had feared, the trial by a panel of officers was little more than a longer version of Captain Goodridge's brief interview. Anxious to finish their responsibility on the panel and repair to the officers' ball to be held that evening, they quickly sentenced both men to be transferred to the territorial correction facility in Laramie to await execution by hanging. When asked by the presiding judge if the prisoners wished to make a statement, Varner declined, but Carson stood up to face the indifferent faces of the panel. "First of all, this is a sorry piece of work you call a trial, and I'm gonna tell you one last time, you're wrong as hell. I never stole a cow in my life, and I never shot anybody." He gestured toward Varner. "And he ain't never shot nobody, either." He stood there glaring at the three officers who had so casually sentenced the two of them to death, at a loss as to what more he could say.

"Mr. Ryan," the judge replied, "you've had your say, and we all understand your position, but there isn't a scrap of evidence to substantiate your claim — just your word and Mr. Varner's. And if the court took that into account, nobody would ever be guilty of anything." He nodded to the guards standing behind the prisoners. "We're done here. Take the prisoners back to their cells to await transportation." It seemed plain to Carson that the panel was more interested in seeing that someone was made to pay for the killings than to make sure the innocent were not wrongfully punished.

As soon as the trial was completed, Captain Goodridge wired Cheyenne to send a marshal to take possession of the prisoners. He received a confirming wire informing him that a deputy U.S. marshal by the name of Luther Moody would depart Cheyenne two days hence. Considering that Cheyenne was a good two days' ride from Fort Laramie, that meant Carson and Varner had four more days of the military's hospitality. They were treated pretty well in the guardhouse, so well in fact that Varner hated to see the days go by so quickly. "Looks like they don't wanna waste no time gettin' a rope around our necks, doesn't it?" he lamented.

"I reckon," Carson replied, his mind already working on possible opportunities for escape, having decided that he preferred death from a guard's bullet to that of a hangman's rope. At this point, however, there was nothing he could think of that might give him that opportunity. He had no choice but to wait and hope he recognized his chance when it came. He assumed Varner was of like mind. It was a case of both men having nothing to lose by an escape attempt.

■ ■ ■ ■

Deputy Marshal Luther Moody and two
posse men left Cheyenne early on a Tuesday
morning. Jim Summer and Bud Collins had
ridden with Moody many times before, so
they knew what to expect from the trip. The
distance from Cheyenne to Fort Laramie
was about the same as that between the fort
and Laramie City, so they figured to be out
for five or six nights. Moody considered taking the prison wagon to transport the
prisoners, but the wagon fitted with an iron
cage would take about twice as long. And
he had been told that the two prisoners were
brought in on their own horses and saddles.
So he figured they might as well ride to
Laramie on the same horses.

Wednesday evening found them at Fort
Laramie too late to get a meal at the infantry
mess hall, which was disappointing to Bud
Collins. The army's food wasn't particularly
good, but they were usually generous with
it to visitors, especially when all the troops
had been fed and the cooks were glad to get
rid of the leftovers. Neither Moody nor Jim
Summer was as concerned with missing
mess call as Collins had been, content to
buy a meal at one of the saloons off the

post. At any rate, Moody was willing to delay his supper until after reporting in to the officer of the day and taking a look at his prisoners. After identifying himself to Lieutenant Calvin Thomas, who had the duty that day, he was accompanied by him to the guardhouse where Moody got a look at his charges through the bars of the cell room.

"Young feller and a one-armed man," Moody mused aloud, eyeing them both in an effort to get a notion of how much trouble they might be. He turned to Sergeant Devers, who was on duty that night. "They been givin' you any trouble?"

"Nope," Devers said, "none a'tall."

"The big one looks like he could be trouble if he had both his arms workin'." Then he looked again at Carson and decided he was maybe a little more formidable than he had thought at first, but he had such a youthful appearance a man could make a mistake in underestimating him. Still, he felt the decision to leave the jail wagon was a good one. Calling the two over to the bars then, he told them that they were leaving in the morning as soon as they were fed. "My name's Luther Moody. I'm a deputy marshal come to take you fellers to Laramie. If you don't give me no trouble, we'll have a good two-day ride. You give me trouble and I'll make it hell for you the whole eighty miles. You understand?" He got nothing but a grunt from Varner for an answer. Carson said nothing, sizing up the deputy at the same time he was being evaluated. A man of average height, Moody had traces of gray hair in his sideburns and mustache. Carrying a little more weight than his frame called for, he wore a .44 Colt waist high with the butt facing the front. His expression was one of bored indifference, as if he had repeated the scene many times. Carson decided he was not a man to take lightly. Behind him, his two posse men stood, casually interested, one lean and hard, the other a rather pudgy man with a round face.

Carson's intense concentration was broken when Moody turned away from the cell and asked Lieutenant Thomas a question. "You got any empty bunks me and my two posse men might have for the night?"

"Yeah," Thomas replied. "There's half a dozen empty cots in the cavalry barracks. You can sleep there tonight, and probably catch breakfast in the morning. I'll go over with you and tell Sergeant Mahan."

"That sounds mighty fine to me," Moody said.

■ ■ ■ ■

By the time Moody and his two men finished breakfast, loaded their packhorse, and saddled their mounts, the prisoners were waiting in the guardhouse, their horses tied out front. After signing a release form, Moody took responsibility for the prisoners and set out for Laramie City. It was a more leisurely start than the deputy desired, but he kept his little party at a steady pace, following the Laramie River southwest before stopping to rest the horses at the confluence of the river with Chugwater Creek.

As soon as the horses were watered and left to graze on what grass they could find, Bud Collins set about making a fire and preparing something to eat. While he sliced some bacon to fry, he talked to Moody. "How much farther you thinkin' about ridin' today, Luther?"

"I don't know," Moody replied. "I've been thinkin' about that. It's been an awful dry summer." He was concerned by the dried-up streams they had passed. "Might be a good idea to follow the Chugwater for the rest of the day to be sure we find a place to camp with plenty of water and grass. We'll make better time if we stay east of those mountains, anyway." He pointed to the rugged range west of them. Collins nodded in agreement. There was some rough country on a direct line between where they stood and Laramie.

"You want me to cut 'em loose so they can pee?" Jim Summer asked.

Moody glanced over at the two prisoners seated on the ground, Carson with his hands tied behind his back, and Varner, his one good hand tied to the back of his belt. "One of 'em at a time," he answered. Then he turned to take a closer look at the two. "Maybe the big-gun first. He looks like he ain't feelin' too good." Varner did, indeed, look a little the worse for wear. The wound in his shoulder appeared to have bled considerably more, a result of the morning's hard ride. The cloth binding his left arm across his chest appeared to have loosened as well. "We might wanna put a new wrap on that shoulder, too. The doctor said it needs to be tight enough so's he can't move it. We got some fresh bandage cloth somewhere. Least I think he gave us some."

"It's in my saddlebag," Collins said. "I'll take care of him after we eat."

Summer snorted indifferently. "Don't make a whole lotta sense to be worryin' about that bandage. They'll be stretchin' his neck soon as we get him to Laramie."

Moody shrugged but did not reply at once. What Jim said was true enough, but it was the decent thing to do to ease the man's discomfort if they could. After a moment, he said, "Bud can change his bandage after we eat." He swung his rifle around to cover Summer when Jim untied Varner's good arm.

When the wounded prisoner's arm was free, Summer backed away, his .44 aimed at Varner's belly. "Get up if you need to take a piss," he said. "Walk over yonder a ways." He pointed away from the creek with his pistol. Unable to respond with any degree of quickness, Varner struggled to roll over on his knees before being able to push himself unsteadily to his feet. Watching his efforts, Carson wondered if the big man had lost more blood than he thought. "Well," Summer prodded, "are you goin' or not? I ain't gonna wait all day for you."

Finally Varner responded, "I'm goin', damn you."

"Don't you go cussin' me," Summer was quick to warn. "I'll let you set there and pee in your pants next time."

Varner responded with a deep scowl, the only weapon left to him, and Carson could imagine the frustration he felt, having been the bully of the gang he previously rode with. He also observed that Varner walked noticeably slower and a bit unsteadily. The thought crossed his mind that he might not make it to the hanging. It caused him to wonder if the prison physician would bother to spend much effort in treating him. He turned his thoughts toward the man they called Jim, and his obvious disdain for his prisoners, and he wondered if the deputy's posse men were picked for their particular role. Luther Moody seemed a reasonable man, almost easygoing. Summer served as his aggressive strong arm, while Collins was brought along to do the cooking and take care of the camp. It might have been coincidence, but it sure looked to Carson as if it was intentional. Further thoughts along that line were interrupted by the return of Varner from answering nature's call. Summer directed him to a large tree close by the fire and sat him down with his back against the trunk. "Watch him, Luther, while I take his partner."

"I got him," Moody said. "Go ahead."

"All right, young feller," Summer told Carson. "Lean over so I can untie your hands." Carson did as he was told. "All right, get on your feet."

His shoulders and arms stiff from having

been tied back for so long, Carson shrugged several times and swung his arms back and forth. His efforts to rid himself of some of the stiffness caused Summer to take a step back and cock the hammer on his pistol. With no further sign that his prisoner might be thinking of making a move, he stepped back to face Carson. He stood there a moment, eyeballing the young man as if just realizing that Carson was a few inches taller than he.

Ever since he was taken into custody, Carson had been watchful for opportunities to make a move toward freedom. Judging by Summer's quick reflexes, he decided this was no such opportunity, so he dutifully walked to the spot where Varner had relieved himself. When he had finished, he was led to the tree where Varner waited and told to sit down close to him. The idea, Carson supposed, was to have both prisoners with their backs against the tree and close enough together that one of the lawmen could easily watch them both.

"You gonna make it?" Carson asked Varner.

"I reckon," the big man answered, "but there's been times when I felt a helluva lot better."

"No more talkin'," Summer ordered immediately. "You keep talkin' and you won't get nothin' to eat." So they sat in silence and waited for Collins to finish cooking his pot of beans and bacon. When the food was ready, the three lawmen helped themselves and ate while keeping an eye on the two prisoners. At last finished, Moody and Summer sat down a few yards away facing them, to stand guard while they were fed. Continuing with the kitchen duty, Collins filled two plates with food and two cups with coffee. He placed the coffee before them first, then placed a plate in Varner's waiting hand. He then reached across Varner to hand the other plate to Carson. It was only for a second while Collins crouched to pass the plate to Carson, but for that second Varner found himself staring at the handle of Collins's pistol barely a foot from his face. There was no decision to be made. He dropped the plate he was holding and snatched the revolver from Bud's holster. Collins jumped back, grasping at his empty holster, then dived for cover when the gun went off. The shot was not directed at him, however, for in Varner's mind, Jim Summer deserved it. In the split second of Varner's revenge, he must have known there would be little time for a second shot, and by the time he cocked the single-action revolver,

64

he was ripped by two slugs in his gut — one from Moody's rifle, the other from the wounded posse man. In his last act of defiance, Varner squeezed the trigger one more time, sending the fatal bullet into Summer's chest. Two more slugs from Moody's rifle slammed into the already dead Varner.

A brief moment followed the gunshots when not a sound was made by anyone. Then Moody sprang forward to pull the pistol from Varner's hand before Carson had the opportunity to grab it. Collins recovered enough to come to his aid as Moody stood over him, daring him to make a move. Carson, fully as surprised as they, was still holding his plate, in no position to do anything but sit. "Watch him!" Moody ordered, and handed Collins's pistol back to him. Then he went to Summer's side, only to find his posse man dead. "Damn," he murmured regretfully.

"I don't know how it happened," Collins pleaded. "I didn't think I was anywhere that close enough for him to grab my gun. I mean, he was just settin' there, one hand, and it holdin' a plate of beans. Poor Jim, you know I'd do anythin' to make it right."

"You just watch him," Moody told him, angry that Collins could have been so careless, but knowing there was nothing to do to change things. Turning his attention back to Summer, he shook his head sadly. "Jim Summer has been ridin' with me, off and on, for over six years, and I never asked him if he had a family. And he never said one way or the other. He was a damn good man, and it's a damn shame to lose him." He got up then and walked back to stand over Carson. "That was a damn good man your friend just killed." His tone indicated to Carson that he held him somehow accountable.

"I didn't have any idea Varner was gonna try somethin' like that," Carson said. "It wasn't a very smart move, 'cause there wasn't a chance he could get away with it. It wasn't as dumb as the move your partner made, though, stickin' that gun in his face. I reckon Varner decided he'd rather take a bullet than stretch a rope. Maybe you'd better not give me a chance like that."

"Maybe we oughta save the hangman some trouble," Collins said, "and string you up right here."

"Maybe you'd better," Carson came back at him, his dander up over this latest incident that had been laid at his feet. "I guarantee you that the first chance I get, I'm gone. I didn't steal those damn cows, and I didn't kill anybody. I tried to tell those army sons of bitches to find Mr. Bob Patterson and he would tell 'em I was with his herd when those cattle were rustled. But they didn't care enough to find out. And, damn it, I didn't tell Varner to shoot your man, so if you're of a mind to hang me, or shoot me, then get on with it, 'cause I'd just as soon not go to prison."

Surprised by the young man's passionate outburst, Moody didn't respond for a moment. "Just simmer down a minute, Bud," he told Collins. "He's probably right about havin' nothin' to do with Jim's murder. He didn't have time to. That don't mean he wouldn'ta done the same thing if you'da stuck your ass up in *his* face. But he didn't, so we'd best do what we can for Jim, dig him a nice grave, and get along to Laramie to turn this one over to the prison." He didn't voice it, but he had to admit that Carson's statement of innocence had a ring of truth to it, and he would just as soon wash his hands of it. Directing his words to Carson now, he said, "Might as well eat your food before it gets colder."

"What the hell was that?" Ed Tice blurted when he heard the gunshots. His automatic reaction was one of anxious concern, lest the shots signaled a posse or a cavalry patrol that might have followed their trail from the wagon they left burning near the stage road. He spilled half of his coffee in his haste to set it down.

"Shots!" Orville Swann exclaimed as he scrambled up the side of the creek bank a few steps ahead of Tice. "Half a dozen or more! Might be a posse!"

Jesse Red Shirt remained by the fire, leisurely sucking the last bits of meat from the leg bone of a rabbit. "Six shots," he stated calmly, "four from a rifle, two from a pistol."

"They came from back thataway," Swann said, still concerned as he pointed upstream. "Reckon what the shootin' was about? Think somebody's already got on our trail?"

"You ain't got the brains of a tick, Swann," Red Shirt snarled. "It's too soon for anybody to be on our trail. Even if they were, they wouldn't be comin' from that direction. They'd be comin' on behind us."

"Yeah, you dumb shit," Tice said, in spite of the fact that he'd jumped to the same conclusion Swann had, "if they was after us, they'd be comin' from downstream." Still concerned, however, he asked, "Reckon what they was shootin' at, Red Shirt?"

"How the hell do I know?" Red Shirt answered. He threw the cleaned bone into the fire and wiped his hands on his shirt. "I aim to find out — maybe somethin' to gain."

Both Swann and Tice knew what that usually meant. It was an expression the half-breed Lakota Sioux used often and, more times than not, meant trouble for somebody. Red Shirt was proud of the fact that he had lived for a while in Sitting Bull's village and often boasted about riding into battle with the Hunkpapa Lakota holy man. "Sitting Bull let the soldiers chase him to Canada, but I never surrendered to the soldiers. I live where I want to live," he was fond of reminding Swann and Tice. Thus far, more than two years after Little Big Horn, he and his two partners had managed to avoid the army and the law while preying upon freighters, settlers, miners, stagecoaches, and any other small expeditions. He had run into Swann and Tice at a shabby little trading post run by Lem Sprool on the North Platte near the Rattlesnake Mountains. Swann, a deserter from the army, and Tice, a wanted murderer from Arkansas, were wandering aimlessly, looking for any opportunity to put food in their bellies. After a night of drinking Lem Sprool's rotgut whiskey, the three decided their odds of success were better if they rode together. From the beginning of the partnership, it was clear to see who would be the leader. Both Tice and Swann were content to follow, which was good, because Red Shirt would not have had it any other way.

"Come," Red Shirt directed his partners. "We'll ride up the creek a ways. Them shots couldn'ta been more'n a couple of miles away." They loped along, single file, close by the heavy brush that framed the creek. Red Shirt kept a sharp eye ahead, for there was very little to hide them in the flat, treeless plain on this side of the mountains. When he saw a small stand of cottonwood trees about half a mile ahead, he stopped and led them down to the creek bank. "You two stay with the horses. I'll work my way up the creek on foot so I can see who it is and what the shootin' was about — maybe somethin' to gain."

Ed Tice strained his neck, trying to see farther up the creek. "How do you know that's where they are? I can't see nothin'."

" 'Cause that's the only spot for a mile where there's trees," Swann said. "Right, Red Shirt?" Red Shirt's response was merely a look of impatience before moving quickly away.

Trotting in a crouch, in an effort not to present a profile along the top of the bank, Red Shirt quickly advanced to within sight of half a dozen horses at the edge of the water. He immediately sank down behind the cover of a thicket of berry bushes, and from that point, he advanced more carefully. After a couple of dozen more yards, he caught his first glimpse of the camp. He dropped to his hands and knees then and crawled closer until he could clearly see the men in the small clearing. He counted two men at first, and one of them was digging a hole with a short-handled shovel. Moving slightly to the side for a better vantage point, he then saw a third man sitting on the ground, his back to a tree. *He must be the boss,* he thought at first, then realized the man was tied to the tree.

He crawled forward a few more feet to the edge of the brush, pausing when a couple of the grazing horses whinnied, but the two men seemed not to notice. So Red Shirt inched a little closer to get a better look. Something crooked was going on, he thought, for now he saw the results of the shooting. There were two bodies on the ground. One of the men, the one watching the other one dig the hole, looked familiar. And then it struck him. It was the lawman from Cheyenne, U.S. Deputy Marshal Luther Moody. It was not difficult to form a picture of what must have occurred. The deputy evidently was taking a prisoner, maybe two prisoners, if one of the bodies was that of an outlaw, to Laramie. So the man tied to the tree was an outlaw, on his way to prison.

An evil smile spread slowly across Red Shirt's face as he realized the opportunity just handed him. Standing unaware, well within the range of his Spencer carbine, was the hated lawman Luther Moody and one of his posse men. Red Shirt pulled his carbine up and rested the barrel on a lump of dirt, piled there by a rodent digging among the berry bush's roots. The two men were standing close enough together to ensure that he could hit both of them before they could react without having to rush the second shot. He laid his front sight on Moody's broad back first, to make sure he got the deputy should something happen to block the second shot. Slowly he squeezed the trigger, enjoying the anticipation of the sudden discharge to come. And then the carbine spoke, and Moody dropped to his knees, remaining there for only a moment before falling forward to land on his side and roll over into the half-finished grave.

Red Shirt quickly ejected the empty shell and chambered a second cartridge. There was plenty of time, however, for Bud Collins stood stunned, confused, and not sure what had just happened. He did not move until Moody's body rolled up against his boots. By that time, it was too late, for Red Shirt's second shot slammed into his chest before he could dive for cover.

As soon as Collins fell, Red Shirt sprang to his feet and screamed a loud war cry in triumph, for he was certain there was no one else in the camp but the prisoner. Before moving into the camp to finish his victims, he turned back toward the creek and yelled, "Come on! Bring the horses."

In the blink of an eye, things had gone from bad to worse for the young man tied to the tree. Helpless, he watched the half-breed trot toward him, the carbine in his hand, and he could only guess when his turn would come. Unconcerned about any trouble from the prisoner, Red Shirt called again for his partners, then turned his attention toward the two men he had just shot. Both were still alive, although mortally wounded. Seeing that Moody was straining to pull himself out of the grave and trying to reach the rifle he had dropped upon being hit, Red Shirt went to him first and kicked the rifle away from his hand. He took a quick glance at Collins then to make sure he was not a threat before concentrating again on the deputy. "Hey, Moody," he taunted, "remember me? You finally caught up with me, you fat ol' son of a bitch." Whether Moody was too near death to respond was impossible to say, but he made no reply. Red Shirt waited a moment, then drew a long skinning knife from his belt and proceeded to take the deputy's scalp. This brought a scream of pain from the dying man, and brought a smile of satisfaction to Red Shirt's face. With his foot, he shoved Moody back into the grave. The deputy made no attempt to crawl out again.

For the two witnesses to the brutal scalping, there was the uncertainty of what was in store for the one tied to the tree, but the certainty of a second scalping for the wounded one in the grave was without question. Whimpering fearfully, with Moody's body pressing him against the side of the shallow hole he had dug, Collins tried to crawl out, knowing he was doomed. Still, in desperation, he tried to crawl toward the bushes by the creek, never thinking to try to pull his revolver from his holster. Red Shirt watched his struggles for a few moments, enjoying his obvious terror. Then he walked unhurriedly to overtake him, grab a handful of his hair, and lift the scalp.

Tice and Swann came up in time to hear

Collins's screams of agony. "Damned if he ain't somethin'," Orville said when Red Shirt went into a short war dance, holding the two trophies up for them to see.

"Gawdam savage," Tice replied, low enough to be sure no one but Swann could hear.

They stood there for a few minutes, surveying the scene to get an estimate of the spoils to be gained — the four bodies on the ground, one lying in a freshly dug hole; the horses by the creek; the man tied to the tree. After a moment, Tice commented, "Looks like you took care of everythin'." Red Shirt grinned in response. "What about him?" Tice asked, with a nod of his head in Carson's direction.

"I ain't made up my mind yet," Red Shirt replied. The question prompted him to walk over to stand before Carson. Swann and Tice followed him.

"He's kind of a young-lookin' pup," Tice commented. "Reckon what they was gonna do with him?"

"That fat one over there is a marshal," Red Shirt said, and pointed toward Moody's body. He directed a question at Carson then. "Where was he takin' you, boy? To the prison at Laramie?"

Carson could not see that he had much

choice but to answer, so he replied, "That's right."

"Why?" Tice asked. "What did you do?"

"Rustlin' and murder is what the court said," Carson answered. "He was takin' me and this one to be hanged." He nodded toward Varner's body lying close by.

"Cattle rustlin' and murder," Swann crowed. "Hell, he's one of our kind, ain't he?"

Red Shirt was skeptical. "Maybe, maybe not," he said. "He don't look so mean to me." The facts were pretty obvious, however, that he had done something bad enough to be captured by Moody and hauled to Laramie City. "Who'd you kill?"

"They said I killed some cowhands and stole their cattle," Carson answered. He made no attempt to acclaim his innocence of the charges. It didn't seem the prudent thing to do under the circumstances.

"I reckon it's your lucky day since we showed up, ain't it?" Swann said.

"Maybe," Carson replied. "I can't say yet. I'm still tied to a tree right now."

"Well, now," Red Shirt commented with a chuckle, "that is a fact, ain't it?" He could not help being amused by the young man's indifferent attitude. He walked from one side of Carson to the other as if judging a horse for sale. "There ain't nothin' keepin' me from givin' you the same those two lawmen got."

"Well, there ain't much I can do about it, unless you wanna untie me and we have a go at it man to man. But I don't hardly think that's gonna happen. So I reckon you're gonna do what you're gonna do. One way or the other, it don't matter too much. I was on my way to a hangin', anyway."

"What would you do if I was to cut you loose?" Red Shirt asked, still enjoying the predicament the young stranger was in.

"I'd get me a cup of coffee outta that pot on the fire," Carson replied unemotionally. "Mine got spilled when the shootin' started."

Red Shirt threw his head back and laughed. "Whaddaya say, boys, think we oughta let him loose and let him get him some coffee?"

"Don't make no difference to me," Tice replied. Carson had nothing of value — at least nothing that Tice would kill to take from him, so he was honest in his reply.

"Me, neither," Swann said, since Tice had not objected, and there was no reason to suspect Carson of attempting any form of retaliation for the killing of the men who were taking him to be hanged.

Red Shirt took the knife he had just used to scalp Moody and his posse man, and cut Carson's bonds. "All right, go get your coffee. And while you're at it, make a new pot and we'll all have some."

"Fair enough," Carson said, and proceeded to do just that while the three outlaws searched the bodies for anything of value.

CHAPTER 4

Out of the frying pan, into the fire — it appeared that Carson Ryan's summer was fated to land him in one tight situation after another. He now found himself seated beside the campfire that Orville Swann had built, eating more of the beans and bacon he had cooked. Across from him the two men who had come up after Red Shirt killed Moody and Collins were noisily gulping their dinner while the half-breed was still inspecting the horses recently gained. The conversation was predominantly an interrogation of the man they had freed. Carson patiently answered their questions, telling them where and how he had been taken prisoner, making his answers as short and vague as possible. He knew it was in his best interest to let them think he rode the same trail as they, and not proclaim his innocence of the charges made against him.

"Hell, it's a good thing we run across

you," Tice said. "We could use another man." This was not what Carson wanted to hear. He had hoped they would leave him a horse and weapons and go their separate ways. "Course, it'll have to be all right with Red Shirt," Tice continued. "He's kinda particular about a lot of things."

"Ha," Swann grunted. "What Ed means is Red Shirt calls all the shots, but I think he must like you. Hell, if he didn't, he'da most likely left you tied up to that tree."

"Yeah," Tice remarked, "and maybe with your throat cut."

Their conversation was interrupted when Red Shirt came back to the fire to join them. "Pretty good horses," he commented as he poured a cup of coffee for himself. "Bring a good price from that ol' son of a bitch on the Cheyenne," he said, referring to a trading post on the Cheyenne River. He grinned at Carson then and said, "I bet you got one of them horses picked out for yourself." When Carson didn't answer, but only shrugged indifferently, Red Shirt informed him, "You can pick out any of 'em you want except that black one. I'm keepin' him for myself." Carson nodded. "Same thing for the guns," Red Shirt went on. "You get yourself a rifle and a handgun, and some cartridges for 'em, but not that marshal's rifle. I want that one for myself." He paused, then remembered. "And that old bastard's badge is mine. I want it. I'll pin it on my scalp stick with his hair."

"I 'preciate it," Carson said. "They took my rifle and six-shooter back at Fort Laramie." He regretted the loss of his father's Henry rifle, but Moody and both of his posse men had been carrying Winchester rifles, so he had hopes of acquiring one of the two left after Red Shirt claimed his. With that in mind, he took note of the weapons carried by his new partners. Red Shirt had carried a Spencer carbine, but both Orville Swann and Ed Tice were armed with Winchesters. So his prospects of getting a Winchester for himself were pretty good. As far as the handgun was concerned, he didn't care that much. Just about anything would do. If he had a choice, of course, he would take a Colt, but a good rifle was the most important requirement. When it came to horses, he was satisfied to keep the bay gelding he had ridden from Fort Laramie. It seemed as stout a horse as those ridden by Moody, Summer, and Collins, and he and the horse seemed to get along fine.

With avoiding a discussion in mind, Carson picked up his saddle and threw it on the bay's back, causing Tice to comment, "You didn't waste much time takin' your pick. We ain't had time to look 'em over ourselves."

"They're all about the same," Carson told him, "and this is the one I rode here on."

"Seems to me we was the ones that took them horses, so we oughta get first pick before he does," Swann complained.

"Like he said, ain't none of 'em much better'n the others," Red Shirt said. "Let him take any horse he wants, long as it ain't that black one there." Like that of a stern father with his children, Red Shirt's word was not disputed. Carson suspected they seriously feared their savage partner, and he could readily understand. Red Shirt was a powerfully built man with wide shoulders and large hands that looked strong enough to crush a man's throat.

"I had a packhorse when they arrested me," Carson said, figuring he might as well try.

Red Shirt gazed at him with a raised brow. "Is that a fact? Well, you ain't got one no more," he informed him. "You'll be ridin' with us, so we'll make up some packs and put 'em on a couple of horses. That oughta do for all of us."

"Right," Carson said, "whatever you say."

Tice and Swann both grinned at him as if he had been accepted into a highly desirable society. He wasn't given any choice about joining them, so Carson's hopes of leaving them right away became suddenly dim.

The issue was settled, as far as Red Shirt was concerned, so he turned his mind to other things. "We might as well camp right here tonight. It's gettin' along toward evenin', so it don't make no sense to start out, then set right down and make camp again."

"How 'bout all them dead bodies?" Tice asked. "They'll be gettin' to stinkin' and bringin' a flock of buzzards down here, maybe coyotes, too."

"We ain't gonna be here that long," Red Shirt told him. "We'll be leavin' in the mornin'. They ain't gonna start stinkin' that quick." When he saw Tice wrinkle his nose as if he already smelled the bodies, he said, "Drag 'em off in the bushes yonder if it turns your belly that much, you damn woman." He turned to Carson then. "What about you . . ." He paused, then asked, "What the hell is your name?"

"Carson," he replied.

"Carson, huh? Well, what about you, Carson? Does the smell of dead bodies turn your belly?" His question was punctuated by a contemptuous smile.

It was obvious the half-breed was looking to amuse himself, and maybe test the fiber of the new member of his little gang of cut-throats. Carson labored to hide the feeling of disgust he felt, one caused by the savage disregard for human life demonstrated by this squat, broad-shouldered murderer more so than the bodies lying about. "I reckon not," he finally answered. "Like you said, they ain't hardly had time to get ripe yet." His answer caused Red Shirt to laugh again, obviously pleased with Carson's attitude.

"Maybe you can help ol' Tice drag those bodies into the bushes," Red Shirt suggested.

"All right," Carson responded, got to his feet, and signaled to the sour-faced Tice. "Come on, partner, and we'll get rid of 'em."

"I ain't your partner yet," Tice immediately replied, "not till I see how good you are when the shootin' starts." He followed him to Varner's body, however, and the two of them cleared the camp area of the dead.

Once they settled down for the day, Carson spent a great deal of thought trying to evaluate his chances of ridding himself of the three outlaws. He had no doubt that any attempt to part company peacefully was out of the question. Red Shirt would never permit anyone who had witnessed his murder of a U.S. deputy marshal to ride off alive. No, he decided, he had no choice but to go along with them and hope they didn't put him in a position where he was unable to fake his participation. Before long, he was bound to get an opportunity to slip away and head for Montana, as had been his original intent. In the meantime, he would let them think he was a willing participant in whatever crimes they were planning.

The evening was spent sitting around the fire, consuming much of the provisions that Luther Moody had brought, and talking about which direction to head when morning came. Carson learned that their destination had been the Black Hills before they happened upon the deputy marshal. Red Shirt held that there was no reason to change his mind. There were more miners staking out claims now that the Indians were not as big a threat. And small camps of one, two, or more men could be found on every little stream that emptied out of the hills into the prairie. These little camps were easy pickings, and it was unlikely anyone would ever find the bodies. "We'll get rid of some of these horses at Crazy

Jack's," Red Shirt said. He knew the old man who ran a trading post on the Cheyenne River had no use for horses, but he would trade for them because he knew they would be cheap. Red Shirt did not want to be bothered with driving extra horses. Crazy Jack knew that, and Red Shirt knew he knew it, so the trading of horses usually went fast.

When Carson asked Swann who Crazy Jack was, Swann told him the origin of the man's name. "Damned old fool built him a tradin' post up on the upper end of the Cheyenne River, back up in the hill country. It ain't no place for a white man in the middle of all that Injun country, and nobody but a crazy man woulda done it. The Injuns knowed he was teched in the head, so they never bothered him. Jack says they'll come around once in a while to trade some skins or somethin', mostly three or four at a time, and he'll give 'em a biscuit or a piece of peppermint. Then they go on off and leave him be. I expect that's who he trades the horses to."

When it came time to turn in, Carson rolled out his blanket a good way back from the fire with the thought in mind that he might take a chance on departing during the night. As he spread his blanket, he glanced up to find Red Shirt watching him. "Don't pay no mind to ol' Swann there," Red Shirt told him. "He don't sleep so good. He gets up all night to piss."

"I can't help it," Swann spoke up. "Somethin's wrong with my pee bag. It don't hold the water no more."

"That's cause he's gettin' too old to be worth a damn for anything," Red Shirt said scornfully.

"Now, you know that ain't so," Swann replied in his own defense. "I ain't slowed down a hair."

His immediate response seemed to amuse Red Shirt. It seemed a pointless conversation to Carson. Unless, he thought, it was a hint from Red Shirt that someone would be watching him during the night. Looking at the smirking half-breed, Carson could well imagine that to be his intent. He decided then that he might have to wait until they became comfortable with him before he made an attempt to desert.

The next morning, they ate a breakfast of more of the late Luther Moody's food supply, then saddled up and headed north, following the same trail Carson had ridden south the day before. Instead of following the Laramie River to its confluence with the Platte, however, they veered to the west far enough to stay well clear of Fort Laramie before crossing the North Platte and heading north again. They were in the saddle three and a half days before striking the Cheyenne River. The journey was time enough to allow Red Shirt and his partners to feel more comfortable with Carson. By the time they approached the rough log structure that was Crazy Jack's trading post, they were convinced that he was a willing recruit, and equally intent upon victimizing any poor soul who crossed their path.

It was almost nightfall when they rode into the clearing where Jack's cabin sat near the bank of the river. Leading the extra horses, they rode right up to his front door before hauling back hard on the reins and dismounting amid the cloud of dust their arrival had created. Their abrupt arrival was enough to bring Jack storming out the door, shotgun in hand, expecting a cavalry raid. His reaction pleased Red Shirt, who favored him with a contemptuous sneer.

"Red Shirt!" Jack blurted, matching the half-breed's look of contempt. "You're damn lucky I didn't blow a hole in you, charging in here like that."

"You old fool," Red Shirt responded, "you couldn't hit nothin' with that damn shotgun if I gave you the first three shots."

"There's a helluva lot of Injuns and half-breeds that made that mistake," Jack shot back. "You wouldn't be the first to learn not to rile my patience." He handed the shotgun to a woman standing just inside the door, and walked out to look over his visitors. "You picked up a new man," he observed aloud. "Looks like you picked up some horses, too. I expect you're hopin' I'll take some of 'em off your hands." He stepped up to take a closer look. "Mangy-lookin' bunch of crow baits, ain't they?"

"You don't know good horses when you see 'em," Red Shirt countered. "I don't know if I'll even let you make an offer. I might take 'em to Spearfish — get top dollar there."

"Yeah, you could do that, 'cept they'd arrest you on sight. There was a cavalry patrol come by here about a month ago lookin' for you and them two beauties you got ridin' with you. You'd best not go anywhere there's law or soldiers." He walked all around the extra horses, looking them over, then paused when he came to Carson. Still directing his talk toward Red Shirt, he asked, "Where'd you get this fresh one?" Then not waiting for Red Shirt's answer, he aimed his comments at Carson. "You studyin' to be as big a backstabbin' cutthroat as these two beauties?"

Carson didn't answer, but Tice spoke up. "You got a mouth on you that's just beggin' for a bullet, old man."

"From who?" Jack demanded. "You? Shit, my woman will cut you down before you clear leather." The claim caused Carson to notice the cabin door standing ajar. He decided Crazy Jack wasn't just making noise. Tice scowled but did not push it further.

With the preliminary insults apparently over, the talk turned more to a civil tone. "Put them horses in my corral," Jack said, turning again to Red Shirt. "We can talk trade in the mornin'. I'll have Sarah rustle you up some grub if you've got any money."

"Tell her to get her ass movin'," Red Shirt said. "My belly's growlin' somethin' fierce while we're just standin' here jawin'."

It seemed a strange way to conduct business. Aside from that, Carson found it surprising that Red Shirt even considered legitimate trade. It was Carson's impression that the savage simply robbed anything he needed and left bodies behind to tell no tales. Carson halfway expected Sarah to be an Indian woman, but she was, instead, a big-boned redhead who stood nearly as tall

90

as her husband, and although she spoke with a heavy Irish accent, there was definitely no twinkle in her eye. In fact, Carson was reminded of the lifeless eye of a wolf when she fixed her gaze upon him. The .44 single-action Colt pistol she wore strapped around her waist seemed right at home as she worked at her stove.

Sarah proved to be an adequate cook, nothing special, but filling, with the standard fare Carson expected in a place like Crazy Jack's — beans cooked in a pot with slices of sowbelly, mixed up with small chunks of meat that Carson suspected was muskrat — and something that looked like wild turnips. To round it out, she brought out a loaf of sourdough bread, baked fresh that morning. It was washed down with the always necessary black coffee. It was the best meal that Carson had had in quite some time, so he made it a point to compliment her and thank her for it. She said nothing in return, but stared at him as if he had said something degrading. Carson's compliment caught Red Shirt's attention as well, and he paused in his eating to study the young man intently. After a moment, he shrugged and continued eating his beans, using a slice of bread as his spoon.

After the table was cleared, Jack brought

out a bottle, and the drinking began. Several rounds were downed before he produced a deck of cards, so old and worn that Carson imagined that the gruff old man probably knew each card by touch. He declined the invitation to sit in a game of poker with the excuse that he didn't have anything he could afford to lose, so he sat at the end of the table and watched. As he had figured, Jack seemed to have the luck that night, so much so that Carson wondered when the violence would begin. It never did, however, even after Jack won hand after hand. All of the other players complained and cursed the cards, but no one challenged Jack's luck. This caused Carson to speculate on the reason. After giving it some thought, he decided Jack's was the only place Red Shirt could go to trade and play cards. Jack was, no doubt, aware of this and played it to his advantage. There was no telling how much stolen merchandise had passed through Jack's business to be traded with the Indians.

As the night wore on, Carson became tired of watching the poker game and announced that he was going to turn in. Swann promptly threw his hand in and said he was going to bed, too. "That damn crooked old man ain't gonna let nobody have a fair hand. I might as well go with Carson before I lose every cent I got." He got up from the table and followed Carson out the door. Carson couldn't help wondering if Swann's decision might in actuality have been an effort to keep an eye on him. True, Carson had considered the opportunity to possibly ride out while his three companions were deep into their whiskey and cards. He might have given it serious thought if Swann had remained in the game. To add to his suspicions, when they bade each other a good night, Swann picked up his bedroll and moved it over by the horses. Coincidence or just happenstance? Carson couldn't say for sure, but he decided tonight was not the night to make good his escape. There were bound to be better opportunities. He picked up his blankets and moved closer to the river.

He had barely settled in to go to sleep when he heard a soft footfall on the sun-baked ground above his head. Without thinking, he immediately rolled over on his belly, snatching his Colt revolver up as he did, ready to fire at the dark form standing over him. "Don't shoot," a soft voice whispered. "It's just me, Sarah."

Fairly astonished, Carson put the pistol back where it had lain beside his blanket.

"Well, I'm sorry, ma'am," he sputtered, purely bewildered by her appearance at his bedside, "but I swear, I almost shot you."

Sarah knelt down beside him. "I brought you a couple slices of bread. A young boy sometimes gets hungry during the night, and this will soak up some of the whiskey you drank." Still puzzled, he started to thank her, but she interrupted. "How old are you?"

"Seventeen," he told her as he began to have uneasy feelings about the clandestine visit from the older woman.

"Seventeen," she repeated, "about what I woulda guessed." He could see her nodding in the darkness. "How long have you been riding with this gang of murderers?"

"Just a few days, ma'am," he answered.

"How many men have you killed?"

"I've not shot anyone," he replied.

"Good," she said at once, "then you still have a chance to make something better out of your life than riding with scum like Red Shirt and the others. I knew I saw something decent in you right from the first. But you need to run as far away from those three as you can."

Feeling somewhat relieved now, he said, "I am, ma'am. I'm plannin' on runnin' first chance I get, but I'm waitin' for a time when

I can get a good head start. I think they've been keepin' a pretty close eye on me 'cause I saw Red Shirt kill a U.S. marshal."

"Good for you, boy. You take leave of these bastards before they get you mixed up in some of their evil doings." She got up then, apparently satisfied that she had accomplished what she had come to do, and left Carson staring at her dark figure as it vanished in the dark. Thinking he was too wide awake at this point to ever get to sleep, he lay back and stared up into the starless night. It seemed like a year since he had bade Mr. Patterson farewell in Ogallala and started out on the first leg of a journey that he figured would find him in Montana. In actuality, it had been only a few weeks.

He had no idea when he drifted off to sleep, but he awoke in the morning to find the sun already sending its fingers probing the shadows in the trees by the river. After breakfast inside, most of the morning was wasted away while Jack and Red Shirt argued over the value of the horses. Carson sat on the ground with Tice and Swann beside a small fire Swann built in a corner of the yard and waited for the trading to be finished. Leaning on one elbow, absent-mindedly feeding the fire with small twigs, Swann finally sought to satisfy his curiosity.

"What was goin' on between you and Jack's wife last night?" he asked Carson. "I saw her talkin' to you after we turned in."

Not surprised that Swann had seen them, Carson replied, "She brought me some leftover bread, thought I might get hungry, so she offered it to me before throwin' it to the hogs."

"Huh," Swann grunted, "she coulda throwed some of it my way." He sat back, apparently satisfied with Carson's answer. "Probably thinkin' about her boy," he said.

"She's got a son?" Carson asked.

"Did have," Swann said. "He's dead now, got shot down by a part-time sheriff on a bank robbery that went bad — up at Deadwood. I reckon he was about your age, just a young feller."

His comment caused Carson to turn to look at the solemn woman who came out of the cabin just then to throw the breakfast dishwater out in the yard. He understood now why she had come to talk to him last night. She met his gaze for a moment before turning away to return to her kitchen, giving no response by her expression. It was easier to understand the woman's concern for him now, and he hoped that he had convinced her that he had no intention of falling to the same fate.

It was late in the morning before Red Shirt and Jack reached final agreement on the trading. As usual, according to Tice, Jack got the better side of the trade. "I reckon we can saddle up now." His guess was confirmed moments later when Red Shirt stalked past them on his way to the horses, cursing Crazy Jack for a cheating skinflint, and telling the three lounging men to get saddled. Less than an hour later, they were on their way, the one packhorse they kept loaded with supplies and cartridges Red Shirt had traded for the extra horses. Crossing over the fork of the Cheyenne, they continued north. According to Red Shirt's reckoning, they could anticipate striking the Beaver River in half a day.

Feeling as much a prisoner as he had felt while in the custody of Deputy Marshal Luther Moody, Carson rode silently, his thoughts of escape interrupted frequently by bantering between Tice and Swann. There was plenty of time to consider the two outlaws who followed their savage boss's whims without protest, riding along behind him like brainless servants. The two men were as different as night and day. Tice seemed to always have something eating away at his insides that caused him to be constantly irritated. He was a tough, wiry man, whose face seemed to never have experienced a smile. Swann, on the other hand, wore a foolish grin for most of the time, seeming to be amused by most everything that happened. The trait the two men had in common was a callous disregard for human life and sympathy for no one. *Fine lot I'm riding with,* Carson thought, recalling Sarah's words. Then it occurred to him that he would hate to have his grandmother see him riding with such evil vermin.

It was the first time he had thought about his grandmother in many years. He didn't recall very much about the woman who gave him birth, for he was only four years old when his mother died trying to give him a younger brother. The baby, a girl actually, didn't make it, either. His father was hit pretty hard by the loss of his wife and, finding it too much to bear, left his four-year-old son with his grandmother and went back to work herding cattle. So Grandma Ryan raised the boy until she passed away when he was fourteen. With no reason to stay, Carson followed his father into the business of punching cattle. In the three years since he had gone to work for Mr. Bob Patterson, he never crossed paths with his father.

■ ■ ■ ■

Upon reaching the Beaver, they decided it was still a little too early to camp for the night, so they stopped for a short while to rest the horses before continuing on. "We'll just follow the river a ways yet," Red Shirt decided. "We've got a good two hours of daylight left, so if we stay with the river, we'll have a camp with plenty of water and grass." They had not gone on for more than a couple of miles, however, before striking a fresh trail where a small party had crossed the river. Red Shirt immediately dismounted to study the tracks in the soft sand at the water's edge. "Five horses," the half-breed decided, "or four horses and a mule, maybe." He stood up and looked to the east and the dark mountains called the Black Hills. "They came from the hills, headin' west. Maybe some prospectors headin' west with some gold." His eyes narrowed, hiding the gleam that always came with the thought of a potential victim. "Maybe something to gain," he announced.

"More likely some damn jackass that finally gave up and is headin' for home with his pockets empty," Tice remarked.

"Tice is probably right," Carson quickly

99

commented, alarmed that he might find himself involved in an attack upon some innocent prospectors. "Most likely a waste of our time."

Mildly surprised that Carson had offered an opinion, Red Shirt cocked an eyebrow as he gave the young man a sharp eye. "Won't hurt to take a look," he said. "Maybe something to gain."

There was no point in trying to argue, so there was nothing Carson could do but hope the party was long gone. This hope was crippled when Red Shirt said the tracks weren't but a few hours old. It gave him a sick feeling inside to think that he might be a part of a robbery, but he resigned himself to the inevitable. It was a waste of time lamenting the fact that he had not made a run for it while they were still camped at Crazy Jack's.

The trail appeared to be a commonly traveled one and led them across a low hill, thick with pines. Soon the sun dropped behind the trees, leaving the forest around them to begin to close in as they made their way carefully now. Suddenly Red Shirt held up his hand, directing them to stop and dismount. When the three behind him caught up, he pointed to a glow filtering through the trees ahead. "It looks like a stream up ahead," Red Shirt said softly. "You stay here. I'll go take a look."

He was gone for about twenty minutes before reappearing out of the darkness. "Two men and a woman," he reported. "They look like prospectors, maybe. Don't know what else they'd be, comin' outta the hills. I don't know if they'll amount to much of a payday, but maybe something to gain." He checked his rifle to make sure it had a full magazine. "We'll ride in peaceful-like. It'll be like shootin' fish in a barrel. They don't look like they could give us much trouble."

"Well, let's get at it, then," Tice said, checking his own rifle.

"What did the woman look like?" Swann wanted to know.

"Let's give 'em time to settle down for the night," Red Shirt said. "Might as well make it easy on ourselves." He turned his gaze to settle on Carson then and studied the young man for a moment. "No," he said then, "we'll leave the horses here and walk into their camp and hit 'em before they know what's what."

"What did the woman look like?" Swann repeated. "She old, young, or what?"

"Whaddaya care?" Tice scoffed. "When did you get so picky?"

101

"Damn it, I just asked," Swann came back, his hackles up.

"I couldn't tell," Red Shirt finally told him, "just a woman." Unlike Swann, he was not interested in the woman, only the possibility of acquiring the party's possessions. "After we take care of the two men, then you can worry about the woman."

The bickering over for the moment, they sat down to wait and to anticipate the attack to come, eager to see if their intended victims might be some of the fortunate ones who had found gold in the mountain streams — all except one. Carson was almost frantic inside, caught in the evil web of Red Shirt's intentions. He could not blindly go along with the savage half-breed's raid on an innocent party. As he sat waiting with them, he glanced from one face to another, seeing the eager anticipation in both Tice and Swann, and the patient countenance of the calculating half-breed. It almost made him sick inside to know what was planned for the party of prospectors, and the fact that he didn't know how he could prevent it. He knew that he could not stop all three of them, even if he decided to attack them. But he also knew he had to do something to stop a conscienceless massacre. When it was time to move on the camp, he was handed another setback that he had not expected.

"All right," Red Shirt said, "it's time to go get 'em." When they all rose to their feet, he caught Carson by the arm. "You stay here with the horses. When the shootin' starts, we don't want 'em runnin' all over hell and back." From the beginning, Red Shirt had questioned the resolve he read in the young man's eyes, and he decided it best not to take a chance on Carson doing something crazy in the heat of a gunfight.

Further distressed over this recent turn of events, he was not sure what he should do. In that moment, however, he decided it was time to pick between right and wrong, and he knew he sure as hell couldn't side with Red Shirt and his two murderers. Even with his mind made up, he couldn't bring himself to take the coward's way and start shooting them in the back. Trying to decide, he waited too long for that opportunity, anyway, for they were already fading into the night. Suddenly he saw his best course of action. He ran to his horse and sprang into the saddle. Raising his rifle, he fired three quick shots into the air, then guided his horse through the trees at a fast lope, riding in a wide circle, thinking to come up from behind the prospectors' camp.

The three warning shots brought the campers out of their bedrolls, reaching for their weapons. "Get to the creek bank!" Jonah Thompson yelled. "Nancy! Keep down behind that bank!" He knew he didn't have to tell his brother what to do; Frank was already running to the creek, his rifle in hand. The first thought by both brothers was *Indians.*

Some fifty yards back in the pines, there was equal confusion over the sudden rifle shots. "What the hell?" Red Shirt roared when startled by the shattering of the silence. The three of them dived for cover, thinking the shots were meant for them. "That son of a bitch . . . ," he started, but left unfinished as he strained to see behind them, halfway expecting more shots to come.

"What the hell's he doin'?" Tice exclaimed, thinking it an accident, before realizing, had that been so, there would have been one shot only.

"The sneaky bastard's warnin' them," Red Shirt decided. "I knew I couldn't trust him."

"Well, what are we gonna do now?" Swann asked while nervously straining to see through the trees behind them.

"Just sit tight right here," Red Shirt ordered, his alarm having been replaced by red-hot anger. "I'm goin' back to take care of that sneaky son of a bitch. I want his scalp on my scalp stick." He was off then, moving stealthily through the trees. The woods became quiet again, as Tice and Swann were left to watch for signs of Carson. In a short time, they heard Red Shirt's voice telling them to hold their fire. "He took off," he told them. "His horse is gone."

"What about our horses?" Tice asked.

"They're all right. He just hightailed it outta here," Red Shirt said. "I'll run across him one of these days. Then he'll pay up for this."

"Whaddaya think we oughta do now?" Swann asked.

"Nothin's changed," Red Shirt answered. "We're gonna take whatever they've got in that camp."

"If you're thinkin' 'bout chargin' in there blazin' away," Tice said, "I ain't for it. Them folks has had time to get ready to give us plenty of lead."

Red Shirt paused to give that some thought. Tice was probably right, he decided. They might be running into a buzz saw. "We'll try to talk our way in first." That sounded better to Tice and Swann, so they followed Red Shirt's lead and worked their way in closer. "Hello the camp," Red Shirt called out. "We're peaceful folk — didn't mean to scare you back there — rifle went off when I was puttin' it away — damn near shot myself in the foot — don't wanna cause no harm to anybody. Like I said, we're peaceful, just lookin' to maybe share some coffee." All the while, the three predators scanned the clearing before the creek, trying to locate their targets.

"Yonder's one of 'em," Tice whispered when he caught a slight movement along the rim of the creek bank. "They're holed up under the bank."

"Yeah," Red Shirt said when he looked where Tice pointed. "They're dug in pretty good." He knew they had the advantage if he decided to risk charging into them. "Tell you what," he called out again, "we got off on the wrong foot. Whaddaya say we both come out and meet in the middle of the clearing?"

"I don't think so," Jonah called back from the creek. "I think it best if you just go on down the creek somewhere and find your own place to camp."

"Mister, if we was up to anythin' bad, we'da already snuck up on you," Red Shirt tried one more time. "We was just tryin' to be neighborly. So whaddaya say, just me and you to talk it over?"

Jonah was not a fool, and he had had enough. "Mister," he yelled back, "you can go to hell."

"Damn you," Red Shirt cursed, fully angry now, more so with Carson than with his intended victims. "We've got you out-numbered, and we can keep you pinned down in that creek till the damn thing dries up!"

"He might be right," Jonah told Frank. "But I don't think we've got any choice but to fight them." With that resolve, he laid his rifle on the rim of the bank and fired a shot in the direction of the man's voice. It was immediately answered by shots from three rifles. The skirmish continued for several minutes with both sides firing blindly in the dark, with no distinguishable targets other than the occasional muzzle flash. Impatient with the lack of any gain, Tice decided to make a run for a bush-covered mound a dozen yards closer, but at an angle that he thought might give him a look at a target. Running in a low crouch, he left the protection of the tree he had been shooting from. Halfway to the mound, a shot rang out and he tumbled to the ground, mortally wounded.

"Good shot, Frank," Jonah said.

Puzzled, Frank answered, "I didn't shoot

him. I thought you shot him."

"It wasn't my shot," Jonah said. They both turned to look at Nancy, who was still huddled under the brow of the low creek bank. There was no need to ask if she had killed him. "They've gotten around behind us," Jonah exclaimed. "They hit one of their own men."

"That doesn't make sense," Frank replied. "It would have been one helluva poor shot, and how come he didn't keep shooting?"

"Damned if I know," Jonah replied while looking nervously behind him now, halfway expecting a second shot at any moment.

Back in the trees, Swann called out, "Tice! You all right?" But the dark lump lying still between the pines and the bushy mound did not respond. "They got Tice!" Swann exclaimed excitedly to Red Shirt. "He ain't movin'."

"He shoulda stayed behind that tree," Red Shirt replied, angry enough at the way things were going to pump five shots at the creek as rapidly as he could pull the trigger and rechamber another cartridge. His barrage ended abruptly when a rifle slug kicked up dirt near his foot. Jumping quickly back behind a tree, he proclaimed, "That shot came from that slope behind those people!" It didn't take but a moment then to realize that Carson had not run as he had first thought. "That son of a bitch has joined up with 'em."

"What the hell would he do that for?" Swann asked, truly puzzled.

" 'Cause he's a no-account, double-dealin' son of a bitch," Red Shirt hissed. The young pup had thoroughly wrecked what would have been an easy strike, and cost him one of his men. To add to his anger, he glanced over his shoulder to see a full moon climbing over the dark hills behind them. "Damn!" he cursed again, for soon the moon would melt away much of the deep shadow, making it more difficult to move in on the camp. "Pretty soon it's gonna be light as day between here and that creek. We've got to move up to where we can see what we're shootin' at." He paused to decide the best way to approach them before directing Swann. "Slide on downstream a little ways and work your way back to the creek. I'll move upstream and we'll have 'em between us. We oughta root 'em outta there quick enough. Then we'll take care of Mr. Carson Ryan."

Swann was not particularly fond of the idea of moving away from the large tree trunk he had taken cover behind, but he was reluctant to tell Red Shirt no, so he started to inch away to another tree to his right. "And, damn it, Swann," Red Shirt called after him, "be careful you don't shoot me."

Being a more cautious man than his simple companion, Red Shirt remained where he was until Swann safely reached the second tree. Then he moved slowly away from his cover and crawled to a low mound a few yards away, where he stopped and waited for Swann to leave the second tree and head quickly for a clump of small pines closer to the creek. Swann was a few steps away from safety when the rifle on the slope spoke once more, causing him to reel awkwardly before collapsing to the ground. Red Shirt froze. Cursing himself for not killing Carson when they first came upon him, he decided not to test the young man's marksmanship any further. So far, it had proven too deadly to challenge. *There will be other times, my young friend,* he promised himself as he withdrew to the trees once more. Safely behind a tree trunk again, he lingered there for a few moments more, reluctant to leave Tice's and Swann's weapons behind. Both men had carried good Winchester rifles and Colt pistols, weapons he could sell, but he knew he was asking for the same ticket to hell they had purchased if he ventured out into the clearing. *Damn!* He swore to think of leaving valuable weapons for Carson to gather up and make a profit on. *That young coyote pup,* he swore to himself, and vowed to cut his heart out. In spite of his lust for revenge, he could not risk his body in the now moonlit clearing, knowing that he would be an easy target.

Backing carefully away from the tree protecting him, he moved back through the pines to the horses, thankful that Carson had not thought to drive them off. He couldn't say that he would miss Tice or Swann, although they had been useful at times. At least he had gained two good horses and a couple of saddles. It was hard to decide what to do at this point, torn as he was between two choices. His passion to avenge the betrayal by Carson caused him to be inclined to continue to stalk him, looking for a chance to kill him. The downside to this plan was the inconvenience of herding a string of extra horses, and he was reluctant to set them free. In the end, he decided to return to Crazy Jack's in hopes of selling the horses, extra riding gear, and weapons. Another thing he had to consider was the fact that he was now outnumbered four to one, if the woman could handle a gun, and he never liked being on the low end of odds like those. He scowled and cursed again before finally withdrawing, still reluctant to swallow his bitter loss and slink off into the night.

CHAPTER 5

Not sure what was happening, Jonah Thompson moved a few feet closer to his brother, who was straining to search the low ridge behind them. "See anything back there?" he asked.

"No," Frank replied without taking his eyes off the dark ridge, "not a thing. You think it's a cavalry patrol or something?" They had at first thought the shots came from a member of the party who had hailed them from the edge of the pines, and the shot had accidentally killed one of their own. But when the second shot was fired, killing another of the aggressors, they knew it was no accident. The question was who, and what was their motive? Once the rifleman had halted the attack, would he, or they, if there was more than one, then begin to turn his weapon on the three of them? "You think maybe it's Indians?"

Harboring the same thoughts that puzzled

Frank's mind, Jonah said, "Either we've got a guardian angel, come to take care of us, or we're next on his list. But damned if I know which." He turned his head toward the edge of the creek bank. "You all right down there, Nancy?"

"I'm all right," Nancy replied, "but if I could make myself into a tighter ball, I'd be better." She paused a moment, then asked, "What are we gonna do?"

Frank looked at Jonah then. "What *are* we gonna do?"

"I don't know," Jonah answered. "Right now I'm afraid to stick my nose outta this creek." He paused then, knowing his younger brother and sister-in-law were looking to him to make the decision. "I reckon it's best not to risk getting shot. I don't see what we can do but sit right where we are and keep our eyes open. It's some time yet before daylight. Maybe then we can tell more about what's going on. If you've got a better idea, I'd like to hear it."

Frank was just about to say that he had nothing better to offer when the voice came from the scrubby pines at the base of the ridge. "Hello the camp. Are you folks all right?"

Startled, both brothers jumped, then craned their necks in an effort to see from

114

where the call had originated. "Keep your eyes on those trees in front of us," Jonah warned. "It might be a trick." Then he called out, "Yeah, we're all right. Who are you? Are you part of that gang?"

"My name's Carson Ryan. I'm not part of any gang. There were three of them outlaws, but now there ain't but one, but he's the dangerous one." He waited a few moments to see if they were going to tell him to come on in. When they didn't, he asked, "All right if I come into your camp?"

"Whaddaya think, Frank?" Jonah asked.

"Well, he did shoot two of those outlaws and probably saved our bacon. I guess we can trust him, but keep your rifle handy and we'll keep our eyes open. The first hint of trouble from him and we'll cut him down. All right?" Frank nodded. "All right," Jonah called. "Come on in." Frank took a few steps closer to his wife to take a protective stance over her. They waited. Then after a few moments, a tall strapping figure walked out of the pine shadows leading a horse.

"Mister," Jonah said, "you're walking awful casual-like across that clearing. Ain't you afraid you'll get shot?"

"He's gone," Carson replied.

"What makes you think that?" Jonah asked.

"I saw him from the ridge back there, leading three horses toward the river. I can't say for sure that he won't be back for another try, but I wouldn't be surprised if he figures it better to get rid of the horses first. He knows now that it's just one of him against three of us." He stopped short of the fire that had been abandoned when the first shots rang out. "Any coffee to spare in that pot there?"

"What?" Jonah blurted, still confused by the sudden appearance of the lone rifleman. "Coffee?" he echoed, and glanced quickly at Frank to see if he had any objection.

"I think you certainly earned it," Nancy interrupted Jonah, who seemed to be having trouble with the proper response. "I'm sure we can spare some for someone who appears to have saved us from being murdered. If there's none left, I'll gladly make you a fresh pot."

"I'd appreciate it, ma'am," Carson said.

"Sure!" Frank suddenly bellowed after his wife put the situation in proper perspective. "Nancy's right, you damn sure earned it, and something to eat to go with it." He, like Jonah, had been befuddled by the unexpected help that had led to the routing of the outlaws attacking them.

"I'd settle for the cup of coffee," Carson

said. "There's a few more things to take care of before I can think about eatin'." He was thinking of the bodies of Swann and Tice lying on the other side of the creek, and the weapons and ammunition on them. "I'm gonna take a look in that bunch of pines, just to make sure Red Shirt didn't double back, and I'll drag those two bodies out of the clearin'. Ain't no use for the lady to have to look at 'em when the sun comes up."

"We can help you with that," Frank immediately offered.

"Did you say Red Shirt?" Jonah asked. Carson nodded. Jonah turned to his brother then. "Ain't that the name of that Indian who was raiding some of the claims near Custer? It was something like that, Red Shirt, or Red Wolf, or something. He was raiding the small claims, murdering the miners, scalping them." He turned back to Carson then. "Are you saying that's the same one who tried to attack us?"

"It's the same man," Carson replied.

"Well, glory be," Jonah exclaimed, "I'm sure glad you came along when you did. How'd you happen to be here?"

Carson thought a moment before answering. Maybe it might not be best to tell them the truth, that he didn't just happen along, that he had arrived with them. "Just luck, I reckon. I ain't really headin' on any certain trail, just ridin' in the general direction of Montana."

"Well, friend," Frank chimed in, "you picked the right trail as far as we're concerned, and we're beholdin' to you." He paused when Nancy stepped up to hand Carson his cup of coffee. Then realizing it was overdue, he introduced his party. "My name's Frank Thompson. The pretty one there is my wife, Nancy. The ugly one is my brother, Jonah. Welcome to our camp."

"Thank you," Carson said. "My name's Carson. . . ." He paused when it struck him that he was still a wanted man, and maybe it would not be a good idea to tell them his last name. "Carson," he repeated, "John Carson."

"Well, pleased to meet you, John," Jonah said. "I thought you said something else when you first came up, but to tell you the truth, my mind was kinda spinning at the time."

"Sometimes I guess I mumble too much," Carson said. No one seemed to make anything of the misunderstanding, judging by the expressions on the faces of Nancy and Frank, so he drank his coffee, then started to cross over the creek.

"We'll help you with those bodies," Frank

volunteered again.

"Might be better if you let me take a look around over there first," Carson replied, "just in case. I'll give you a holler when I'm sure I wasn't wrong about them all bein' gone." He stepped up in the saddle, having no actual concern about anyone's safety at this point. His real purpose was to strip the bodies of weapons and ammunition. When he had been arrested, he had lost everything he owned, so he wanted to make sure he had plenty of ammunition for his Winchester, and hoped to trade the other weapons for supplies he was now without.

Frank shrugged. "All right, just give a holler when you're ready."

The bodies were lying approximately thirty yards apart. He dismounted when he came to the first one. It was Ed Tice. Looking as irritable and dyspeptic in death as he had looked when alive, Tice caused no feelings of guilt in Carson's mind. The man had held no value for the lives of other human beings, male or female. Carson relieved him of his rifle and handgun and pulled a cartridge belt from his body. He was not interested in anything to be found in his pockets other than the small amount of cash. He then led his horse over to Orville Swann's corpse.

119

Looking down at the relaxed features of the simple man, Carson felt the first hint of regret, and it struck him only then that he had killed two men. It could be easy to justify and say that he had done the world a favor, maybe even have saved lives that might have been their future victims. It did not cancel the fact that he had taken the lives of two human beings. That fact could never be reversed, no matter what happened from this point forward. Back on the darkened ridge, the two men had been nothing more than targets, and he hadn't hesitated a moment to knock them down. As he looked now at the results of his marksmanship, they conveyed a sobering thought for him to deal with. He, too, was a killer, a murderer. It was not something that he could take lightly, no matter the guilt of those he had killed. *It had to be done,* he thought. *Those innocent folks might have been killed if I hadn't.* There had been no choice left to him, and right or wrong, the boy in Carson Ryan also died on this fateful night.

He took Swann's weapons and cartridges and tied them on his saddlebags with Tice's. *I'll have to come up with a better way to carry these,* he thought as he led the bay toward the trees where the other horses had been. The packhorse would be sorely missed. He didn't know what he expected to find, but he scouted the woods anyway. When he was sure there was nothing there, he called out to Frank that it was all right to come for the bodies.

"Be right there," Frank called back, but before crossing the creek, he paused to confer with Jonah and Nancy. "Whaddaya think about this fellow? You reckon he's got any tricks up his sleeve?" He was especially concerned for his wife, who was still visibly shaken by the events that had occurred on this night, even though she had done her best to appear in control.

"I don't know," Jonah replied, making an effort to keep his voice down. "He just showed up out of the blue and says he ain't going anywhere in particular. But, hell, he seems like a nice enough young fellow. Wouldn't hurt to have him ride along with us, as handy as he is with that rifle, especially if that devil Red Shirt decides to get on our trail. That is, if he ain't got anything up his sleeve."

"He's got an honest face," Nancy remarked. "I think he'll be all right."

"All right," Jonah decided. "We'll see what he says about traveling with us. Heck, if he had murdering us in mind, he could have shot us in the creek when he was shooting those two in the clearing. Let's go, Frank."

It didn't take long to dispose of the two bodies lying in the clearing. When they had been dragged away into the pines, the three men returned to the camp, where Nancy had built the fire up again. There were a few hours left before sunrise, but there was very little sleep in the waning darkness except for Carson. He was tired and still felt the weight of his conscience, but he was secure in the belief that he had nothing to fear from these people. As for the two brothers and the woman, sleep was out of the question. They had heard of the atrocities carried out by Indians and outlaws in the Black Hills, but this was their first exposure to it personally. The experience tended to convince them that extra protection would be a very good thing, considering the distance they had to cover. All three tried to sleep, but soon gave it up, Nancy first, and then one by one they joined her sitting by the fire where they talked in hushed tones until the sun rose above the distant hills. When Carson threw his blanket back and walked downstream to take care of nature's business, the Thompson family roused themselves to get ready for the new day.

While the men saddled the horses and

loaded the packs, Nancy prepared breakfast. Nothing had been said to Carson concerning a parting of the ways, so Jonah broached the subject. "What are you figuring on doing now, John?"

His attention concentrated primarily on the cup of fresh coffee in his hand, Carson did not respond immediately, until he glanced up to find Jonah waiting for a response. Realizing then that the question had been aimed at him, he silently reminded himself that his new name was John. "I was just thinkin' about that. I reckon I'll just set out for Montana country again."

"Sounds like we're all heading in the same direction," Jonah commented. "It might work out for all of us if we traveled together. It would be handy to have you and that rifle of yours along with us, and it would be handy for you to have somebody to do your cooking. And three guns are better than two. That's for sure." He gestured toward Carson's horse. "We've got two packhorses, so maybe we could carry some of those extra weapons for you, too. Whaddaya think?"

Carson glanced at Frank and Nancy, who had both paused to hear his response. From their expressions, he could see that they were in favor of it. "It might be a good thing at that," he replied, "if you folks are sure you can put up with me." He saw smiles on all three faces. "I don't have any supplies to amount to much. I lost my packhorse in a river crossin' on the way up from Texas," he lied. "But I'm a pretty good hunter. Maybe I can supply us with some fresh meat." He shrugged apologetically. "About those extra guns and such, I was fixin' to ask you if you needed to trade for any of 'em. There's a couple of good Winchester '73s there."

"I might wanna take a look at one of 'em at that," Frank said. "I got a better chance of hitting something with my shotgun, though."

After a night that had threatened disaster, the Montana party set out with a new sense of optimism. Even though their new member was younger by half than Jonah, he presented himself as quite capable and obviously more experienced in life on horseback. As Nancy had fittingly expressed to her husband, "When John gets on his horse, it seems like the horse just becomes a part of him." When they came to a small creek in the middle of the day, they decided it was a good place to rest the horses and fix the midday meal. While the men waited for Nancy to cook the bacon and beans, Carson took the opportunity to learn a little more about the party he was now riding with.

"I've been tryin' to figure out how you folks happened to be in the Black Hills, and why you're headin' to Montana."

"To tell you the truth," Jonah offered, "we started out for Montana, but we got a wild notion to see if first we could strike it rich with the other dreamers that rushed to the Black Hills." He went on to explain that they were going to join Nancy's father near Big Timber, and hopefully help him expand an already sizable cattle ranch. But when they had reached Fort Laramie, there was so much talk about the mining prospects near Custer and Deadwood that they decided to wire Nancy's father and tell him they were going to join the gold rush in hopes of providing a bigger investment in the ranch.

"He wired back and said we were crazy," Frank chimed in. He looked at Nancy and laughed. "He thinks Nancy married a crazy man, anyway, so it didn't matter much to me what he thought about our gold digging."

"Oh, he doesn't think you're crazy," Nancy protested.

"Well, anyway," Jonah went on, "that's how we ended up near Custer. We didn't make any investment money, but we made grub money, and so far, we've still got our hair. How about you, John, how do you happen to be here?"

Carson shrugged, reluctant to say much to avoid making statements that might end up contradicting earlier remarks. "Like I said, I came up from Texas with a herd of cattle. We dropped 'em off in Ogallala and I came on up this way, figurin' on goin' to Montana."

"Why are you going to Montana?" Nancy asked.

" 'Cause I ain't ever been there," he answered, just as he had answered Duke Slayton when Slayton asked him the same question. In truth, Carson could not really say why he wanted to go to Montana Territory. It was a calling inside him, as if he were going home, even though he had never been there. There was a deep need to see the vast plains of rich bunchgrass, and a natural desire to feel the mystique of the rugged mountains that reach all the way up to heaven's backyard. These were the reasons he wanted to go to Montana, but he could not put them in words.

"Do you have family in Texas?" Nancy wanted to know.

"No, ma'am, not anymore. They're all gone."

"Oh," she responded, sensing that he didn't care to volunteer any additional information. He was an interesting young man, she decided, and she suspected he was a lot more complicated than the simple facade he presented. "You might find Big Timber a good place for you, since you've worked with cattle before. My father has a large ranch, and he might need someone with experience."

"Yes, ma'am," Carson replied. "I know how to run cattle. That's about all I know how to do." He had one more question that had puzzled him since he joined them. "How far is Big Timber from here?"

"I don't know for sure," Jonah answered. "But I'd guess about three hundred miles, maybe a little more."

"And you know how to get there?"

"Near enough," Jonah replied. "I went out there with Mathew Cain, that's Nancy's father, when he got his first herd up there. That was the only time I've been there, and that was a couple of years ago. We went up the old Bozeman Trail that time and it was still a little bit risky, what with the Sioux and the Cheyenne on the warpath. It ought to be a whole lot quieter now since the army's taken care of that."

"If you went up the Bozeman," Carson said, still uncertain, "you musta gone through Fort Laramie."

"That's right, we did. But I'm pretty sure we can still head northwest and eventually strike the trail up to the Yellowstone. And once we get there, it's just a simple matter to follow it to Big Timber."

Carson nodded thoughtfully. *Well,* he thought, *I wanted to see the country. I might see a hell of a lot more of it than I'd planned.* He had no real concerns, however. He figured that if they got lost, they could always head straight north until they struck the Yellowstone.

A little before noon on the third day, they reached the Belle Fourche River. The horses were showing signs of fatigue, so much so that Jonah thought it best to camp there the rest of the day and start out again in the morning. Carson was not surprised. While his bay was still fresh, the horses Frank and Jonah rode were of poor quality in comparison. It caused him to wonder if the brothers knew any more about cattle than they did about horses — or panning for gold, for that matter. The delay was of little consequence to him, however. He was in no particular hurry, as long as they reached Big Timber before heavy snows set in. Besides that, he welcomed the opportunity to do a little hunting. He was already craving a change from the steady diet of bacon, and he had noticed deer sign along the trail into the river. So after he had given the brothers a hand with the horses, he rode off up the river to test his luck.

There was a feast that night of roasted venison and, since she had plenty of time to make them, fresh biscuits to go with it. It was a welcome change of diet for everyone. In fact, it was the first time that Nancy had ever eaten venison, a fact that left Carson shaking his head in wonder. "She always said that deer were too pretty to kill and eat," Frank said. "She most likely wouldn't be eating right now if she had watched you kill it and do the butchering." She pretended to give him a stern look as she sliced off another portion for herself.

It was an enjoyable evening for Carson as well as the Thompsons. He almost felt like one of the family, and thoughts of Duke Slayton and his gang of outlaws and Red Shirt and the others were left behind. The future looked promising with notions of working with Jonah and Frank in the cattle business. He decided that meeting up with them was a genuine stroke of good luck.

CHAPTER 6

Leaving the Belle Fourche, they rode another full day, reaching another river in the early evening. "I'm hoping this is the Powder River," Jonah commented as he pulled a roughly drawn map from his saddlebag and spread it out on the ground, so they could all see. From the Belle Fourche, he had pointed his little party in a general northwest direction. "If it is the Powder, then we should strike Crazy Woman Creek by noontime tomorrow, and if we do, then we'll be close to the old Bozeman Trail." He paused then to look around at the faces hovering over the map as if expecting an argument. There was none, for the country was new to everyone.

"How will you know the Bozeman when we reach it?" Nancy asked. "Is it marked or something?"

"No," Jonah replied patiently. "It's not like there's a regular road there, but I think I'll be able to recognize it, even if it has been a couple of years."

"Seems to me like there oughta be a lot of old horse tracks, and wagon tracks, too," Carson said. "We should be able to tell when we strike it, but I reckon we'll figure it's time to turn north if we run slap into the Big Horn Mountains." The country was new to him, but he at least knew that the Bozeman Trail ran east of the Big Horns.

"I suppose you're right, John," Jonah said, and laughed. "Another day's travel oughta get us to the Bozeman." The thought seemed to raise the spirits of everyone as they prepared to feast on more of the deer Carson had shot the day before.

Carson sat with his back propped against a sizable cottonwood, downing the last few swallows of his coffee. Watching Frank playfully teasing Nancy about some private joke between them, then glancing over at Jonah propped against another tree, his eyes closed, his belly full, Carson realized that they had totally accepted him. The subtle looks of caution that had followed him the first couple of days were now gone. It made him feel comfortable, a feeling that all the unfortunate things that had happened to him were in the past and were of no further concern. He looked forward to Montana now more than ever.

As Jonah had predicted, they came to a sizable creek before noon the following day that had to be the Crazy Woman. They stopped there to rest the horses and prepare a noon meal before pushing on to search for signs of a well-traveled trail to the north. They were unsuccessful in finding a marked trail of any kind and, after some disappointment, decided to turn north anyway. They had reached the foothills of what had to be the Big Horn Mountains, so as Carson had said before, why not ride north until reaching the Yellowstone? "I was so damn sure I would recognize the way I had come with Nancy's father," Jonah said, scratching his head.

"Hell," Frank said, "it doesn't matter how we get there, as long as we get there. Right, John?"

"I reckon," Carson answered. By noon the following day, they discovered old tracks left by a train of wagons when they crossed over a creek to travel the other side, redeeming Jonah and his map. Now all were sure they were traveling the Bozeman Trail.

"You'd all be dead if I was a soldier," he mocked. The three Lakota warriors, sitting around the half-eaten carcass of a calf, were

133

startled by the sudden voice above them on the edge of the bank. They stumbled over each other as they scrambled to get to their weapons to defend themselves against they knew not what. Their wild panic greatly amused the man watching, and he laughed as they dropped pieces of meat and half-gnawed rib bones on the ground in their panic. "You call yourselves Lakota? I think maybe you are Crow women."

"Red Shirt!" Cut Hand exclaimed when he recovered enough to see who had spoken. He lowered the old single-shot rifle he had managed to grab. "Don't shoot!" he warned his two companions. "It is Red Shirt."

"Ha!" Red Shirt spat. "I could shoot you all before any of you had time to pull a trigger. He remained squatting on his heels, the late Luther Moody's Winchester '73 cradled across his thighs, watching contemptuously while the startled threesome tried to regain their composure.

"There are no soldiers around here," Walking Fox stated in their defense. "We had no reason to be careful."

"There is always a reason to be careful," Red Shirt said. "It's a wonder you three are still alive." Although he was talking mainly to insult them, there was a great deal of truth in his comments. Crazy Horse and

Sitting Bull had been defeated, and many of the survivors had escaped to Canada with Sitting Bull. A few, like Cut Hand, Walking Fox, and Lame Foot, had managed to escape the army patrols and continued to make sneak raids on settlers, stealing anything of value, and slaughtering cattle, like the one they feasted upon today. Red Shirt was well known in Cut Hand's village before his people were scattered and forced to go to the reservation. Although a half-breed, Red Shirt claimed to be Lakota and professed to be always at war with the whites, so he had gained a begrudging degree of respect among the Indians. Much of this was due to the fact that the territorial policemen had put a reward on his head. So the three Lakota warriors tolerated his verbal abuse.

"Why do you hide out here on the river," Red Shirt asked, "stealing a cow now and then to keep from starving?" He held his rifle up for them to see. "Look at this rifle. I took it from that fat marshal, Moody, after I killed him and took his scalp. I killed the men he had with him, too. It is a Winchester, the newest model. I took many horses, too, because I don't fight with weapons like those pitiful rifles you carry. My medicine is strong. I know where there are more rifles like this one, and cartridges to go with them. And there are only three men and a woman to guard them." He paused to let that sink in, but he could tell by their envious eyes that he had captured their interest. As soon as he had come upon them feasting on the stolen calf, he knew it had been the stroke of luck that he needed to seek his revenge against Carson Ryan and the three people he was traveling with. With three warriors, he could easily turn the odds in his favor. "I'm on their trail now and I will hunt them down and take more weapons and cartridges."

Walking Fox spoke up then. "Maybe if we went with you, it would make it easier to kill the white men."

"Maybe we could get better weapons for ourselves," Cut Hand suggested.

"Maybe," Red Shirt said, pretending to think deeply on the idea. He affected a noble pose then and nodded solemnly. "It is the right thing to do. I will help my Lakota brothers get weapons and cartridges. We must not linger here, though, for they are two days ahead of us." He knew they would have to ride hard to catch up with Carson, but he was determined now more than ever.

After Swann and Tice were killed, Red Shirt had wasted no time talking trade with

Crazy Jack, and practically gave their horses away, but he didn't care. The defeat at the hands of the young traitor had caused his hatred to fester in his mind until he couldn't know peace until he had settled the score. It had taken some careful scouting, but he had found their tracks crossing the Belle Fourche. They had continued on a steady course to the northwest, and he followed their trail to the Powder, near the place where Cut Hand and his companions had slaughtered the cow. He had been just about to cross when he had smelled the aroma of beef roasting over a fire. Less than two hundred yards upstream, he had found them. Again, he congratulated himself for his luck. If the wind had come from the other direction, he would not have found Cut Hand and the others. This was a good sign that his medicine was strong. He would find young Carson Ryan and he would add his scalp to his scalp stick.

While Red Shirt unsaddled his horse and left it to graze, the three Lakota warriors talked quietly among themselves to make sure joining him was a good thing for them. "He is respected for his war against the whites," Cut Hand said, "and he is said to have killed many of them."

"And we need these guns he speaks of,"

Walking Fox commented. "I say it is wise to ride with him."

Lame Foot had not had much to say since Red Shirt surprised them. "All we have heard about his medicine as a great fighter has come from his mouth. Some in our village don't think he is an honorable man. That is all I know. But we will join him if that is your wish."

When he evaluated his war party the next morning, Red Shirt found that it was not as strong as he had hoped. All three warriors were capable, but their weapons were worse than he had at first thought. To be exact, Cut Hand had an old trading post single-shot rifle, while Lame Foot had a double-barrel shotgun, with only a few shells, and Walking Fox had only a bow. He would give one of them his Spencer carbine to use, but that still left them at a disadvantage in a gunfight with the white men. The difference would be made up, he decided, by the superior skills in tracking, stalking, and fierceness of the Lakota Sioux. He would find these people, and he would be avenged. Of that, he was certain.

Although it was still late summer, the mornings were quite chilly and already there were signs of frost along the lower streambeds.

Traveling through rolling foothills, with the rugged Big Horn Mountains reaching up just west of the trail they now followed, the travelers were struck by conflicting emotions. There was a feeling of growing excitement on the part of the Thompsons as they felt they were not far from the Montana border. At the same time, they could not help being concerned by the cooling weather. As Frank put it, "I swear, I wouldn't be surprised if we got caught in some snow by the time we get to the Yellowstone."

As for Carson, he could feel the heartbeat of the mountains, pulsing in rhythm with his own, and the call to explore those rugged peaks to the west was stronger than ever. The possibility of early snow did not concern him, for he had complete confidence in his ability to adapt to whatever conditions befell him. He might have decided to say good-bye to his new friends and follow the call of his heart had it not been for the feeling of responsibility that had come over him to see them safely to Big Timber.

One afternoon they came upon the ruins of Fort Phil Kearny. The fort, built on a high plateau between the forks of Little Piney Creek, had been burned by the Indians when it was abandoned by the army. There were a few hours of daylight remaining, but Jonah and Frank decided to camp there that night near the burned remains of the palisade walls of the fort. On the high bluffs, it looked to be an ideal place to camp for the night with a good view of a large segment of the Bozeman Trail. A little extra time to rest was welcomed by everyone, including the horses.

Although accustomed to life alone, Carson had to admit that he enjoyed the family atmosphere of traveling with Jonah, Frank, and Nancy. All three were older than he, and he almost regarded them as aunt and uncles. Nancy came very close to mothering him, even though there was not *that* much difference in their ages. Watching her preparing their evening meal, he was prompted to ask Nancy if she knew what the date was. "Why, no, I can't rightly say," she replied, after pausing to think for a moment. "It's got to be sometime in the middle of August. Ask Jonah, he keeps a calendar."

"Ask me what?" Jonah asked as he walked up to place more wood by the fire.

"The date," Nancy said. "John wants to know the date."

"August twenty-eighth," he replied at

once. "I checked my calendar this morning. Why?"

"No particular reason," Carson answered. "I was just wonderin', that's all." In fact, it was of some significance, but only to him, for tomorrow would be his birthday, his eighteenth. He wondered what had prompted him to think about it. His seventeenth had slipped by him unnoticed while he was on a cattle drive. But this one had triggered something in his memory. Maybe it was because it was his eighteenth, and maybe tomorrow would be a lucky day for him and his friends. At any rate, he planned to keep it to himself.

The morning began as every morning had begun before that. They roused themselves out of their bedrolls before sunup and saddled the horses while Nancy made the one pot of coffee they would drain before starting out again on the now well-defined Bozeman Trail. They would stop to eat breakfast when it was time to rest the horses. On this morning, however, they were a little later than usual getting started, because one of the packhorses decided it would not accept the packs. Carson gave Jonah a hand with the reluctant animal, and between the efforts of the two, the horse finally called off the rebellion. By the time all were ready to climb into the saddle, the first rays of the sun were already tipping the leaves in the tops of the cottonwoods down by the creek. "Let's get started," Jonah said, and climbed up into the saddle. Carson heard the dull thud of the bullet as it impacted with Jonah's back at almost the same time he heard the crack of the rifle that fired it. Jonah sat straight up in the saddle as the second shot thudded against his back. Then he slumped to the side, falling into the arms of his brother, who rushed to help him.

"Get down!" Carson yelled, and threw himself at Nancy, who was standing motionless in shock, knocking her to the ground. Realizing they were both stunned by the sudden horror, he grabbed Frank, who was staggering under the weight of his brother, and pulled him to the ground as several more shots zipped over their heads. He made a quick check of Jonah, but he was already dead. "Crawl over behind those timbers!" he directed, pointing toward a low corner of a building about three logs high that the Indians' fires had somehow spared. "I'll get the horses!" Moving as quickly as he could, he gathered the reins of all the horses and ran inside what was once a seventeen-acre compound, but was now a burned outline where there had once been log walls. With no prior plans for defense, he looked around hurriedly for a place to leave the horses. The only possibility, a stack of burned timbers that had once been a cavalry barracks, was the closest thing he saw, so he made for them, calling out to Frank as he did, "Get that rifle workin'! I'll be right back!" He led the horses behind the pile of timbers and tied them, pulled his rifle from his saddle sling, grabbed the extra rifle and a cartridge belt from one of the packhorses, then got back to Frank and Nancy as quickly as possible. The return trip was a good bit hotter since he no longer had the string of horses to use as cover.

With bullets flying all about him, he dived for cover beside Frank, cocked his rifle, and immediately threw shot after shot at the low shrubs by the creek when he saw a muzzle flash. "Could you see any of 'em?" he asked Frank.

"Jonah," Frank responded. "We've gotta get Jonah."

Carson realized then that Frank was still in a state of shock over having seen his brother shot down, and had not fired a shot at the creek. Carson reached over and felt the barrel of the Winchester he had given him. The barrel was cold. "Frank," he said roughly, "Jonah's gone. There ain't nothin' we can do for him now, so we've gotta keep throwin' lead at that patch of bushes down by the creek, and maybe we can scare 'em off." He felt Nancy move up beside his arm.

"Give me the other rifle," she said. "I'll shoot it."

He laid the cartridge belt between them, and she wasted no time in firing at the shrubs he had pointed out. Following her lead, Frank finally put his rifle to use. Carson took a moment to evaluate their position. There was nothing but open space between them and the people shooting at them, so they were not likely to charge them, but he was concerned about their rear. From the shots fired so far, he figured that it was a small party attacking them, but how small? Big enough to split up and send half their force to circle around behind them — maybe to make a try for the horses? He had to make sure. "Can you two keep an eye on that fork of the creek down yonder? I don't think it's a very big party, and I doubt they wanna try chargin' across that open bluff. I need to check behind us in case some of 'em's thinkin' about gettin' us caught in a cross fire." He figured that was what he would do if he was in their shoes. "We can't let 'em get to the horses."

144

Nancy answered for them. "We can do that. Frank and I will shoot anybody who tries to run across that clearing. But you be careful. Don't you get yourself shot and leave us to fight the Indians alone."

"I won't," Carson said. "Just be sure to keep your heads down." Then he withdrew, trying to keep his head low as he crawled backward. When he felt the contour of the plateau inhibited their line of sight, he got to his feet and ran to the horses. He found them where he had left them, pulling against the reins that tied them to the scorched timbers. Frightened by the sound of constant gunfire, their natural instincts told them to run. He took a few minutes to try to calm them down before finding some protection for himself while watching the open parade ground behind them. As he settled in behind a partially burned doorsill, he couldn't help worrying about the two guarding the front. Frank seemed visibly shaken by the surprise attack. Carson supposed it was mainly the loss of his brother that had gripped him with such paralysis, but he appeared to have come out of it when Nancy stepped up. Picturing the determined woman, he was at once reassured that she could handle the situation.

■ ■ ■ ■

"Damn the luck," Red Shirt cursed. "If we had attacked them at night, we wouldn't have had to sit back under this bluff and shoot at 'em at this range." It was frustrating to have caught up with them and yet be unable to advance close enough to kill them. All the sign he had read during the previous day had told him that he was almost upon them. It prompted him to ride on late into the night until the horses became so tired they were forced to make camp. And then to catch up with them only in time to see them leaving their camp was too much for Red Shirt's patience. So when the shot presented itself, even at a fairly long range, he could not resist the temptation to take it. He had succeeded in killing one of them, but the others escaped, including the one he really wanted. He slid back down from the bank to confer with his partners after making sure Carson and the other two were not going to make an attempt to ride out the other end of the fort.

"I think it would be a good thing to get around behind them and steal the horses," Walking Fox said.

"That would not be easy in the daylight,"

Lame Foot said.

"What you say is true," Walking Fox countered. "But there are enough old beds where the buildings were burned that if a man is a skillful scout, there is a good chance he could find the horses. And without their horses, they would be at our mercy. I am such a man."

Red Shirt nodded. "I've been thinking the same thing," he said. It had occurred to him, but he had discarded the idea because the fort behind Carson was just as open as that expanse before them now. Maybe Walking Fox was right. Maybe there were enough old beds to use for cover. He tried to picture the *beds* Walking Fox spoke of, knowing he was referring to some old foundations where buildings had once stood. "It is possible," Red Shirt said, "but it would be dangerous, and would take a man who could move quickly and carefully."

"I am such a man," Walking Fox repeated, drawing his shoulders back proudly.

"Yes," Red Shirt said, "you are such a man. Go, then, and we will keep them pinned down from here."

"I will go with you," Cut Hand offered, "to help with their horses."

Red Shirt smiled. "It's a good plan. Cut back near the forks of the creek and come up the other side. Me and Lame Foot will keep 'em busy."

With no sign of anyone coming up from the other side of the parade ground, Carson took the time to drag a couple of charred timbers over to lay on top of his doorsill in an effort to build a higher barricade for him and his rifle. The sun was starting its daily climb into the prairie sky. It made him wonder if Nancy and Frank had a canteen of water with them. If not, they might get mighty thirsty if the siege lasted all day. He thought of Frank then, and the tragic killing of his brother, and wondered if he had been in any way to blame. Maybe he should have routinely been scouting their back trail each night to make sure no one was following them. It had never occurred to him to do so. Then he wondered if it was Red Shirt who was shooting at them. *If it is,* he thought, *he sure got himself some help awful fast.* But the more he thought about it, the more likely it seemed to him. These and other thoughts raced through his mind, and it occurred to him then that he had definitely assumed the responsibility for seeing Frank and Nancy safely to their destination in Montana. Thinking of the long day of waiting before them, he wondered if he should take the canteen from his saddle and sneak back to them. "Hell, I don't know," he mumbled, realizing that he didn't like the role as the person in charge. Further thoughts were curtailed for the moment when a slight movement near the old officers' row caught his eye.

Immediately back in the moment, he laid his rifle across one of the timbers he had dragged into position and strained to see what had prompted him to become alert. There was nothing for several minutes, causing him to believe it had been the wind blowing the sage that had grown up along the old palisade wall. He was about to shift his gaze to scan the empty parade ground again when he saw them. First one, then a second figure crawled from behind the scorched rubble of a building to take cover behind the ruins of a house that had stood next door. His instinct had been right on. They were making a play for the horses.

He quickly checked his rifle to make sure it was ready to fire, then shifted his focus back to the ruins of what appeared to have been a row of small buildings. With his rifle aimed at the space between the houses, waiting for the two to appear, he cautioned himself not to fire until they had made their way a little closer. In a second, they reappeared, and he could definitely identify them as Indians, and it was obvious that they planned to gain the protection of the pile of burned lumber that had once been a large building of some sort. From there, it was a distance of perhaps fifty yards of open ground to the horses gathered behind him. Although he had a shot, he told himself not to take it, not sure if he would be able to get a clear shot at both stalkers. And he needed to get both, because now that he had seen that only two had circled around behind them, he was sure it was a very small party of Indians. If he could kill both of these two, it might discourage the others from pressing their losses and maybe convince them that they had chosen the wrong camp to attack. So he waited.

After what seemed to him to be an unusually long wait, the two warriors evidently decided to make their move. Only one of them appeared from behind the pile of rubble, however. He ran in a crouched lope across the open space, covering about half the distance to the horses when the other warrior followed him. Carson didn't take time to puzzle over the interval between the two. Maybe it was to determine if there was anyone watching the horses. Whatever the reason, it meant Carson's reactions were going to be tested if he was to kill both warriors, so he flattened himself as best he could behind his charred breastworks, hoping the first warrior could not see him.

Walking Fox loped past the timbers piled low across the burned-out sill at a distance of perhaps fifteen yards, never noticing the man lying flat behind them. Carson waited until he had run past; then he slowly raised his rifle to sight in on Cut Hand, who was still only a few feet from the protection of the ruined building. Taking careful aim, he squeezed the trigger. When the Winchester fired, he didn't wait to see Cut Hand fall, instead reversing his position at once to bear down on Walking Fox, who spun around at the sound of the gunshot. The Winchester spoke again, slamming a slug against the Lakota's chest before he could raise his carbine to fire. It had happened so fast that Carson did not remember cocking the rifle between the first and second shot.

Back under the bluff on the other side of the fort, Red Shirt cursed, for the two shots he heard were unmistakably from a Winchester rifle, and they were the only shots heard. There were none from the old single-shot rifle Cut Hand carried, or the Spencer carbine he had given Walking Fox. "Damn him," he spat, knowing that Carson had gotten both of them. His frustration with the young man was beyond control, so much so that he rose and fired half a dozen reckless shots at the corner where Frank and Nancy had taken refuge. Two answering shots prompted him to duck down again.

Like Red Shirt, Lame Foot realized the two shots they had first heard were not from the weapons his two friends carried, but he had not come to the same conclusion that caused Red Shirt to curse. "Maybe they were not able to get to the horses," he said. "Maybe we will have to wait until night. Then we can slip in, kill them, and take the horses."

"Walking Fox and Cut Hand are dead!" Red Shirt spat back at him. He knew it to be true, just as sure as if he had witnessed the shooting. "That damn coyote pup does not miss with that rifle of his. He was sent here to devil me!" Oblivious of Lame Foot's questioning stare, Red Shirt fumed on. "I had him once, tied to a tree. I set him free to let him ride with me, and the devil turned on me. I should have killed him when I had the chance."

"Maybe they not dead," Lame Foot insisted, not ready to concede to Carson's invincibility, in spite of Red Shirt's ranting.

"They're dead," Red Shirt pronounced

emphatically.

"I go see," Lame Foot said, not at all happy with Red Shirt's lack of concern for his friends' fate. It had been several minutes now with still no sound of shots from the Lakota warriors. "I go see," he repeated.

"You ain't gonna find nothin' but two dead Injuns," Red Shirt called after him as Lame Foot scrambled back down the bluff to follow the same path his friends had taken. He needed to kill someone so badly that he was tempted to raise his rifle and shoot Lame Foot in the back. *He still hasn't won yet,* he thought, referring to Carson Ryan. *Lame Foot and I can still keep them pinned down with me in the front and him in the back.*

Carson remained where he was, watching the parade ground to make sure there were no other raiders trying to close in on them. He felt sure Frank and Nancy were probably nervous, wondering about the two shots he had taken. When he heard the barrage of rifle shots from below the bluff, and the shots fired in response, he wanted to run back to support them, but he stayed a few minutes longer before deeming it safe to abandon his post even briefly.

"We were wondering," Frank said when

153

Carson crawled in beside them.

"Two of 'em tried for the horses," Carson said. "I got both of 'em. I heard a lot of shootin' from back here. What was that about?"

"I don't know," Frank replied. "One of them just took a notion to pop up and blaze away. We both took a shot at him, but I don't think we hit him."

"I know we didn't," Nancy added.

"I got a feelin' there ain't but two or three of 'em left, and I'm hopin' they might decide to give up on us since they just lost two. If you can hang on here for a while longer, I'll go back to make sure there ain't nobody else tryin' to get behind us. If there ain't, we might be able to slip out the back and find a better place to hole up." He paused. "Is that all right with you?" They both nodded enthusiastically, more than ready to abandon Fort Phil Kearny. "All right, then, I'll go back to the horses."

The first thing he noticed when he returned to his makeshift breastworks was that the body of the foremost Indian had been moved several yards. Possibly Walking Fox had not been dead and tried to drag himself back, but the thing that puzzled him most was the fact that the carbine he had carried was missing. He looked back at the

154

other body and it appeared to be in the same place it had fallen. He paused only a moment to consider the risk, then decided there were no others behind the rubble of the large building, so he went out in the open parade ground where the body lay. There were footprints around the body and back toward the ruins where the other body lay. He didn't hesitate to follow them, certain that the Indian who had left the tracks was in full retreat. When he got past the remains of the back palisades, he stopped. The tracks went on down toward the fork of the Little Piney Creek. It was a sign to him that it was his party's chance to slip out the back of the fort, so he immediately turned around and went back to Nancy and Frank.

Red Shirt had been right, and Lame Foot thought about how certain the half-breed had been that Cut Hand and Walking Fox were dead. From the beginning of their chance meeting with Red Shirt, Lame Foot had been the one who had uneasy feelings about joining the notorious renegade. The death of his two friends told him that Red Shirt's medicine was bad, and they should not have gone with him to hunt this white devil with the medicine gun. Lame Foot believed now that Red Shirt knew this man, Carson, would kill his friends, otherwise he would have warned them not to go after the horses. So he decided to leave before he, too, was sacrificed to the medicine gun.

His first thought had been to recover Cut Hand's and Walking Fox's bodies, since the white man had gone when he found them. But he soon realized that he could not carry both bodies without the horses, so he returned to the fork of the creek where they had tied the horses. He had a change of heart when he got there, thinking that he should forget the bodies and save himself from more of Red Shirt's bad medicine. He decided it was also wrong to leave all the horses with Red Shirt, so he jumped on his pony, took the reins of their horses, and rode out to the south, leaving Red Shirt to deal with his own fate.

Farther up the bluff, Red Shirt paused suddenly to listen. *Someone was stealing the horses!* In a panic, he backed away from the edge of the bluff and raced down toward the creek in time to see Lame Foot galloping away, leading two horses. Enraged to think he had run out on him, he raised his rifle and fired, but Lame Foot was not an easy target as he rode behind the high bushes on the bank of the creek. It was only then that Red Shirt realized that his horses were still there. That was still not enough to quell Red Shirt's anger. He sprinted toward the horse and was in the saddle within a few minutes' time, flailing the blue roan mercilessly as he set out after Lame Foot.

Above him, running through the ruins of the fort, Carson arrived at the edge of the plateau just in time to see their assailant ride away. "Red Shirt!" he exclaimed when he saw the black horse that had once belonged to Luther Moody. The evil half-breed was still stalking them. For a moment, he was torn between two choices: go after Red Shirt immediately or get Nancy and Frank away to a better place to defend themselves. This was the second time he had tangled with Red Shirt, and the second time Red Shirt had suffered the loss of men. The half-breed was not likely to accept his defeat and call it a day. Carson knew it was simply a matter of time before it had to be settled between them. He looked back at Frank, who had taken a few steps out from the charred timbers, and now stood watching him, waiting to be told what to do. He was clearly unable to make sensible decisions yet, so Carson again felt the responsibility for the couple's welfare and quickly made his decision.

"Frank!" he yelled. "Get Nancy ready to ride. We've got to get out of here now while we've got the chance. Sooner or later that son of a bitch is gonna try to get on our trail again, so we need to put as much distance between us and him as we can."

"Right!" Frank yelled back, then hesitated. "Jonah. What about Jonah?"

"We'll put him on his horse and take him with us," Carson answered. "When we get to a safe place, we'll bury him there. All right?"

"All right," Nancy answered for her husband. "Come on, Frank." They ran toward the ruins where Carson had left the horses.

Carson watched them for a brief second before turning back to look in the direction he had last seen Red Shirt. He was distracted then by the sound of a horse's whinny, and his attention was called to a lone packhorse standing near the edge of the creek below the bluffs. Red Shirt had galloped away in such a fury that he hadn't spent the time to take it with him. The mental image of the furious murderer caused Carson to make sure he didn't lose any more time himself. He paused another moment to decide, however, then ran down to the forks of the creek and untied the packhorse. An extra horse could afford them the advantage of distributing the load on their packhorses, not only lightening the load, but speeding up their flight as well.

Red Shirt had even added to their convenience by leaving the packsaddle on the horse. Carson did not bother to search through the packs, but there was a sack of grain he was glad to find. He kept it and dropped the other packs to the ground, but one item caught his eye. Strapped to one of the packs, a small wooden rod about five feet long with wisps of various shades of hair had fallen from the pack strap to land at the edge of the water — *Red Shirt's scalp stick.* Carson picked it up with a gnawing feeling of disgust when he remembered the half-breed adding Luther Moody's and his posse man's scalps to his coveted trophy. In a moment of anger, he propped one end of it on the ground and stomped it with his foot, breaking it in two. Then as a sign for the savage, he stuck the two broken halves in the sandy shore. With that small feeling of satisfaction, he led the horse back up to the fort.

Frank and Nancy were working frantically to make sure everything was ready to travel, and when Carson arrived with the extra horse, he found them struggling with Jonah's body. "Here," Carson said to Nancy, and handed her the lead rope on the pack-horse. She stood back then and watched while Carson and her husband loaded her brother-in-law across his horse. Once the corpse was settled, Carson took a length of rope from the saddle to make sure Jonah stayed put after telling a teary-eyed Frank to go shift some of the packs to the spare horse.

When all was ready, they said good-bye to the ruins of Fort Phil Kearny with no regrets in leaving. Carson led them across the western branch of Little Piney Creek and set a course for the Big Horn Mountains. He could not estimate how much time they had before Red Shirt would pick up their trail, but he figured their best chance of losing him was to leave the Bozeman Trail and take to the mountains.

CHAPTER 7

Carson set a fast pace toward the mountains with two of the packhorses trailing behind his bay gelding. Nancy led the other packhorse and followed, with Frank bringing up the rear, leading his brother's horse. Watching Carson sitting tall in the saddle ahead, Nancy found it hard to believe that he was so young. His coolness under pressure and his ability to assess the situation, then take charge of it, were nothing short of a godsend when she and Frank had been plainly devastated. She forgave Frank his moments of indecision, for she could hardly blame him when seeing his brother struck down so suddenly. She was not so compassionate for her own actions, however. She had held Jonah in high esteem and certainly had fond feelings for Frank's older brother, but she had always prided herself in her ability to respond strongly to any test of will or strength. She had a feeling that she had better not have any more of those moments of indecision, because they were not out of danger yet. She looked beyond the tall young man to the mountains where they hoped to find refuge. They had been riding toward the lofty, foreboding peaks for what seemed like hours, yet they seemed to be no closer than they had been when they first crossed the river. Then they followed a narrow valley through the hills and came out to find the mountain suddenly looming right before them.

Carson let up on the bay and allowed the horse to set its own pace for a while as he rode parallel to the base of the mountains. When he came to a wide stream coming down from the slopes above, he stopped and told Nancy and Frank what he wanted them to do. "Ride straight into the water, like you were goin' straight across. Make sure those horses you're leadin' go straight after you. Then when you get all of 'em in the middle, turn downstream and stay in the water. Don't let 'em leave any prints on the banks. Just do like I do."

"You mean turn upstream, don't you?" Nancy asked. "I thought we were trying to get to the mountains."

"We are," Carson replied. "I'm just hopin' we can buy us a little more time. If Red

Shirt follows us this far, he might figure we're tryin' to hide in the mountains. He'll see we never crossed over the stream, and know we're tryin' to hide our trail. If we're lucky, he'll ride the stream up into the mountains, lookin' for the place we came out of the water. It'd be a whole lot easier if we weren't leadin' horses, but if we're careful, we can do it without leavin' tracks." He gave his horse a nudge and entered the water. He had to ride almost to the other side before the two packhorses were both in the water, but after that there was no problem in leading them downstream. Nancy and Frank followed his example and all the horses filed after him.

The stream began to narrow after about a quarter of a mile, so Carson watched for a good place to come out of the water. A stone shelf that extended into the stream was the answer, so he led them out at that point, onto a grassy slope, and headed north once again. He looked back to check on his followers and received a smile of confidence from Nancy.

The sun was settling down in the western sky when they came to a likely path into the mountains. Carson chose a game trail that led up a ravine, because it appeared to have a gentle rise that would not tax their horses greatly. By this time the horses were in need of rest, and their riders were past ready to make camp and prepare something to eat. As they rode in the heavy shadow of the mountain, it seemed to be later in the day than it actually was, so Carson took extra care while guiding the bay up the narrow game trail.

Frank and Nancy rode silently behind their young guide, never questioning his choice of trails or suggesting alternative plans. Without consciously thinking about it, both had put their complete trust in the man they had known for such a brief amount of time. They were sure Carson would find the right place to camp, and their confidence appeared to be justified when the game trail they followed leveled off at the top of the ravine and took a sharp turn to follow a ledge that led them to a narrow stream. A small meadow was bisected by the busy stream, and just below it, a belt of evergreen trees circled the foot of the mountain. It was a perfect campsite, Nancy thought, and she marveled at Carson's instincts to find such a place. It not only provided grass and water, but more importantly, it appeared that the only access to it was to follow the narrow trail along the ledge. It would be hard for Red

Shirt to get across that ledge without being seen.

The same thoughts were alive in Carson's mind as he assessed the campsite, with some slight difference in viewpoint. He had had no idea where the game trail would lead them when he started up it, and he was fully as surprised as Nancy was when they saw all that it offered. He had suspected that the night might be spent with no grass or water for the horses, but because of the lateness of the hour, he had had to pick someplace while there was still enough light to make camp.

After Carson and Frank lifted Jonah's body from his horse, all three helped in taking care of the horses. No one voiced it, but neither Frank nor Nancy could think about preparing a meal before burying Frank's brother. Looking around her, she picked a spot near the upper end of the little meadow and pointed to it. "That would be a good place to lay Jonah to rest," she suggested.

"Yeah," Frank said. "Jonah would like that. Nice and high. He can look out over that little valley below."

"We'd better get to diggin' a grave before it gets much darker," Carson said.

"Right," Frank replied. "I'll get a shovel and a pickax from the packs."

"I'm going to need wood for a fire," Nancy said when Frank returned with the pick and a short-handled shovel.

"There oughta be plenty of it down in those trees," Frank said. "I'll go scare up some for you before we start digging."

Nancy looked uncertain as she glanced at Carson. "Do you think it's all right to burn that wood? Pines and firs make a lot of smoke, don't they?"

"Well, yeah," Carson replied. "I reckon they do, but I don't think anybody would be able to see it, dark as it is back in this hollow. They'd be more likely to smell it, but I doubt it, as high as we are above the prairie, and I don't think Red Shirt is anywhere near enough this soon. I'll go help Frank gather wood."

It was not an easy task, digging in the hard, rocky soil under the grass. The short-handled shovel was especially irritating to work with for someone with a long, lanky frame like Carson's. It was well after dark when the job was completed, the final dirt excavated by lantern light. Nancy's bacon and beans, having been set to warm at the edge of the fire, had already dried out to the extent that a little while longer wouldn't cause much more harm. So they decided to go ahead and lay Jonah to rest and then eat.

Nancy asked Frank if he felt like saying some words over his brother's body before they lowered him into the Wyoming mountainside, but he declined, saying he didn't know what to say. So she offered a prayer for Jonah's safe passage to heaven, and promised that she and Frank would never forget him. Carson stood to the side and watched, waiting to fill in the grave. It was a short ceremony, but one with proper mourning, especially for Frank, who had looked to his older brother to make the important decisions for him. When it was done, they retired to the campfire to eat.

There was a sense of relief in the camp that night, with a feeling of safety in their mountainside meadow. Carson alone seemed concerned about the possibility of a night visitor in the person of a revenge-seeking savage. He had seen the brutal hostile up close and knew the passion to kill that drove him relentlessly. Having no idea when Red Shirt would return to Fort Phil Kearny to pick up their trail, he could not guess how much time they had before he came. But even if it was right away, it would be impossible for him to catch up with them tonight. And if they were lucky, he might not find their trail after they left the stream. They had left the water onto a rock ledge and ridden across a grassy rise. By the time he was on their trail, the grass might have recovered enough so that their hoofprints were no longer visible. All that considered, he figured they could count on a peaceful night. However, just in case, he decided he would spread his blanket at the head of the ledge and tether his horse beside him to help alert him if anyone came calling.

The night passed without incident, and the sun woke the camp early when it shone brightly on the east side of the mountain. Carson led his horse to the stream and watched him drink, his mind turning over the options available to the party of three. He knew they could return to the base of the mountain the same way they had come up, and start again to the north. But the adventurer in him caused him to wonder where they would come out if they continued to follow the game trail that led them to this place. When the bay finished drinking, he dropped his reins and walked to the other side of the meadow near the freshly dug grave and looked out across the mountain as far as he could see. The trail appeared to lead deeper around the mountain, toward another mountain. *Maybe,* he wondered, *there's a passable valley between them.* He was still contemplating the possibility when Frank and Nancy came up behind him.

"We're ready to go," Frank said. "I guess we'll have to ride back down that ravine the same way we came up here."

"Yeah," Carson said, hesitating. "Or we could keep followin' this game trail around the mountain and see where it takes us."

"Wouldn't that just take us up the mountain?" Nancy asked, wondering how that would help them when their goal was to reach Montana.

"I don't think so," Carson replied. "I would guess that it's a trail through the mountains. The only tracks I've seen on it are deer tracks, and they ain't likely wantin' to climb up to the top of this mountain. I'm thinkin' this trail might lead us through to a valley or someplace where we can just head straight north again for the Yellowstone, and leave Red Shirt to keep lookin' for us on the Bozeman Trail." He paused to hear their thoughts on the idea. "I ain't sayin' I'm right, but it would make Red Shirt's job a lot harder, and we can always turn north somewhere, even if we're deep in the mountains."

Frank looked at Nancy and shrugged. From the look on both their faces, Carson could see that they had no strong objection to the gamble. He did not realize that they had no notion as to a good plan or a bad one. After Jonah's death, the two of them were lost. Jonah was the older brother who always led, and he was the only one of them who had actually been to Big Timber. So now they looked to Carson for leadership. It didn't matter that he had never been in this country before, because they both had the feeling that he would find a way. They feared Red Shirt, but a bigger fear would be the possibility of losing Carson. Frank and Nancy were prone now to follow Carson's instincts. "It might be the right thing to do, at that," Frank said. "I like it better than going back down the way we came and maybe running into that murdering Indian on his way up."

So it was decided. Frank and Nancy said a final farewell to Jonah, and the travelers started out again, following the narrow game path farther into the rugged Big Horn Mountains.

As peaceful as the night had been for the party of three white people, it had proven to be one of desperation for the Lakota, Lame Foot. He had not been lucky enough to escape without having been seen by Red Shirt. Racing over the rolling prairie, he had whipped his laboring pony mercilessly, but the angry avenger's blue roan was steadily closing the distance between them. In desperation, he released the two horses he was leading, hoping Red Shirt would go after them, and let him go. Red Shirt ignored the two horses and continued after Lame Foot, his anger too strong to allow Lame Foot to escape after having betrayed him.

Up a dusty draw and over a gentle rise, dotted with sagebrush, Lame Foot pushed the exhausted horse, knowing he had to find a place to make a stand. Another quarter of a mile and he saw a line of bushes that defined a small creek, and he knew that was going to have to be the place, so he whipped the failing pony and headed toward it. He could defend himself now that he had the Spencer carbine Red Shirt had given him. He was a Lakota warrior; he should not fear the notorious killer. The thought had no sooner entered his mind than he was startled by the snap of a rifle slug passing close beside him. Red Shirt had closed to within range of the Winchester he carried. Lame Foot shrieked involuntarily and whipped his horse again. The wind-broken horse made it to the creek, where it collapsed, sliding through a crop of berry bushes and throwing Lame Foot from the saddle to land in the middle of the shallow creek.

On hands and knees in the water, Lame Foot looked around him frantically, trying to find the carbine that had been tossed somewhere in the bushes when the horse went down. It was nowhere in sight. In a panic, he scrambled out of the creek just as Red Shirt pulled his spent horse to a stop twenty yards away and dismounted. Seeing that Lame Foot had no weapon, Red Shirt stood watching the frightened man, savoring the advantage he held. Short in stature, but powerfully built with wide shoulders and muscular arms, he looked to be the devil incarnate as he stood holding the Winchester in one hand, leering wickedly at the hapless Lame Foot.

They stood motionless for a few moments, staring at each other, one with a sickening expression of fear on his face, the other with the gloating smile of an executioner. "I got no use for a cowardly dog who betrays me," Red Shirt scorned.

In fearful anticipation of the bullet he knew would be coming to claim him, Lame Foot began to sway slightly from side to side, and he began to chant his death song. The mournful notes from the frightened man served to please Red Shirt even more, and he let Lame Foot suffer the anticipation of his death several minutes more before he slowly raised his rifle and ended his song.

His thirst for vengeance satisfied, only then did he pause to assess his situation. His horse was spent, it was already late in the afternoon, and he was several miles from his packhorse. Thinking that the three white people he was determined to kill might have taken the opportunity to escape, he knew that he had no time to waste. There was no choice but to walk back to the fort and lead his horse. He looked quickly back behind him to see if the two extra horses Lame Foot had released were anywhere in sight. They were not, and he cursed them for running away. He looked then at Lame Foot's horse and knew that it was spent. Angry again, he took the time to take Lame Foot's scalp before turning to glimpse his carbine a few yards away in the bushes. He put the Spencer in his saddle sling, and with his Winchester in his hand, he took the blue roan's reins and started back.

He reached the forks of Little Piney Creek in the fading light of day to find his packhorse gone and his packs spilled upon the ground. His horse went immediately to the water to drink. Red Shirt, furious that he had to admit to himself that he should not have chased Lame Foot, was now faced with the loss of many of his supplies. He could not carry them all on one horse. He needed a packhorse, and in his anger he had left Lame Foot's horse behind. It would have been no more trouble to lead the horse along with his. The thought caused his fury to rise to a level he could not contain. Then he looked at his horse drinking from the creek and discovered the two broken pieces of his scalp stick, stuck unceremoniously in the sand at the water's edge. He threw his head back and howled like a wolf, thinking it a challenge from the young white man. "I will cut your guts out and eat your liver!" he roared out at the dark and silent fort on the plateau above him.

To confirm what he already knew to be true, he went up the bluffs to the deserted army fort. They had gone, but there was enough light remaining to see the direction they had taken. He followed a difficult trail on the baked-out dirt until reaching a portion of the parade ground that was knee high in grass and weeds. Even in the growing darkness, the trail left through the weeds by seven horses was plain to see. It told him that they had left in a hurry, taking no time to hide their tracks. Unfortunately for him, he could not follow their tracks until morning, no matter how anxious he was to catch them. But he promised himself that he would follow Carson Ryan to Canada, if he went that far.

As Carson had hoped, the game trail led them around the mountain and descended to pass between the mountain they had camped on and a higher one north of it. The trail wound back to the west, where they appeared to be approaching a dead end at the foot of the rock face of yet another mountain. To their surprise, there was a small passage on the south side of the mountain that the game trail entered. It brought them to a narrow canyon bisected by a wide stream. Since it had been a hard morning's work for the horses, they decided it best to rest them there. With the steep walls of the mountains on either side of them, they settled down to eat their midday meal. There was a sense of protection within those high walls, shutting out the evils of the surrounding prairie grassland. It was almost enough to lull the small party of travelers into a false sense of safety, so much so that Frank suggested staying there for the rest of the day. "Our horses are looking real tired, and I'm thinking they sure need a little more time to rest up." Carson had to agree with his assessment of the horses' condition, even though the bay he rode appeared much stronger than theirs. He was not enthusiastic about delaying their escape that long, but justified it for the simple reason that the horses would serve them better in the long run. So they stayed where they were, gave the horses an extra ration of grain, and let them rest for the balance of that day.

Nancy gave voice to the feeling of security. "As many twists and turns as we've taken today, I don't think anyone could have followed us."

Carson reminded her that even though the way had been difficult at times, they had been following a game trail. "Anybody else could follow the same trail," he said. "And Red Shirt can follow where there ain't no trail."

"I declare, John, you sure know how to spoil a perfectly good picnic." She stood over him, about to refill his coffee cup. "I've a good mind not to give you any more coffee until you can show us you can smile." She nodded to her husband then. "And the same goes for you, Frank. I know you're hurting. I miss Jonah, too, but we've got to turn our thoughts toward making a new life in Montana."

"I know what you're trying to do," Frank said. "It's just a little bit too soon for me to start kicking up my heels and singing a song. We only laid Jonah to rest last night. I need a little more time to get over the fact that he's gone."

She said no more, but proceeded to fill the cups of both men, then busied herself with the chore of washing their plates in the stream. Her life had been nothing less than one terrifying moment after another ever since they had left Custer City in the Black Hills. And she was terribly afraid of the vengeful murderer who seemed determined to kill them all. But she was reluctant to tell Frank of her fears, for she felt that he was as afraid as she, and she was trying to maintain a brave and cheerful front to encourage him. *God help us if anything happens to John,* she thought. She paused then to look back at their young guide, sitting by the small fire they had built to cook their food. *He's so serious.* Then another thought entered her mind. *Some guide, he doesn't know where we are, or where we're going.* That bit of irony made her chuckle in earnest.

As they expected, the night passed peacefully with no guests.

Back in the saddle the next morning, Carson led them along the stream until he found the point where the trail began again. They followed it between two more mountains and out onto a broader valley. At this point, the game trail took a sharp turn and headed almost due south, following the valley. Carson pulled up to confer with his fellow travelers. "It ain't gonna do us no good to stay on this trail." He pointed to the sun, then back to the trail. "We need to keep the sun on our left shoulder. If we follow that trail any longer, the sun'll be on our right shoulder, and that ain't the way to the Yellowstone."

"Well, whaddaya wanna do?" Frank asked.

"If it was up to me, I'd say stay with this valley till it runs out," Carson answered. "It's headin' in the right direction for one thing."

"Well, it is up to you," Nancy quickly remarked, "so I guess that's the best thing to do." There was no argument from Frank, so they turned north and followed the valley.

They were still following the valley when nightfall caught up with them, and they made their camp in a small cluster of trees near the edge of a creek that flowed down from the mountains beside them. There was good grass, and the water was swift and clear. Since there had been little opportunity during the last few days to do so, Nancy decided it was time to take a bath. After they had eaten their supper, she announced her intention to do so.

"Not me," Frank said. "You're liable to freeze to death in that water."

"I don't care," Nancy replied. "I declare, I'm downright grimy. I've got to have a bath, and I need to get out of these clothes and give them a good cleaning."

"Well, don't say I didn't warn you," Frank said, "when you come down with pneumonia." He looked at Carson then and shook his head.

Carson figured this was one decision he had no say in, but he tended to side with Frank, and he wondered how Nancy could even think of taking a bath with Red Shirt lurking out there somewhere. "Well, if you decide that's what you're gonna do," he said, "I reckon I could take a little ride back down the valley just to make sure we ain't got no company. That would give you a little privacy to take your bath." He had planned to scout their back trail, anyway, just to be safe. With the trail they had ridden since leaving Fort Phil Kearny, it seemed damn near impossible for anyone to follow them, but he didn't trust Red Shirt. He was halfway convinced that the half-breed was part devil.

"You don't have to leave," Nancy said. "I can just go on the other side of those bushes hanging over the creek. You can stay here and talk to Frank."

"I was gonna take a look around behind us anyway," Carson replied. He finished his coffee and rinsed the cup in the creek. As he did, he couldn't help commenting, "That water is a mite cold, though." He picked up his rifle and started walking back the way they had come. "I'll sing out when I come back in."

When they thought he was out of earshot, he heard Frank say, "I'd better watch you take your bath in case there's some bears or something around."

"You stay right there by the fire," she told him. "You don't need to be looking at me. If any bears come around, I'll send them over to you."

"Ah, shoot," he replied. "It's not gonna hurt just to look."

"Now, Frank," she scolded playfully, "you know it's not good for you to start thinking those thoughts when we're in a place where you can't do anything about it."

Walking back through the trees, Carson couldn't help chuckling to himself. They might need a little time to themselves, because there certainly hadn't been any since he had joined them. Leaving the creek, he walked back along the valley they had ridden along, looking for signs that might tell him they were still being followed, but expecting none. It seemed more unlikely now that Red Shirt had picked up their trail. If he had, he would have caught them by now, since they had lost almost a full day when they took extra time to rest the horses.

As he walked, he was struck by the heavy silence of the broad valley, especially in contrast with the noisy hum of insects back by the creek. And he was reminded once more how much he enjoyed the nighttime. He had never even minded riding nighthawk when he was driving a herd. Nighttime was a good time to think on the many things there was no time for during the day. He wondered then what had become of Duke Slayton and Johnny Briggs, and Bad Eye — and Lute. It struck him then that Lute might have come close to warning him that day. The old man was not at all anxious to ride to the support of his friends. And he thought to himself how much he would like to run into them somewhere in the future, so he could thank them personally for the fine mess they made of his life. Maybe it made no difference now, for he never planned to visit Wyoming Territory again. Then he laughed at himself for having been taken in for a fool, and he remembered thinking they were the worst drovers he had ever ridden with.

His thoughts returned to the couple back in the camp, and he wondered if Nancy enjoyed her cold bath. He was prompted to wonder then why Frank and Nancy had no children. He had no idea how long they had been married, but they didn't act like newlyweds. *Well, ain't none of my business,* he thought. *Maybe Frank ain't figured out how to make a baby.* He grinned at the thought. Frank seemed not to know how to do a lot of things. Feeling at peace with himself for the first time in quite a while, he looked up when a three-quarter moon popped up above a mountain peak, seeming to rest atop the mountain. The scene caused a craving in him to see more of the mountains of this wild country. *I best be getting back to the camp,* he told himself, realizing that he had walked for a couple of miles. *As cold as that water's bound to be, she ought to be finished with her bath by now.*

■ ■ ■ ■

Shivering so hard she could barely pull on the clean pair of Frank's trousers that she favored to her skirts and petticoats, Nancy would not admit it to Frank when she returned to the fire, but the water had been so cold that it stung when she waded in up to her knees. That was as far as she could force herself to go. Washing her torso and arms with a cloth dipped into the fast-moving creek, she had almost lost her breath and her very bones ached with the cold. She finally finished drying her back and arms, although she would not be comfortable until back by the fire. Pulling on a heavy shirt, she was about to leave the cover of the bushes that had ensured her privacy when she detected movement in the shrubs on the other side of the creek.

That dog, she thought with an impish grin, but immediately had second thoughts. Frank would hardly have crossed over to the other side of the creek to annoy her. Then she realized that Carson had been gone for a long time, and she was at once bitterly disappointed in the young man she had become so fond of. That he would slink around in the bushes to spy on her told her that he was lacking the character she had given him credit for. Maybe he thought it was a funny joke, spying on a lady. Angry now, she pulled her coat over her shoulders and picked up the pistol and holster she had become accustomed to carrying. Leaving the screen of bushes, she stopped suddenly when she saw the dark form across the creek moving back toward the fire. "Well," she yelled, "did you get a good eyeful?"

Startled, Red Shirt turned at once and fired, his shot passing inches from Nancy's head and clipping a large branch from the bush she had just left. Terrified, Nancy dived to the ground, her fingers trembling as she tried to pull the revolver from its holster. Finally she freed it and shot at the place where she had seen the form, although it was no longer there. It immediately occurred to her that now he knew where she was, but she no longer knew where he was. Her only impulse was to run, and run she did, leaving her soiled clothes on the ground where she had fallen.

"Nancy!" Frank screamed out when he heard the shots. He dropped his coffee cup, grabbed his rifle, and ran to meet her on the dark bank of the creek.

Seeing her husband, Nancy exclaimed breathlessly, "He's found us!" She rushed to meet him, but wasted no time in an embrace. "We've got to hide!"

"Over there!" he said, pointing to a clump of larger pines, which offered greater protection than the bushes by the creek.

On the other side of the creek, Red Shirt retreated quickly to take cover behind a thicket of younger pines. When he had been startled by the woman's sudden challenge, his reaction was to assume that they had somehow spotted him and had managed to get around behind him. He counted himself lucky that she had foolishly called out instead of shooting first. In the darkness, he could not be sure if his shot had hit anyone or not, but he removed himself as a target immediately. He cursed his luck in having been spotted before he had the chance to look over the camp and see where everyone was. Now his task was going to be much more difficult and many times more dangerous with Carson lying in wait for him to make a move. There was danger from the woman and the other man, but he felt it paramount to locate Carson, for his rifle seldom missed. Red Shirt would have to work his way in closer to try to spot him, so he left the thicket and moved quickly to a low mound closer to the creek. Since there were no shots fired when he moved, he decided that they didn't know exactly where he was, either. Encouraged by that thought, he moved again, closer still to the camp, this time to a place of protection behind a large log. From here, he could see the deserted camp and the horses picketed beyond. He decided to wait there awhile to see if he might spot one of the three.

Carson guessed that he was about half a mile from the camp when he heard the two shots, and he immediately feared the worst. So far, there were only the two shots as he broke into a run. What did it mean? Red Shirt? Other Indians? He raced to find out. Something told him it could be no one but Red Shirt, and he blamed himself for agreeing to stop to rest the horses for over half a day. He couldn't deduce anything from the two shots, one a pistol, the other a Winchester, for Red Shirt had a Winchester, but Frank did, too. He feared what he might find when he got back.

The moon had freed itself from the mountain peak behind him and was now high enough to cast shadows among the trees by the creek. Carson stopped running when he was within fifty yards of them and began to move with extreme caution, darting from one point of cover to the next: a hummock, a bush, whatever was available. When he reached the trees without daring fire, he dropped down behind a pine and crawled up to a spot where he could see the camp. There was no one to be seen. Frank and Nancy must have fled. At least there were no bodies in the small clearing, but the mystery was yet to be solved. He had to think for a few moments before deciding whether to call out to them or to remain in the shadows and try to work his way all around the camp, searching for Frank and Nancy or what or who had caused the gunfire. He decided it best to choose the latter and refrain from announcing his presence.

Withdrawing to the trees once more, he rose to his feet and began a careful circle around the campsite on the other side of the creek. The pines were thick enough in most places to allow him to move rapidly while allowing enough moonlight for him to see what was ahead of him. Still, there was no sign of anyone and he was approaching the point where he would have to cross over the creek if he was going to complete the circle around the camp. At the water's edge, he hesitated to listen. There was nothing but the sound of the water running over the rocky bottom and the clicking of the insects. He stepped into the water and started across, placing his feet carefully on the slippery rocks. When he got to the other side, he reached up and grasped the branch of a bush to help him out of the water. Halfway out, he looked up to see the short, compact body and wide shoulders of the demon Red Shirt.

"Howdy, Carson," Red Shirt growled with an evil grin of anticipation. It was only for an instant, because as soon as he spoke, his body was hurtling through the air to impact with Carson's and they both landed in the icy water. It had all happened so fast that Carson had no time to raise his rifle. It was now somewhere on the bottom of the creek. Both men struggled to regain their feet with Red Shirt clawing at the young white man, trying to get a firm grip on him. But Carson was quick enough to avoid the thrusts of the vengeful half-breed, and managed to gain a few feet of separation. Confident in his ability to overpower the lanky younger man, Red Shirt had dropped his rifle back on the bank and pulled his scalping knife. His evil grin promised the pleasure he anticipated with the methodical killing he planned. "You put me to a helluva lot of trouble to take your scalp," he taunted, "but there ain't no place for you to run now."

Carson did not reply, but drew his skinning knife and moved cautiously, trying to set his feet squarely under him on the slippery rocks. He did not underestimate the solidly built half-breed's ability when it came to hand-to-hand fighting. Like the fight he had had with Varner, his survival depended on his quickness to avoid the powerful arms and the thrusts from the deadly knife. He knew that, despite his thick torso and wide shoulders, Red Shirt was quick also. Who was the quicker was about to be decided, and it was going to be the ultimate penalty for the one who came in second. They slowly circled for a few moments, Red Shirt still grinning with confidence while Carson waited warily, not sure if he was a match for the savage half-breed, but determined to make it costly for him either way.

Finally, unable to wait any longer, Red Shirt made the first move, lunging at Carson and grabbing the wrist of Carson's knife hand while slashing at his belly with his knife. It was quick, so quick that Carson was unable to block him entirely, but succeeded in protecting his gut and taking the blow on his arm. He felt the bite of the blade on his forearm. Unable to free his knife hand from the viselike grip that held him, he sought to disable Red Shirt's knife hand as well. He suffered another slash across his forearm before he was able to clamp down on the powerful wrist, and the two combatants strained against each other in a contest of strength. Neither man could gain an advantage as he pushed and pulled in an effort to free a hand. It evolved into a sheer test of physical dominance that would seem likely to go to the sturdy half-breed. The knee-deep water close to the bank negated the use of feet as weapons, which might have played a part if the battle had taken place on dry land, but Carson knew it was to be decided by upper-body strength, and he was not sure but that he might have met his match. He strained against the sneering outlaw in desperate determination, knowing he could not allow himself to weaken under this supreme test, but there was no indication that Red Shirt was weakening, either. He realized at that moment that his fate might lie in the next few seconds in his life, for he was beginning to feel his strength draining. He suddenly felt his brain spinning in his head as he reached deep down inside his body for more strength, and he heard a sudden explosion in his head. Not sure what it had been, he then felt a weakening of Red Shirt's grip on his wrists. He stared into the half-breed's eyes and discovered a look of surprise and despair, and he realized then that the explosion he had heard was the crack of a rifle shot.

His strength failing rapidly, Red Shirt tried to fight on, even though blood began to spread on his shirt from the hole in his side. Knowing he was seriously wounded, he jerked his wrists free from Carson's exhausted hands and staggered back toward the center of the creek, where he collapsed in the deeper water. His strength nearly spent, Carson still tried to go after him, but he was not quick enough to reach him before the hated half-breed's body was carried away by the current to disappear in the darkness. With the last ounce of his strength gone, Carson waded back to the bank and crawled out to drop on the ground.

It was done. The ominous cloud that had followed the three travelers was at last dispersed. A dozen yards upstream, Frank and Nancy Thompson stood shaken and staring in disbelief of the deadly struggle just witnessed. Frank still held the rifle in his hand, having been afraid to shoot a second time, lest he might hit Carson. Frozen for the moment before, but free now, they hurried to the bank to help him. "John!" Nancy cried. "Are you all right?"

Slowly, he got up on his hands and knees and crawled up the bank. "I reckon," he replied. "I ain't sure. I ain't ever been this tired before, though. I know that for a fact." He rolled over on his back and lay there for a few moments. "I don't know how it woulda turned out if you hadn't shot that son of a bitch — pardon me, ma'am."

"Frank shot him," Nancy said, proudly now that the danger was past.

"I'd have shot him again, but I wasn't sure I wouldn't have hit you," Frank said.

"You're bleeding," Nancy exclaimed, just then noticing the blood on Carson's sleeve. She knelt down at once to look at his arm. "You've got a couple of bad-looking cuts on your arm I'll need to take care of."

"I ain't worried about that right now," Carson said. "First, I've gotta find my rifle. It's on the bottom of this creek somewhere."

Carson waded around in the knee-deep water for several minutes, but he had no luck in finding his rifle. It was too dark to see the bottom, and he wasn't really sure exactly where it might have flown when Red Shirt lunged at him. "Doggone," he commented. "I didn't notice the water was this cold when I was tryin' to keep him from cuttin' my throat."

"I reckon I can understand why," Frank

said, and prepared to wade in. "I'll help you look."

Carson stopped him. "No use you freezin' your feet off, too," he said. "I'll just wait till daylight and maybe we can see it. It can't get no wetter than it is now." He waded back over to the shore. "It sure ain't gonna do it any good." Then he remembered. "I've still got a good one, though." He walked a few feet down the bank and picked up the Winchester Red Shirt had tossed there, a Winchester '73, with the letters *L. Moody* carved on the stock.

"What are you gonna do about the body?" Nancy asked, thinking Red Shirt's corpse might somehow contaminate the water, picturing it snagged on a root or a rock a few feet downstream. It was a little too close to their camp to suit her.

"John and I can look for him in the morning," Frank said. "It's too dark tonight. Besides, he's downstream from our camp."

"Good," she said. "Then you can sit by the fire and get dry while I look at John's arm. I've got some old shirts I've been keeping for bandages." She started back toward the fire, then stopped to exclaim, "I declare, I can't believe we can stop worrying about that devil chasing us." She paused again to pose another question. "How could he have caught up with us so quickly?"

"I've been thinkin' about that myself," Carson replied. "And the way I figure it, he knows the country, and he figured we were headin' for the Yellowstone. So while we were roamin' around in the mountains tryin' to lose him, he rode straight up the valley and got ahead of us. It pays to know the country."

Although they had already had their supper, Nancy decided a fresh pot of coffee was called for to celebrate their freedom from pursuit. They stayed by the fire later than usual that night, talking about what the future held for them when they reached Nancy's father's ranch in Big Timber. It was a topic that had not been discussed on recent nights because of the threat hanging over their heads. After Carson's boots had dried out a little, and his arm was freshly bandaged, he made a search in the trees to find the black horse Red Shirt had ridden. He found it tied to a bush some fifty yards from the camp.

They started out again a little later the next morning, since they had stayed up so long the night before. Carson walked almost a quarter of a mile downstream, looking for Red Shirt's body, but it was nowhere to be found. It was enough to worry him some.

He would have felt better had he been able to confirm the kill, but there was no sign anywhere along the banks that would tell him the savage killer had pulled himself out of the creek. Recalling the instant the night before when Frank's shot had slammed into Red Shirt's side, he remembered the look in the half-breed's eyes. It had been the stare of a man looking into the eyes of death. If he was not dead at that moment, then he surely was by now. Carson stood there by a turn of the creek where the water formed a little pond before continuing out to the prairie. Thinking of the powerful hands that had trapped his wrists seconds before the fatal shot, he reached down and picked up a sizable piece of a dead limb and tossed it into the water. It swirled around for a few moments before the current took it away downstream. Satisfied, he returned to the scene of the fight to look for the rifle he had dropped in the water.

He searched for his rifle for quite some time before giving it up for lost. It confounded him that he couldn't find it in the clear-running creek. He knew it sure as hell didn't float away like Red Shirt's corpse, but it had somehow vanished, so he finally gave up and rode away with Luther Moody's Winchester rifle and his blue roan gelding

— his own rifle snagged on a root under the bank, right where he had started to pull himself out of the creek when Red Shirt attacked him.

CHAPTER 8

It took a full day to find their way out of the mountains. Referring to the rough map that Jonah had brought with them was not helpful, for they had no known point to start from. With nothing more to count on, they followed the valley to its end, which left them with still more mountains to find their way around, trying always to keep a northern heading. Striking a river that snaked its way out into the rolling hills and plains, they consulted Jonah's map again and decided that it might be the Little Big Horn, so they decided to follow it. The river took so many turns Carson soon decided it would take them until Christmas if they stuck strictly by the banks, so he picked out points in the distance and rode straight toward them. It seemed that the river always came back to them. Without the strain of having to always hurry, they allowed themselves to take a day of rest when Carson spotted a herd of antelope and was fortunate enough to get a shot at one as they crossed the river. They camped one night at the confluence of the river they had been following with a larger river. Carson decided to call it the Big Horn, whether it was or not, and he felt sure that whatever river it was, it more than likely would eventually lead them to the Yellowstone. His assumption turned out to be accurate, for they finally struck the Yellowstone one afternoon about three hours before dusk.

They were sure the wide river they came to was none other than the Yellowstone, if only by its size. The river they had been following emptied into it at what appeared to be the beginnings of a small settlement. It had the same effect on the weary travelers as if it had been a metropolis. There was a small trading post of some kind and a sawmill, plus a couple of cabins and a blacksmith shop, all on the south bank of the river. Gazing across the river at the rough bluffs, one could guess why no one was looking to settle on that side. Carson's horse, as well as the blue roan Red Shirt had ridden, was in need of shoeing, but with supplies running short, they decided to go to the trading post first.

"Well, howdy, folks," the proprietor sang

out cheerfully when they pulled up before his store. "The name's Gabe Loomis. Welcome. Where are you folks headin'?"

"Howdy," Frank returned. "We're on our way to a place called Big Timber. You ever heard of it?"

"Well, sure," Gabe replied. "I've heard of it — 'bout a hundred and fifty miles from here, I reckon, give or take a few miles. That's a far piece to go yet, and you folks look like you're a little tuckered out. Where'd you start out from?"

"The Black Hills," Frank said.

"My stars," Gabe commented, as if impressed. "You folks come on inside." He turned to Nancy. "Would you like a cup of water, ma'am? Ridin' that country between here and the Dakotas must be hard on a lady. I've got a jar of nice cool water settin' in the spring box." He sent a towheaded youngster down to the spring to fetch a drink for the three of them. Nancy graciously accepted and took the opportunity to sit down in a real chair to enjoy it. Getting down to business then, Gabe asked, "What can I do for you folks?"

"We need to buy some supplies," Frank told him, and proceeded to call out the items needed.

While the cheerful merchant fetched the

items requested, he continued to question the strangers. "What's in Big Timber that pulls you folks up that way?" He went on before Frank had a chance to answer. "If you're lookin' for a place to put down some roots, you oughta think about staying right here. We're fixin' to build us a nice little town. There's good land for crops on this side of the river that ain't been claimed yet, and there ain't been no Injun trouble for some time now." He set a sack of flour on the counter and tied it with a string. "What's in Big Timber that's got you ridin' all that way?" He repeated the question.

"My father-in-law's in the cattle business up there, and we're on our way to join him," Frank replied. "Otherwise, we might have been interested in looking over your little town."

"Oh well," Gabe said. "Couldn't hurt to ask. We're hopin' to attract families that are lookin' to settle down here and help us build a town. What about the young feller with you? Kin of yours?"

"No, that's John Carson. He's a friend of ours." Then remembering his manners, he said, "I'm Frank Thompson, and this is my wife, Nancy."

"Glad to know you," Gabe said. Nodding in Carson's direction, he commented, "He don't say an awful lot, does he?"

Frank laughed. "Oh, he can talk, but I guess he doesn't waste words at that."

Carson had not been paying much attention to the conversation between Gabe and Frank. He had been thinking about something else. Frank was restocking supplies for him as well as the two of them, and he couldn't help feeling guilty about not paying his fair share. The problem was he didn't have any money, so he paid attention when Gabe totaled up the cost of Frank's supplies and rounded it off to twenty-seven dollars. He didn't remember much of the long division he was taught in the few years of schooling he had received, but he was pretty sure one-third of that sum was nine dollars. Since there were three of them, he thought that was fair, so he filed that ay in his mind to take care of at the first opportunity. He was not without means. He had things to trade: a fine horse, an extra Winchester rifle, a Spencer carbine, two Colt revolvers, a good saddle. The ammunition he would keep. You couldn't have too many cartridges.

When the supplies were loaded, they bade Gabe Loomis farewell and rode over to the blacksmith, since Carson's horses were in bad need of new shoes. Nancy and Frank waited by the gatepost while Carson talked to Aaron Cox, the smithy. Their horses had been shod before they left the Black Hills. Carson and Cox came out of the shop in a few minutes and after a respectful nod to the man and woman at his gatepost, the blacksmith looked at the hooves of the two horses. "Yes, sir," Cox said, "they need shoein', all right." He dropped the bay's hoof and straightened up. "You want me to shoe 'em?"

"I ain't got any money right now, but if you're willin' to trade, we can do some business. I've got a fine-workin' Colt .45 handgun here I'll let you have if you shoe these two horses and give me nine dollars cash to boot. Whaddaya say?"

Cox had to pause to think about it. He took the gun belt and drew the revolver to examine it. "It is in good shape," he said, "but I've got a pretty good pistol already. I'll tell you what, since you say you're short on cash, I'll take it off your hands for the shoes and two dollars cash."

Carson shook his head. "Nope, I've got to have nine dollars."

"Five dollars?" Cox countered.

"Nine," Carson replied.

"You drive a hard bargain, mister, but I reckon the gun is worth it. All right, I'll do it."

By the time the blacksmith finished shoeing the two horses, it was getting late enough in the afternoon to begin thinking about finding a place to camp. They rode down the river a short distance until they came to a stream that emptied into it, and decided it was as good a place as any. After the horses were taken care of and Nancy was cooking their supper over a cheerful fire, Carson sought to pay for his share of the supplies. Handing Frank the nine dollars he got from Cox, he said, "Here's money to cover my share of the supplies you bought back there. I think that's fair. Tell me if you think it ain't."

Frank was taken by surprise. Busy over her kettle, Nancy paused to hear the exchange between them. "My goodness, John," Frank said, "I didn't expect you to pay anything for the food."

"Well, I'm sure as hell eatin' my share of it, and there'd be a whole lot more for you and Nancy if I wasn't with you."

Nancy commented at that point, "If you hadn't been with us, I doubt Frank and I would still be alive to eat it. Don't take his money, Frank." Looking directly at Carson then, she said, "I don't recall you charging us anything for that antelope we just finished."

The bantering went on for about ten minutes longer, before they agreed to accept two dollars as Carson's part in the food bill. Once that was agreed upon, they settled down to eat and celebrate their arrival at the Yellowstone River, having survived the more risky portion of their journey. They would start out in the morning, riding west along the river. Aaron Cox had recommended following the trail on the south bank, and figured the distance to be more like one hundred and thirty-five miles, instead of the hundred and fifty Gabe had estimated. "You'll strike Coulson in about two days," he had said, "and that's more than halfway to Big Timber. You'll recognize it when you get there. There's already a good-sized town started, right on the river, and if you ain't crossed over to the other side by then, Coulson's a good place to do it."

Their journey along the Yellowstone was as uneventful as they had hoped, and Cox's estimate of the distance to Coulson was accurate, for they arrived at the new settlement at the end of their second day from Gabe Loomis's trading post. At a rate of ten cents each, they crossed to the north bank of the Yellowstone on a ferry just west of the town. Although not in existence for a great length of time, Coulson was a thriving town, already boasting a two-story hotel, several saloons, a post office, and a few other stores. They did not linger in the town, but camped on the river a few hundred yards west of the ferry and continued their journey early the next morning.

Another day and a half on a well-traveled trail found them at last in the settlement of Big Timber, located where the Boulder River flowed into the Yellowstone. With the Absaroka and Beartooth mountains to the south, the Crazy Mountains to the northwest, and the beginning of an endless prairie stretching northward, Carson was convinced that this was the country he had a yearning for.

They were not home yet, however, for there was still the task of finding Mathew Cain's ranch. Jonah's map was not very detailed at this point, showing the ranch somewhere north of the confluence of the Boulder and the Yellowstone. Frank reasoned that the most likely place to get directions would be in the general store, so they tied the horses up there and went in. They were greeted by Albert Smith, the proprietor. "Mathew Cain? Sure, I know him. He buys most of his supplies from me." He favored Nancy with a warm smile and said, "So you're Mr. Cain's daughter. He said he had a daughter back East somewhere. I'm right pleased to meet you, ma'am." After all the introductions were made, Smith told them the best way to find the ranch house. "There's a lot of prairie out there, so I think the way for you folks to find it is to go back east about eight miles till you come to a good-sized creek that empties into the river. That's Sweet Grass Creek. Just follow that creek about seventeen or eighteen miles, and you can't miss your daddy's house. It's right on Sweet Grass Creek. There ain't no sign or gatepost, nothin' but the brand, M/C, carved on a tree."

"Much obliged," Frank said.

Outside, they decided there was not enough daylight left to make the entire trip, but they would ride the eight miles back to find Sweet Grass Creek, then follow it as far as they could before having to stop to rest the horses. As Carson suspected, the horses gave out before the daylight did, so they picked a spot where a pair of cottonwood trees stood guard on either side of the creek and made camp there.

It was difficult for Nancy to contain her excitement during the evening, being so close to seeing her family again. It had been six years since the rest of her family had left Omaha to follow her father's dream of breeding cattle. Nancy had remained in Omaha with an aunt on her mother's side, planning to join her family when she had completed her schooling. She had been delayed in coming west when she met a friend of her father, Jonah Thompson, who had helped her father drive a small herd of cattle up into Montana. More importantly, she met Jonah's younger brother, Frank. The two were attracted to each other right from the start, and after a short courtship, they decided to marry. They built a small house in Omaha where Frank worked in a hardware store. Times were hard for the young couple, so when Jonah received a letter from Mathew Cain telling him that he had prospered in Montana and inviting him to come back out to help him expand his business, Jonah didn't hesitate to accept. When he announced his plans to Frank and Nancy, they decided to go with him. Now, finally, they had reached Montana, but, sadly, without Jonah.

It was a difficult night for Nancy to sleep. She would see her family again tomorrow. They would meet her husband. She wondered how much everyone had changed. Would she even recognize her younger sister, Millie? She had been only ten when Nancy last saw her. And her brother, Lucas, was only eight years old when she saw him waving to her from the back of her father's wagon. They were both grown up now. Then a distressing thought occurred. *Will I look so old to them now?* She looked over at Frank, already asleep. *Oh well, not much I can do to make myself look younger.* She turned on her side and tried to go to sleep.

She was up earlier than usual the next morning, and was the first to revive the dying fire. Eager to get started, she roused Frank from his blankets and sang out to Carson, "If you two want to eat before we get started, you'd better get out of those blankets."

"Damn, honey," Frank replied, "it ain't even daylight yet."

"I don't care. I've come all this way to see my family and I don't plan to lie around here waiting for the sun to come up. Now get yourself up!"

Not waiting for her to start on him, Carson rolled out of his blankets and pulled his boots on. "I'll start saddlin' up the horses right after I walk down the creek a ways to see if everything's all right behind those bushes."

"Me, too," Frank said, and fell in behind

Carson as he slipped between the bushes and headed down the creek. Less modest than Carson, he stopped to do his business right outside the circle of firelight while Carson continued on to find more privacy. By the time he returned to the campfire, Frank was in the process of saddling up, with Nancy badgering him to hurry. Breakfast was already on the plates and coffee poured. Frank glanced up at Carson and winked. "You'd best not drag your feet today, John. Nancy's ready to see her pa, and she ain't likely to spare the whip."

"I can see that," Carson said with a grin.

"Listen, you two, I haven't seen my family in six years, and we're sitting here only a few miles away. I can't wait any longer."

Not wishing to delay the reunion, the men ate quickly, loaded up the packhorses, and got under way immediately. Frank commented that they broke camp quicker than they had done during the time when Red Shirt was chasing them.

Mathew Cain, owner of the M/C Ranch, stepped down from the saddle and handed the reins to his son Lucas, who had ridden in from the south range with him. Lucas took the reins and had started leading the horses toward the barn when the riders caught his eye. "Pa," he called back to his father, then pointed to the three. "Riders comin' in." They were leading five horses. *Probably wanting to sell Pa some horses,* he thought. It was not an unusual occurrence.

Cain turned to look in the direction Lucas pointed. He waited until they had come a little closer before speaking. "Ain't none of the boys," he said when he didn't recognize any of the three. "Looks like one of 'em's a woman. Wonder where in the hell they're goin'." He did not see many strangers riding across his ranch, and whenever he did, they were usually lost. "I'll tell Lizzie she might have to feed some extra mouths." He stepped up on the porch and stood waiting for the strangers to arrive. "You go ahead and put the horses in the corral." He stared hard at the woman riding between the two men. Something about her looked familiar. He was reminded of his daughter. Then the thought struck him. *Nancy? Could that be you?* It had been at least six years since he had seen his elder daughter. He walked back down the porch steps to stand in the yard. The two men with her were both strangers to him. He was sure he had never seen either of them before, so he spent no time in studying them. His attention was pulled back to the woman, who was now smiling broadly. *It is Nancy!* He started walking to meet her. She threw her leg over and hopped down from the saddle when still several yards from him. Carson reached over and took her reins.

"Papa!" Nancy squealed as she ran to greet her father, causing him to stagger back a couple of steps from the impact when they met. She locked her arms around his neck and they embraced for a long moment before she stepped back.

"Nancy, darlin', I don't know if I can believe my eyes. Is it really you?"

"It's me, all right, and we've gone through one helluva time to get here," she replied, beaming broadly. "This is Frank," she said then.

"Frank?" he responded, unable to remember at the moment.

"My husband, Frank," Nancy exclaimed.

"Oh, Frank," Cain replied, somewhat awkwardly. "Course it's your husband." He turned to face Frank, who stepped forward with his hand out.

"Glad to finally meet you, Mr. Cain," he said. "I guess we fell in on you kinda unexpectedly."

"Not a'tall," Cain quickly assured him. "I'm so tickled to see my eldest daughter. I'm just wonderin' why it took you so long to decide to come out here." He turned to take a longer look at Carson, who was holding the horses. "And who's this you got with you?" Then he remembered. "Where's Jonah? I was expectin' him. Did he decide not to come?"

"My brother's dead, Mr. Cain," Frank announced solemnly. "He was anxious to come help you, but he didn't make it." He went on to tell the circumstances that had cost Jonah his life.

"I swear, I'm sorry to hear that," Cain said. "He was a good man and a good friend. I'm real sorry for you, too. I know it was a terrible tragedy." He turned back to Nancy then. "Sounds like you folks had a rough time of it." Then remembering, he said, "You never told me who this feller is," nodding toward Carson.

"This is John Carson," Nancy said. "And if it wasn't for him, Frank and I might not have made it." She went on to tell of their chance meeting with Carson and his part in leading them to the Yellowstone.

"Nancy's telling it straight," Frank offered. "We might not have made it if he hadn't come along."

"Well, I reckon I owe you some thanks," Cain said with a wide smile. He offered his hand. Carson didn't say anything; he just shook the outstretched hand. "Well, if this don't tie my day up with a ribbon," Cain went on happily. He took another look at his daughter. "I swear, if you ain't lookin' more and more like your mother." He gave her a wicked wink. "And she was the prettiest woman in the state of Nebraska. God rest her soul." He put his arm around her shoulders and gave her a hard squeeze. "Let's get you folks settled." He paused then and yelled out toward the barn, "Lucas! Get up here and say hello to your sister."

"Well, get over here and give me a hug," Nancy told her brother when he came up from the barn, but only stood there, gaping at the three visitors. A shy boy of eight when she last saw him, and now a strapping boy of fourteen who only vaguely remembered his big sister. With an embarrassed grin, he stepped forward to submit to a hug, and waited patiently until he was released. "My goodness," Nancy remarked, "you're almost full grown, almost as big as Papa." Lucas grinned anew and stepped back to gawk at the two men with his sister. "This is your brother-in-law, Frank," she told him.

"Pleased to meet you, Lucas," Frank said, and offered his hand.

"Me, too," Lucas returned.

"Where's Justin?" Nancy asked then. Justin, her big brother and eldest of Mathew Cain's offspring, was always the serious one, perhaps because of his role in helping to raise his younger brother and sisters after their mother died.

"He took a couple of the boys over toward the mountains to round up a bunch of strays," her father said. "He oughta be back for supper. He's sure gonna be surprised to see you."

"Well, what about me?" The voice came from the porch as a young girl stepped out the door and stood squarely with hands on hips. "Don't I get a hug?"

"Millie!" Nancy exclaimed delightedly. "Come here!" After a long hug, Nancy stepped back to look at her. "I declare, you're a grown lady. I wouldn't have recognized you."

"Trying to take care of this wild bunch will make you grow up fast," Millie replied. "Either that or kill you." She smiled at Frank then and said, "Welcome to the family, Frank." Back to Nancy, she remarked, "You look as good as the last time I saw you. I believe married life agrees with you." She cocked an eye in Carson's direction, lingered for an instant, but said nothing.

"Well, let's get you all in the house so you

can rest a spell," Mathew Cain suggested. "Millie, you'd best tell Lizzie we're gonna have extra mouths around the table."

"I already told her," Millie said. "I sent her out to the smokehouse to cut some off one of those hams we smoked last fall."

Standing apart from the reunion, patiently watching, Carson said nothing until the family started to go up the steps to the porch. "I need to take care of the horses, Mr. Cain. Is it all right if I let 'em out in the corral?"

"Oh, sure, young feller," Cain replied, having forgotten about him in the midst of all the greeting and hugging. "Lucas, go help the young man with the horses. What was your name again?"

"Carson," he answered, "John Carson."

"Right, John," Cain said. "You and Lucas take care of your horses, and then come on back and we'll get you somethin' to eat."

"Thank you, sir," Carson replied, then spoke to Frank. "I expect you'll wanna unload your packhorses here at the house, won't you?"

"Oh, I guess that would be the smart thing to do, wouldn't it?" Frank responded, having forgotten about it amid all the excitement of the reunion.

An interested witness to the exchange of

words, Millie commented, "Why don't you just unload it and leave it on the porch? We can take it in later, and Mr. Carson can take the horses to the corral." She looked at him in an appraising manner, the way a buyer might look at a horse he was considering.

"Yeah, Millie's right," Cain said. "Just unload it on the porch. We can do somethin' with it later." Carson got the impression right off that it was Millie who ran the house, and when he locked his gaze on hers, her expression told him he had guessed right.

While the men unloaded the horses, Millie locked arms with her sister as they ascended the steps to the porch. "So, how well do you know this stray you picked up on the way out here?"

Nancy told her that Carson had just appeared one night when they were camped on a creek near the Beaver River. "We were in a terrible fix until he showed up."

"Like an angel out of the blue," Millie said, facetiously, "just sent down to rescue you and Frank."

"He happened to be in the right place for us at the time, that's all," Nancy said.

"I just wonder what he's after," Millie insisted.

"He's after a job working with cattle,

216

that's all. Why are you so suspicious?"
Nancy said. "John's really a nice fellow, and
he's worked as a drover on several trail
drives. And he's certainly handy with a rifle.
Papa would do well to hire him."

"Maybe he'd be more comfortable eating
in the bunkhouse with the other men,"
Millie said. "I mean, if it's a job he's after,
that's where the hired hands usually eat.
Justin can talk to him about working on the
M/C when he gets back tonight. He does
most of the hiring."

"Well, tonight he can eat with us. He's
our friend, and he's certainly earned our
courtesy," Nancy insisted, finding it hard to
understand Millie's attitude toward someone she didn't even know. After what she,
Frank, and Carson had been through together, she found it difficult to think of him
as simply a hired hand. *She'll see when she
gets to know him,* she told herself.

When Frank and Nancy's belongings were
unloaded, and the horses were taken to the
barn to be unsaddled and fed, they were
turned out in the corral for the night. "We
can let 'em out to graze with the rest of the
horses in the mornin'," Lucas said.

"Good," Carson responded. "I was gonna
suggest the same thing." He could tell that

he was going to like the fourteen-year-old boy. Lucas seemed to have his head on straight, and he appeared to be pretty good with horses. Carson couldn't help seeing a little of himself in the boy when he was about the same age.

Leaving the corral, they saw a few of Cain's ranch hands riding in. They gave Carson a nod, which he acknowledged as they passed by on their way to the barn. When they returned to the house, they went in the back door to a large kitchen where Lucas introduced Carson to Lizzie Krol. Lizzie, a slight German woman with streaks of silver running through her long black hair pinned up in a large bun, nodded politely to Carson. Sitting on a chair in the corner was the small towhead who had been sent to the spring to fetch water. Carson was to learn later that he was Lizzie's son, Karl. When Carson said he hoped he hadn't put her to too much trouble, having another mouth to feed, she responded with a pleasant chuckle. "It makes no difference to me. I cook for five people in the house and six in the bunkhouse. A few more don't make no difference."

"Well, it sure smells mighty good, whatever you're fixin'. I appreciate it," Carson said. He followed Lucas into the parlor where the others had gathered.

They walked into the room in time to hear the end of the story Nancy was telling her family about their meeting with Carson. "And then, when it looked like these outlaws were going to sneak up on us, all of a sudden we hear a rifle go off behind us, and one of the outlaws fell dead."

"Nancy and Jonah thought it was me that shot him," Frank interrupted.

"That's right, we did," Nancy continued. "Then another one of the outlaws tried to sneak up closer, and bang! Down he went. It turned out that there were only three of them, and the other one ran."

Mathew Cain turned to greet Carson as he found himself a chair in the corner of the room. "Well, that was a good piece of work, young man. I'm glad you came along when you did. You certainly have my thanks."

Carson acknowledged his comment with a slight nod of his head, unaware of the appraising eyes of Millie as she continued to study the young stranger. "Yes, sir," she finally remarked, "like a guardian angel watching over them."

Her remark was puzzling to them all, and especially to Carson. Why, he wondered, did she gaze so suspiciously at him? She had eyed him the same way when he was still standing out in the yard when they had just arrived. Feeling he should reply in some fashion, he said, "I don't reckon I'm much of an angel. It's just lucky I was there at the time."

"Pretty handy with a rifle, are you?" Millie asked boldly.

"I get by," Carson said matter-of-factly, wondering where her questions were going to lead, and what he had done to get on the wrong side of the cynical young woman.

"Nancy says you came out here looking for a job," Millie went on. "Is that right?"

Carson was growing more uncomfortable by the moment. He had hoped to get an opportunity to talk to her father about that at the appropriate time, instead of applying with his young daughter, who looked only a year or two older than her brother Lucas. "Well, miss," he replied, "I expect I was fixin' to talk to your daddy about workin' for him, but I reckon that'll be between me and him."

At that point, Millie's father interrupted the interrogation. "For goodness' sake, Millie, let the young man be. I'll be glad to talk to him about goin' to work for the M slash C, but now ain't the time. We're fixin' to eat some supper in a minute, just as soon as Lizzie gets it on the table."

Millie was not willing to abandon her curiosity without at least one more comment. "I'm just hoping we hire men who know something about working cattle, and can help us out. We've already got too many gunmen in the valley who are handy with a rifle."

The conversation had gone a little too far by now to suit her father. "That'll be enough from you, young lady," he warned her sternly. "Right now Mr. Carson is a guest in our house, and what he does or is thinkin' about doin' is none of our business." He looked at Carson then and offered an apology. "I'll have to ask you to forgive my daughter's lack of hospitality. She ain't really saddle broke yet and sometimes she likes to buck a little bit too much."

"No harm done," Carson responded. "But I'd like to let her know that I know how to work cattle. That's all I've ever done since I was Lucas's age. I can drive 'em, rope 'em, brand 'em, ride roundup, and most everything else except chuck wagon. I ain't much of a cook. I ain't sayin' I'm better'n anybody else at it, but Mr. Bob Patterson thought I was good enough to hire for three years."

His statement brought broad smiles to the faces of Nancy and Frank, and a grin to

Cain's square jaw. "Well, I might have use for somebody like that," Cain said, although he had no idea who Bob Patterson was. "We'll talk after supper." He paused to cock an eye in Millie's direction. "That is, if it's all right with my younger daughter." That brought a few chuckles from everyone but Millie.

"Horse feathers," Millie said in disgust. "I'll go see what's keeping Lizzie from getting supper on the table. Lucas, don't you go getting yourself settled down just yet. Lizzie oughta be about ready for you to carry supper down to the bunkhouse." She left the room.

"I know it," Lucas called after her, then added, "Boss." It was a regular chore since there wasn't a cook shack and a separate cook for the ranch hands, and he didn't have to be reminded by his sister.

It was rather obvious that the young boy objected to his sister's authoritative manner. Carson couldn't help wondering if she was always this abrasive to every stranger who showed up at the ranch, or was it just him? He made up his mind at that moment that he would attempt to stay out of her way as much as possible.

Supper that night was a grand affair from Carson's point of view, his having become

222

accustomed to suppers on the trail. Not surprisingly, there was beef, but there was also ham, potatoes, beans, onions, huge biscuits, and plenty of hot coffee. Carson helped himself as each bowl was passed, and lit into his plate with total concentration. Judging by the meal put on the table on his first night, he decided that he and Lizzie's cooking were going to get along just fine in the event he was hired. He was engrossed in the process of trying to cut a large piece of tough beef in two when he suddenly glanced up to find Millie's eyes focused on him. It gave him pause to wonder if his table manners were in need of polishing. He glanced around the table to see if anyone else was watching him, but everyone seemed to be busy with their own eating, and he couldn't see any difference between their manners and his. When he glanced back in Millie's direction, she looked away. *That girl just flat doesn't like me,* he thought.

After supper, the men retired to the porch while the women cleared the table and Lucas went to the bunkhouse to retrieve the empty pots. The gracious host, Mathew Cain brought out a box of cigars and offered them. "Albert Smith gets these shipped in from San Francisco," he said, referring to the owner of the general merchandise store in Big Timber. After everyone was lit and a heavy cloud of smoke hung over the porch, Cain opened the subject of employment for Carson. "I can use a good man," he said, "if you're as good as you said you are in the parlor. I want you to talk to Justin, though. He's been doin' all the hirin' for the last couple of years. It would have to be all right with him." He turned his head to look down in the direction of the barn. "I'm surprised he ain't back yet. I suppose he'll show up before long. I don't see no reason why he wouldn't hire you. We need a couple more men — lost one last month, got bucked off a horse and broke his neck." He paused as if to observe a moment of sympathy, but it was no more than a moment, and then he continued. "Anyway, you can grab you an empty bunk in the bunkhouse — there's a few — and we'll see what's what in the mornin'. All right?"

"Yes, sir," Carson said. "I appreciate it."

Justin had still not shown up when it was time to think about calling it a night, so Cain announced that it was past his bedtime, which signaled an end to the men's smoking session. Carson left to pick up his possibles from the tack room and transfer them to the bunkhouse. "I'll walk down with you and introduce you to the men,"

Cain said.

Frank said good night and went to find Nancy. He found her and her sister in the bedroom, but Nancy told him she needed a moment more with Millie, and sent him to wash up for bed. When he had gone, Nancy sought to finish her conversation with her younger sister. "I want you to understand something, Millie. I know I'm your older sister, but I fully appreciate the fact that you've been the woman of the house ever since Mama died. And I know you've done a good job. I didn't come out here to try to take over your job or your position with Papa. Frank and I came all this way to get a new start in life, and work with you and the family. We hope to build our own little house close by, and I certainly don't want to take your place. I probably couldn't do as good a job as you've done, anyway."

"Oh, Nancy!" Millie cried in alarm. "I don't think that way at all. I apologize if I gave you that impression. I certainly didn't mean to. I'm so happy to have you come home, and I wouldn't care one bit if you wanted to be the woman of the house. I hoped that you and Frank would live with us here in this big house. There's certainly room for you, and I know Papa would be pleased if you did. You're my big sis, and you can pull your rank any time you want. Whatever did I do to make you think I wasn't glad to see you?"

"I don't know." Nancy hesitated. "Nothing, I guess. I just thought you might feel that way. I should know you better than that. Maybe it was the way you sort of attacked John, like you resented all of us piling in on you." She paused then to look hard at her sister. "Why do you dislike John so much?"

"I don't know," Millie said. "I don't really dislike him. Like you said before, I really don't even know the man. I just wanna be sure he's not another one of those gunmen that have been riding through here every once in a while, I guess."

Nancy still puzzled over her sister's reaction to one who had been of such service to her and Frank. Then it struck her. A suspicious smile spread slowly across her face, and she said, "He is good looking, isn't he?"

"What?" Millie sputtered. "I don't know. I hadn't really noticed, and I certainly don't care whether he is or not." She turned on her heel then and left the room, saying, "I'd best get out of here so you and Frank can get ready for bed."

Nancy stood there smiling as she watched

her leave the room, thinking that there might have been a reason for Millie's behavior that she had not even considered. Millie might have felt a threat with their arrival, but it was not from Nancy. Maybe she was in fear of a weakness in her resolve to function in a man's world on equal terms. Perhaps she had convinced herself that she was better off if she never allowed herself to become interested in a man, and maybe John Carson presented a challenge. If that were the case, then she might be determined to fight any attraction to the tall young man.

CHAPTER 9

The four ranch hands whom Carson met in the bunkhouse all seemed friendly enough. One of them, who looked to be quite a few years older than the other three and introduced himself as Mule Simpson, showed Carson which bunks were unclaimed. "Two of the fellers is out with Justin," Mule told him, "so you won't wanna get one of theirs, especially Pruett's." All of the bunks, except for those of the four men present, had straw tick mattresses rolled up, with a blanket and pillow stacked on top. Carson assumed this was the procedure followed whenever the men were away from the ranch for a while. "Pruett's a little fussy about his things. His name's Pruett Little, but there ain't nothin' little about him, so it's best not to rile him."

"I appreciate it," Carson said, recognizing the subtle warning that Pruett was the one who liked to throw his weight around. There always seemed to be one. "I'll try not to aggravate him if I can help it."

"I don't expect they'll come in tonight, since they ain't here by now," Mule said. "They'll make camp and come in in the mornin' about breakfast time."

There wasn't much time for conversation beyond introductions, since it was almost bedtime for the men. Morning came early on the M/C, so everyone was soon ready to kill the lantern and hit the hay. Carson rolled out the straw mattress on one of the unclaimed bunks, shook the dust out of the blanket, tested the pillow for any signs of vermin life, and settled in for the night.

He was awake the next morning before sunup while the other men were still sleeping, a habit formed by his many days on cattle drives. He moved quietly out the door and walked a dozen yards or so behind the bunkhouse to empty the coffee consumed the night before, shunning the outhouse located behind the main house. When he returned to the bunkhouse, the other men were just stirring. "I swear," Mule said, "I thought you'd hightailed it durin' the night — decided you didn't wanna work here after all."

Carson shrugged in response. "I wasn't gonna leave before breakfast, if the chuck's as good in the mornin' as it was last night."

Shorty chuckled at the remark. "The chuck's the main reason we work for Mr. Cain." A man whose nickname was for an obvious reason, Shorty had had very little to say the night before. "So we'd best go take care of the stock so we ain't late for breakfast."

"Come on with me, John," Mule said. "I'll show you what chores have to be done before breakfast." He stood aside when Shorty and the other two men passed out the door. "Don't wanna get run over by the younger fellers," he said with a chuckle. "They're in a hurry to get to the feed room in the back of the barn. Miss Millie comes down to the barn every mornin' to milk the cow, and sometimes she don't take time to put her robe on over her nightgown." He paused when he stepped outside the bunkhouse door. "As cool as the weather's gettin', I don't suppose they'll get many more mornin's to get a look."

"I don't think she likes me very much," Carson said. "Last night she looked at me like I was a weevil in the flour bin."

Mule looked surprised. "Is that a fact? Millie's pretty much friendly with all the men. She runs the ranch with an iron hand, but she gets along with ever'body. Ol' Lizzie's the one that's got a temper on her, if you set her off. She'd be quick to come after you with one of those butcher knives of hers. But as long as you don't aggravate her, she's sweet as a peach." He lowered his voice to almost a whisper, even though there was no one around to hear what he said. "She must be sweet some of the time, 'cause everybody thinks that little boy of hers looks a helluva lot like Mr. Cain. Don't tell nobody you heard that from me. I'm just sayin' what everybody thinks."

It didn't matter to Carson, one way or the other. He figured what Mathew Cain did with his cook was his and Lizzie's business. He smiled to himself when he realized that he hadn't even signed on yet, and already he knew Pruett was the bully and Mule was the gossip. He appreciated the fact that Mule had made an effort to make him feel welcome, however. Curious, he couldn't help asking, "How come they call you Mule?"

"I don't know," Mule answered. "My name's Merle, and somehow over the years, it got changed to Mule. No particular reason, I reckon." Carson nodded but made no response. He would have guessed, however, that the name might have been inspired by Mule's long face and his larger-than-normal ears.

■ ■ ■ ■

As Mule had predicted, Justin and the two men showed up at the ranch in time for breakfast. They had found about thirty head of cattle that had bunched up in a narrow ravine near the foothills of the mountains. By the time they had driven them back with the other cattle, it had gotten too late to start back that night. Justin, as was his habit, came straight to the bunkhouse to eat with the crew. He was surprised to find a strange face at the long table at one end of the building.

"Looks like we got us a guest, boss." It was Pruett who spoke first.

"Looks that way," Justin replied, eyeing Carson with curiosity.

Mule spoke up then. "This here's John Carson. Mr. Cain hired him on yesterday."

"Is that right?" Justin said with no show of emotion as he continued to study the stranger.

Carson got up from the bench to face Mathew Cain's elder son, who was almost an exact duplicate of his father, even to the square jaw and the thick head of hair. The main difference was the generous infusion of gray in the father's hair, but the heavy frame and long arms were all a direct inheritance. "I wasn't exactly hired on," Carson said. "Your father said I could bunk here last night and talk to you this mornin' about hirin' on."

Justin nodded, understanding the situation, and also aware that his father wouldn't have told the man to stay overnight had he not been convinced that he was worth hiring.

"Tell him, if you don't hire him, he's gonna have to pay us for the grub," Pruett joked, and winked at Clem Hastings, the man who had ridden in with him and Justin. He made a place for himself on the bench between Mule and Shorty. "Move over some, Shorty, and pass that platter of bacon."

Carson was immediately reminded of Jack Varner. Pruett was about the same size. Carson hoped that was where the similarity ended.

"Let's eat some breakfast first," Justin said. "Then we'll talk about it." He sat down at the end of the bench, and all hands turned their concentration to focus on the breakfast. When it was finished, Justin took a few minutes to assign his men the work he wanted done that day, and then he took Carson to the corral where he had instructed Shorty to drive in some of the horses from the remuda. "You got your rig in the tack room, I reckon?" Justin asked. Carson nodded. "Go on and get it."

When Carson returned with his saddle and bridle, Justin told him that all of the horses now in the corral had worked cattle, so he was to rope one, saddle it, and move the rest of the horses out of the corral and drive them back with the others on the range. Recognizing it as a test, although a fairly simple one as far as he was concerned, Carson took a coil of rope hanging on a post and fashioned a loop, then paused a moment to look over the group of horses bunched at the upper end of the corral. His selection made, he walked toward them, his approach causing them to move around the corral in a circle. He took a couple of turns over his head with the rope, then threw it at a red roan. The loop landed neatly over the horse's head and Carson drew it up tight. Using a post in the center of the corral for leverage, he pulled the roan up to a halt and calmed it down with a few strokes of his hand while he put the bridle on it. In a short amount of time, he had the horse saddled and he climbed aboard. Watching with a good measure of interest, Justin walked over and opened the gate. The horses immediately passed out of the corral, with Carson following behind. Outside, he quickly headed them off and turned them toward the herd grazing on the range, driving them easily to join the others.

It was enough to convince Justin, as well as Clem Hastings, who had paused to watch with him. It was plain that the new man had, in fact, worked as a drover before. When Carson loped comfortably back to the corral and dismounted, Justin met him with the news that he was hired. "You're just in time for the fall roundup," he said. "We'll be startin' before long. Might be a good idea for you to spend that time gettin' to know our range. I'll send one of the boys out with you to show you where our range runs into the Bar-T's. Thirty dollars a month, bed and board, is that all right with you?" He didn't wait for Carson's answer. "Hope it is, 'cause that's as much as I pay."

"That'll do fine," Carson said. " 'Preciate it. I'll throw my other saddle in the bunk-house with the rest of my possibles. I rode in on a bay, leadin' a black. They're grazin' with your horses, but I expect I'll bring the bay back here to the corral. The black's a good horse, but he ain't ever worked cattle before."

"Fair enough," Justin said, and offered his

hand. They shook on it. "Like I said, we're gonna be startin' roundup in a few weeks, so we need to get some chores caught up around here before we go. There's a pile of logs over on the other side of the smokehouse that's gonna have to be sawed in lengths and split up for firewood. I figure that's a good job for you and Shorty. He already knows he's gonna be doin' it, so go on over and work with him. Maybe you can cut that pile down some."

"All right," Carson said, and turned to go right away. He figured that this was another test to see if he had any objection to doing ranch chores. Chopping firewood was probably a job that was always given to a new man. He had to wonder why Shorty got stuck with the job. Justin watched him walk away for a few seconds before turning to go to the house.

"Well, look who he sent to help me," Shorty sang out when he saw Carson come around the smokehouse. As chilly as it was, he had already shed his coat. "Ain't you got no gloves?"

"Nope," Carson replied. "Reckon I'll have to do without 'em."

"We got a heap of wood to cut up. You're gonna wish you had 'em."

"I do already," Carson said matter-of-factly. "Let's get at it."

They lifted a log and propped it across the sawhorse, then got on either end of a crosscut saw. That's how the morning was spent, sawing logs into lengths that would fit in the fireplace and Lizzie's kitchen stove, staying hard at it until the noon meal was called. Shorty proved to be a talker on a par with Mule, so Carson didn't have to say a lot, and in the process, he learned some things he had not been sure of about running free-range cattle. There were several ranches in the valley that grazed their cattle on the free range. Since there were no fences, ownership of the cows was determined by the brands they wore. The job at roundup was to separate every ranch owner's cows from the other brands and drive them back to his home range for the winter.

When young Karl Krol sounded the angle iron announcing the arrival of the noontime meal at the bunkhouse, Carson and Shorty had no more logs to saw and a small mountain of lengths ready for splitting. "We done all right," Shorty commented as they both pulled their shirts on, having shed them earlier. "We mighta outdone ourselves, might be more'n we can split before supper."

"We'll just have to hump it this afternoon," Carson said. Feeling eyes upon him, he turned to see Millie standing at the back steps of the house watching him. As soon as he turned to see her, she spun on her heel and went in the kitchen door. *That's one strange girl,* he thought.

"Well, here come the woodcutters," Pruett announced when Carson and Shorty walked into the bunkhouse. "You boys about finished choppin' that firewood?"

"No," Shorty replied, "but we will come suppertime. Ain't nobody can chop wood like me and John."

"I'm glad we finally found out what you're good at," Pruett needled. "We knew it wasn't cowpunchin'." He laughed at his joke. "And you got you a helper, too."

"You wait till suppertime," Shorty fired back. "Me and John'll show you and the rest of the boys what two good men can do when they set their mind to it. That'll shut that big mouth of yours."

"Don't go gettin' too big for your britches," Pruett warned. Shorty knew he was in little danger of trouble from Pruett because of the great difference in size. The other men wouldn't stand for any physical retaliation on the bigger man's part. Knowing this as well, Pruett turned his japing upon the new man, who looked more capable of accounting for himself. "How 'bout it, John Carson? You think you can outwork anybody on the M/C?"

Carson, already focusing on his dinner, paused to consider his response. He didn't want to get started with Pruett as he had with Jack Varner, but he didn't want to give Pruett the idea that he could be bullied. "What I think," he finally answered, "is that Shorty can outwork anybody on the M/C. I'm just helpin' him do it." Pruett didn't know how to respond to that, but he didn't want to let Shorty have the last word, so he forced a chuckle and said, "I'll bet you two don't get halfway through that woodpile before supper."

Unwilling to back down, Shorty responded, "How much?"

Pruett didn't expect to be taken up on the bet, and he hesitated for a few moments before replying, "Why, I'd bet you two dollars you don't split half of that wood."

Caught up in his pride, Shorty was not willing to back down. "I'll bet you five dollars me and John cut up the whole damn pile."

Now Pruett was interested for sure. "By suppertime?" he stressed.

"By suppertime," Shorty responded confidently.

"You got a bet," Pruett said, and looked around at the others present. "You heard that didn't you, boys? The whole damn pile by suppertime."

Returning to the woodpile after dinner, Carson commented to his work partner, "Looks to me like we're gonna have to work like hell if we're gonna split all this wood by suppertime."

"Yeah," Shorty replied somewhat contritely. "Sometimes my mouth is bigger than Pruett's. I reckon we'll get done what we can, and I'll have to hear him bray like a donkey about it."

Carson picked up an ax, tested the weight, and said, "Why don't we split every damn piece of this wood, and you can bray like a donkey?"

Shorty grinned. "Now, that'd be somethin', wouldn't it? Shut his big mouth then."

So they waded into the huge mountain of sawed lengths, both men with axes swinging at a steady pace, with no pauses between lengths, with no sound other than that of a soft grunt as the ax came down on the round section of tree trunk, followed by the splitting sound of the wood. A stack of stove-ready firewood soon began to pile up between the two men, who now seemed to be caught up in the accomplishment of their goal. Very few words passed between them, only a determined smile now and then as the pile grew to waist high. Before long, they could no longer see each other when the pile became higher than Shorty's head, but the steady blow of ax blade against wood never stopped until a sharp crack signaled a broken ax handle. "I'll be right back!" Shorty exclaimed, and ran to the barn to get another ax, knowing that would be quicker than taking the time to put a new handle in the one he had just busted. "I'll fix that handle later," he announced when he returned to the woodpile.

Sheer determination kept the two men at it throughout the afternoon, and as the pile of lengths waiting to be split steadily diminished, their will seemed to gain strength. By this time, most of the others in the house and around the barn were aware of the attempt to claim the woodcutting title of the M/C. The contest drew spectators to stop and gawk from time to time, most of them calling out encouragement. The two participants seemed to pay them no mind. They just kept chopping.

"He sure knows how to swing that ax, doesn't he?" Lucas said.

Millie jumped, startled when he came up behind her as she was standing looking out the kitchen door. Recovering quickly, she responded, "Huh, anybody can chop wood. Men," she scoffed, "have to make a game out of everything, even chores." She spun on her heel and left him standing there.

When Lizzie called Lucas from the kitchen door to come carry supper down to the bunkhouse, he reluctantly left to do her bidding, for the two woodcutters were down to only a few lengths left to split. For the two men, it only caused them to work harder, for Shorty's boast had been that they would finish it all by suppertime. Lucas seemed to sense the significance of that. Whether or not this was the reason he tarried a little on delivering the food to the bunkhouse, no one could say. They were down to one length by the time Lucas set the pots on the table and signaled the men. Carson and Shorty both attacked the last one with a triumphant vengeance. They threw their axes aside then and shook hands, both men drenched with sweat. Shorty looked down at the blood on his hand after they shook, and knew the price Carson had paid to back him up.

It was a triumphant entrance that Shorty made in the bunkhouse, amid the cheering of his fellow cowhands. In a fitting response, he paused in the doorway to take a deep bow. Then going straight to Pruett, he held out his hand. "Five dollars, I believe we agreed on."

Flushed with embarrassment, Pruett responded irritably, "You're gonna have to wait till payday. I ain't got five dollars."

His response couldn't have pleased Shorty more. He gave the big man a stern look and said, "I'll wait, but let this be a lesson to you, don't go makin' bets you can't back up."

"You go to hell, Shorty," Pruett replied, much to the amusement of the other men.

Shorty threw his head back and laughed delightedly. "Hell, let's eat," he exclaimed. "Come on, partner, set yourself down by me."

Carson, who had silently watched Shorty's moment of triumph from the corner of the room, sat down beside him. He enjoyed some measure of pleasure from the victory won that day, but it was not without a price. His hands were blistered and bleeding, and the muscles in his arms and back were stiffening up. Still, it was worth it to see Shorty collect on the bet.

An interested spectator, Justin Cain had entered the bunkhouse in time to catch Shorty's entrance. It appeared that his new hire was not afraid of physical labor, and it looked as if he had made a fast friend of Shorty. Justin decided to send Shorty out to ride the boundary lines with Carson in the morning. He told them as much at the supper table. He had talked to Frank and Nancy about the quiet young man who had accompanied them from Dakota Territory, and there was little doubt that they thought he was something special. *Well, I can use a man who's something special,* he thought. *If he can use a rifle like they say, he might come in handy right now.* He had not even talked to his father about it yet, but when he and Pruett and Clem found those strays in that ravine near the mountains the day before, it almost looked as if someone had herded them into that narrow pocket. Clem had commented that it sure looked like a strange place for cattle to gather. There was nothing to attract them, no grass, no water. He remembered Pruett's remark as well. "You talk like cows have got sense," he had said. "You can't depend on a damn cow to do anythin' on its own." But Justin wasn't ready to rule out the possibility that someone had driven those cattle up to the head of that ravine, figuring on changing the brands. Maybe he was just being overly suspicious, but he had come up a little short on the head count lately, and he wasn't at

244

all confident in Lon Tuttle's integrity. Lon, the owner of the Bar-T range, had hired a rough-looking bunch of drifters to work his cattle. His herd was much smaller than Mathew Cain's, and Justin wouldn't put it past ol' Lon to increase his stock with a branding iron. After supper was over, he told Shorty what was on his mind. "I can't send all the boys up there to look around, so I want you and John to take a good look along the river. Drive any of our strays back where they belong, and keep an eye out for any of Lon Tuttle's men on this side of the river."

Carson and Shorty rode out to the north before breakfast the next morning, planning to cover a little ground before stopping to rest the horses and boil some coffee to drink with the jerky they carried. Shorty gave John a running commentary of the bunchgrass prairie and boasted that it was better than the grass in the lower territories when it came to putting hard weight on cattle. "Them mountains yonder," he said, pointing to the west, "them's the Crazy Mountains. The Injuns called them that because the wind gets to blowin' around those sharp peaks and narrow valleys, and it moans like they was crazy." Carson gazed long and hard at the rugged peaks, already feeling a desire to ride up into them, just to see what was up there. Shorty told him of Justin's concerns about the possibility that they were losing some cattle to the Bar-T. "Our home range runs up to the Musselshell River. That's about twenty miles from here. Lon Tuttle's Bar-T grazes north of the river."

"You think Tuttle's men are rustlin' M/C cattle?" Carson asked. "I thought the Bar-T and another ranch east of here all worked together on the roundup."

"They do," Shorty said, "but Tuttle has been hirin' on some pretty scruffy-lookin' hands lately. I ran into a couple of 'em last month on the south bank of the Musselshell, and they looked more like gunmen to me." He rode on a few minutes before adding, "Justin just wants us to take notice of any cows we see that are sportin' sores that ain't healin' too fast." He didn't have to explain; Carson had seen old brands that had been worked over to look like healing injuries, usually close to a freshly applied brand.

After a ride of about ten miles, they stopped by a tiny stream that came down out of the Crazy Mountains to have their breakfast of coffee and beef jerky. The dry spell the ranchers had endured during the last few weeks had dried the little stream considerably, causing Shorty to joke, "Damn, looks like there ain't gonna be none left if I fill this coffeepot." There was enough moving water for the horses to drink, however. Breakfast was a brief stop, and soon they were on their way again, arriving at the banks of the Musselshell around midday.

There was a small group of cows standing in the shallow water close to the bank when they came up, so Shorty rode into the river to check the brands. "All these cows are wearin' M slash C brands," he called back to Carson. "I'll keep 'em bunched here, and we can push 'em back on our range after we see if there's any more by the river. Why don't you take a little ride down around that bend? There might be more down that way."

Carson acknowledged with a wave of his hand, and turned the bay gelding to the east. He knew the cows would not likely cross the river over to the Bar-T range if left alone, so there was no harm in leaving them there until roundup as long as there was no rustling going on. And because the brands on these six strays had not been tampered with, it was apparent that Mr. Cain's cattle were all right. He had continued along the river for the better part of a mile when he spotted a dozen cows on the opposite bank, the beginning of Lon Tuttle's Bar-T range, according to Shorty. Carson turned to look back the way he had come, but the bend in the river blocked his view of Shorty. To satisfy his curiosity, he decided to cross over to the other side to take a look at the cows.

The first thing that captured his attention as he rode up the opposite bank was the almost uniform epidemic of black spot disease that had evidently afflicted the cows. It was a blatant alteration of the brand, especially this close to roundup. Given a little more time, the mutilated M/C brand might have looked more like an old sore, and the freshness of the Bar-T brand might have faded. When the stolen cattle were scattered among the thousands rounded up, it was hoped, they would be too few to notice.

Carson decided the best thing to do was to drive the cattle all the way back to range headquarters to make sure they ended up where they belonged. He rode around behind them and started driving them down the bank. They were reluctant to cross over, even though it was shallow enough at this point for them to ford without getting in over their heads. It took a while before he pushed a couple of lead steers to find shallower footing on the south side, but it was easier then to get the others to follow. At last, all twelve cows were back on the proper bank of the river, and Carson started them back toward Shorty.

While Carson was busy trying to get a dozen reluctant cows across the river, Shorty had visitors in the form of four riders who suddenly came up behind him from the north side of the river. There was a thick bank of bushes growing between the cottonwood trees that hid the riders until they appeared on the bank. They paused for a few moments while they and Shorty silently eyed each other. Then after a few muttered words between them, the four riders filed down the bank and crossed over to the M/C side of the river.

Shorty watched cautiously as they rode up to confront him. First glance told him that these were not ordinary cowpunchers. They looked as rough as the men he had seen a month back, but they were different men. He was sure of that. Extremely uncomfortable with the position he found himself in, he nevertheless greeted them boldly. "What brings you fellers down this way?"

One of them, a menacing-looking man with dark black hair hanging shoulder length from under a wide-brim Montana Peak hat to fall on the shoulders of a buckskin coat, answered Shorty with a question. "Who the hell are you?"

Rankled a bit by the curt demand, Shorty replied, "I work for Mr. Mathew Cain and the M/C Ranch, whose range I'm settin' on right now." He nodded toward the water behind them. "That river you just crossed is the line between the M/C and the Bar-T. You fellers work for the Bar-T?"

"Yeah," the stranger replied. "We work for the Bar-T. We're lookin' for some of Mr. Tuttle's stock that's strayed over the river."

"I ain't seen none of his cows on this side," Shorty said, "but if there is, you'll get 'em back after roundup."

"I expect we'll get 'em when we wanna get 'em," one of the other men said. He and the other two moved their horses to form a semicircle facing Shorty.

Shorty had a pretty good idea what was coming next, and he backed away a few steps, shifting his eyes back and forth over the grinning faces of the men confronting him. "I reckon it's my job to see don't none of Mr. Cain's stock gets took," he said, and took another step backward.

"That's a pretty damn big job for one man all by his lonesome," Black Hair said with a sneer.

"He ain't all by himself." The voice came from the brush between the cottonwoods behind them. "He's got me and this Winchester lookin' at your backs." He cocked it to emphasize his meaning. All four jumped when they heard it, hands falling onto their gun handles. "First one draws one of those guns is the first one gets shot," Carson warned.

"Hold on!" Black Hair blurted. "There ain't no use in goin' off half-cocked. Ain't nobody done nobody no harm."

"I expect the best thing for you men to do is to get the hell off M/C range and stay off," Carson said, moving out of the trees, his Winchester still trained on the backs of the four men. "If I find any more M/C cattle with those damn round sores on 'em, I'm gonna cut out two Bar-T cows for every one I find. Now get on back across the river where you belong."

"All right, we're goin'." The four rustlers turned their horses back toward the water as Carson came out in the open. Both men stopped, stunned when they were suddenly face-to-face. "Carson Ryan!" Duke Slayton blurted when he found his voice.

Just as startled, Carson exclaimed, "Duke Slayton!" He recognized one of the others then. "And Johnny Briggs," he added softly, his mind spinning in confusion.

Baffled more so than anyone, except possibly the other two men with Duke and Johnny, Shorty could only gape for a moment. Then he hurriedly pulled his Colt from his holster. Duke recovered his senses quickly. "Carson, boy, am I glad to see you got away from that army patrol! We was plenty worried about you and Lute. Ain't that right, Johnny?"

"That's a fact," Johnny replied. "We was plenty worried."

"You son of a bitch," Carson said. "You ruined my life and damn near got me hung!" He was fighting hard to keep from pulling the trigger and knocking the lying murderer off his horse. But he was calm enough to know if he did there was a good chance he and Shorty might catch a bullet in the fight that would ensue. He had never really thought that he might someday run into Duke and Johnny, and when it happened so soon, he wasn't sure what to do about it. "I shoulda just shot you back there instead of warnin' you."

"Now, look here, Carson," Duke implored. "There wasn't never no hard feelin's about you. Hell, all the boys liked you, but it wouldn'ta done no good to tell you everythin'. We was just plannin' to part company when we got up here, and nobody would know the difference. We didn't count on that cavalry patrol ambushin' us. We didn't have no choice but to get the hell outta there. Ain't that right, Johnny?" Again Briggs nodded enthusiastically while Duke continued. "Look at my side of it. I lost a lot of good boys. Some of them fellers had been with me for a long time. Rufus, Skinny, Varner, Bad Eye. I ain't got no idea what happened to Bad Eye, but I heard the marshals run up on Lute all the way back down near Cheyenne. That crazy old fool shoulda had sense enough to head up this way like the rest of us. But hell, it was like losing family, losin' those boys." Almost forgetting, he hastened to add, "And you, of course. I was worried about you. We was hopin' you and Lute had run for it. Ain't that right, Johnny?"

"That's right, Carson, we were hopin'."

It was a touching performance, but Carson wasn't buying it. "Duke, you're a lyin' son of a bitch, and I oughta shoot you down right here, but I'm gonna let you and that trash ridin' with you ride on back to the Bar-T. But if I see you on this side of the river again, I'm not gonna stop to warn you. I *will* shoot you down. There will be no more M/C cattle stolen, or I will come on the Bar-T lookin' for you."

"Them's mighty harsh words from somebody you rode with," Duke said. "There mighta been different things said if you wasn't standin' there with that rifle pointed at me."

"You're wastin' my time," Carson said. "Get goin' and thank your lucky stars that you're able to ride away from here."

"All right, we'll go, and no hard feelin's. I know you think you been double-crossed, but we didn't mean for it to happen like it did." When there was no sign of mercy in Carson's face, Duke said, "Come on, boys, let's get back on our own range."

One of the men riding with Duke and Johnny was not inclined to be kicked off the M/C range. A tall, thin fellow, wearing a bowler hat, and answering to the name Blackie was not willing to retreat without protest. "Just a damn minute, here," he said, "who the hell do you think you are? You don't own this river. We'll go where the hell we please, this side or the other'n."

"Let it go for now, Blackie," Duke warned

him. He had spent a short time with Carson Ryan, but it was enough to know that he didn't make meaningless threats. He also knew that it was highly unlikely that Carson would blatantly execute the four of them unless he was forced to. "There'll be another time," he said softly to Blackie. "Ain't no use in any of us gettin' shot."

The warning was wasted on Blackie. "To hell with him," he said. "He still ain't but one man with a rifle. Him and his partner are two against four of us. If he pulls that trigger, he's a dead man for sure, 'cause one of us is gonna get the next shot."

Carson's patience was threatening to expire. "Shorty," he directed, "make sure you aim that pistol at Mr. Blackie there. If somebody pulls a trigger here, I wanna be damn sure he gets one of the first bullets."

"I got him covered," Shorty replied. "I believe we can get all four of 'em before they can draw their guns. I'll take care of Blackie and that other feller beside him, so we don't waste time shootin' the same one." He suspected that Carson was working a bluff, and he wanted to let him know that he was backing him.

"Fair enough," Carson came back. "I'll take Duke and Johnny. When I count to three, we'll cut 'em down. You ready? One —"

"Wait! Damn it, wait a minute," Duke protested. "We're goin'!" He wasn't ready to call Carson's bluff. Maybe he was wrong. Maybe the young man was bitter enough to take out the revenge he threatened. One thing he knew, however, was the only two with weapons already drawn and aimed were Carson and his partner. And he was damn sure he was not fast enough to pull his weapon and fire before that first bullet hit him, and he had serious doubts that Blackie and Jake were, either. "Come on, boys," he said, and reined his horse back toward the water. As he entered the river, he called back to Carson, "It was good to see you again, Carson. Looks like you won the first round. Next time might be different."

"Keep your eye on 'em, Shorty," Carson warned before answering Duke's warning. "There ain't no need for no next time," he called back to Duke. "You just stay on that side of the river and we'll get along just fine." With his rifle raised against his shoulder, and the front sight resting on Duke's back, he stood ready to fire as the four rustlers made their way toward the north bank of the river. When they were out of earshot, he told Shorty, "We better get outta here pretty damn quick as soon as they get outta sight."

"You don't have to tell me that," Shorty replied, his pistol still aimed at the departing four. "I thought for a minute back there we were gonna be ass-deep in a shootin' war, and I still ain't sure they won't be doublin' back on us."

"I know damn well they will be," Carson responded. "That's why we'd best find ourselves someplace to wait for 'em, someplace with some protection for us and our horses." He had not ridden with Duke and his gang long enough to know the extent of his potential for ruthlessness, since he and the rest of his *cowboys* had tricked him for so long. But he had found out that they had murdered the original drovers of the herd they had stolen. The soldiers who had arrested him told him that, so he thought it in his and Shorty's best interests to assume the outlaws would be coming after them.

They continued to consider their options while both men kept their eyes on the four riders passing through the cottonwood grove on the other side of the river. "Whaddaya think we oughta do about these cows?" Shorty asked. "We can't fool around tryin' to drive cattle while that bunch is sneakin' around, lookin' to get a shot at us."

Remembering then, Carson informed him, "Hell, I've got a dozen head I left around the bend of the river that I drove across from the other side, and they've all got Bar-T brands on 'em — right beside fresh sores where the old brands used to be."

"Damn," Shorty swore, just as the last of the four rustlers cleared the tree line and followed the others across the open prairie, "how we gonna handle that many strays?"

"I don't know," Carson answered honestly. He was reluctant to leave the cattle for Duke and his partners to claim again, but the most important thing was not to get bushwhacked. He stood up in his stirrups and looked around him before settling on a low line of hills behind them. "We've got a little time before they'll take a chance on circlin' back on us. Let's see if we can drive those cows back up in those breaks back yonder and maybe find someplace to keep 'em bunched up for the night . . ." He paused. "Unless you've got a better idea."

"That sounds as good as any to me," Shorty said. "Let's get started."

One final look at the four riders, now in the distance, and the two partners headed the six strays along toward the bend of the river, where they picked up the dozen Carson had left grazing there. The cattle seemed more inclined toward milling around near the shallow water close to the bank, but the two drovers were finally able to herd them away toward the hills to the south. Daylight was fading rapidly by the time they reached the line of rugged, rocky breaks that led up to barren hilltops devoid of trees or grass. It was not an ideal place to bed a group of cattle for the night, but there was grass along the base of the hills and a spring that had almost dried up. "It'll have to do," Shorty said. "We ain't got time for nothin' better."

"We can drive 'em up to the back of that ravine," Carson suggested, pointing to a pocket formed by the narrow walls. "Maybe we can cut enough of that sagebrush over yonder to make a fence to close 'em in. Whaddaya think?"

"Might work at that," Shorty said.

So they set to work building a sagebrush fence across the narrow foot of the ravine. As darkness approached, they drove the cattle inside their enclosure and turned their attention to making a camp. There were very few trees along the base of the hills, but they managed to find enough dead limbs and brush to build a fire. Shorty turned his attention toward making some coffee while Carson climbed up the back of the ravine to the top of the hill to take a look behind them for signs of Duke and his men. When he came back down, Shorty asked, "See anythin'?"

"Nope," Carson answered, "and pretty soon it's gonna be too dark to see much if there is anything out there."

"Well, you'd better try some of this coffee while you've got the chance. That little ol' trickle of a stream is so small that I had a hard time fillin' the pot. I got a little sand and rocks in it from scrapin' the bottom." He took a sip from his cup and smacked his lips. "I swear, though, I believe it gives it a little body."

"Anything would taste pretty good right now," Carson said as he poured a cup for himself. "We'd best lay out our bedrolls and build up the fire a little."

Shorty bit off a hunk from the strip of jerky he was eating and remarked, "Times like these sure makes you miss Lizzie's cookin', don't it?" He changed the subject abruptly then, having had no time before to satisfy his curiosity. "How come you know this Duke Slayton fellow?"

Carson shrugged, not wishing to go into any detail about his past. "I ran into him and his gang back before the end of the summer. They were movin' some cattle up Montana way. We parted company back in Wyomin' Territory."

"From what I gathered, you two didn't get along too good," Shorty said, hoping to learn more details.

"No, we didn't," Carson remarked. "I expect we'd best finish up our supper and get ready for tonight."

"I reckon you're right," Shorty said, although disappointed that Carson was tight-lipped on the subject of Duke Slayton. Still, he posed one more question. "What did he call you when he first saw it was you? He said Carson, but didn't he call you somethin' else?"

"I don't know," Carson replied. "That son of a bitch is likely to call you anything."

There was still enough light to see the cow pies and hoofprints of the twelve cows that Carson had left on the riverbank, although it was fading rapidly. "Here's what happened to that bunch we changed the brands on this afternoon," Johnny Briggs called out to the others.

Duke Slayton rode over to see for himself. "Ain't no doubt about that," he confirmed after he dismounted and took a closer look.

"The son of a bitch went across the river and drove 'em back." Leading his horse, he followed the tracks for a couple of dozen yards before concluding, "They drove 'em back toward those hills."

Blackie stared off in the direction Duke indicated. "Well, I expect they couldn'ta got too far before darkness set in, so let's get after 'em."

"Just hold your horses a minute," Duke said. Unlike Johnny Briggs, Blackie and Jake had not ridden with Duke long enough to know that he called the shots, and it was a source of some irritation to him if you didn't remember that. "If you can see those hills in this light, then they can see you comin' just as good. And I wanna be sure we get the jump on the two of 'em, so we'll wait till it gets a little darker. Then we'll catch 'em while they're sleepin'. It'll be easier to spot a campfire after dark, anyway."

"Maybe you're right," Blackie conceded.

"Sure he's right," Johnny said. "That's why he's the boss." He looked at Duke then and said, "We might as well take it easy. Right, Duke?"

"Might as well," Duke replied. "Might even build us a little fire down under the bank and have a little coffee, give 'em a chance to crawl in their blankets."

"I'll get some wood," Jake volunteered.

It seemed a casual affair as the four outlaws relaxed on the south bank of the Musselshell River, drinking coffee, biding their time. To further enhance the atmosphere, Blackie brought out a bottle of rye whiskey from his saddlebag to spike the coffee. There was no feeling of concern on the part of any of them for what they intended to do — the cold-blooded murder of two men. For Duke, especially, there was no sense of guilt for killing anything or anyone that might hinder his going after what he wanted. There was no choice now as far as Carson was concerned. He had to be killed, because he could identify Johnny and him as rustlers. So his only concern beyond that was the possibility that too much of Blackie's rye whiskey might hamper their aim when the shooting started. For that reason, he halted the passing around of the bottle before it was totally empty. It might have been a little too late, for Jake had already fallen asleep.

Another hour passed before Duke decided it was time to move. He sent Johnny ahead to see if he could find any sign that would lead them to where Carson drove the cattle, knowing Johnny was the better tracker. "Let's go," Duke said, and gave Jake a little kick in the back. "Get up." It took a couple more prods with the toe of his boot before the sleepy outlaw grunted in protest. When Jake stumbled awkwardly upon getting on his feet, Duke demanded, "Are you drunk?"

"Hell no, I ain't drunk," Jake protested, "not on that little bit of whiskey."

"Damn you," Duke warned, "you'd better not be. I don't know nothin' about the feller he's got with him, but Carson Ryan ain't nobody to take lightly, so you'd better be awake." He watched Jake for a few moments more before getting ready to step up in the saddle. Jake and Blackie might not understand why he was so cautious about Carson Ryan, but he remembered how Carson always seemed to be in control of his surroundings. He remembered the quickness of his reflexes, like the time he dueled Jack Varner with tree limbs, and the way he outsmarted the bigger man to keep from getting his ass whipped. No, he told himself, he would not take the young man lightly, and the best way to avoid trouble from him in the future was to put a bullet in his head tonight. To make sure Jake and Blackie understood, he told them again what had to happen. "Mr. Tuttle said to make sure nobody saw us herdin' Mathew Cain's cows. And damn it, Carson and that feller with him saw us, so we can't let 'em get back to tell Cain. So if you wanna keep your jobs, you'd best make sure we take care of those two."

They rode out across the rolling prairie toward the hills, now no more than a long line of dark shadows in the moonless night. Halfway between the river and the hills, they met Johnny on his way back. "I found 'em," Johnny said as he pulled up before them. "They made a camp back up in a ravine. They were tryin' to hide it, I reckon, but I still caught sight of their fire. I worked up the ravine a ways till I could see the camp. Looks like they run them cows up in there, too. I could see both of 'em movin' around the fire, but they were too far away to get a good shot. There ain't no back door to that ravine they picked. It leveled off about halfway up, and ended up at a cliff about fifty feet straight up. The best thing to do is to climb up those hills on both sides of that ravine and trap 'em in a cross fire."

"Then I reckon that's what we'll do," Duke said. "Lead us out."

Duke and the other two followed Johnny to the base of the closest hill, where he stopped to point out the ravine where Carson and Shorty had ridden up to make their camp. "You say they got all them strays bottled up in there with 'em?" Jake asked.

"That's right," Johnny replied.

"Hell, we could just set ourselves up right along here and wait for 'em to come out in the mornin'," Jake said. "We oughta be able to knock both of 'em down before they even know what hit 'em."

"I ain't plannin' to sit down here at the foot of that ravine all night," Duke said. "It's best to take care of business tonight and be back on our home range come mornin'." That should be the end of the discussion as far as he was concerned. "All right, me and Johnny'll go up this side of the hill. You and Blackie cross over to the other side of the ravine and go up that slope. Just get where you got a clear shot down in that camp, but don't start nothin' till I shoot. Everybody got that straight?" When all three acknowledged, he said, "Let's go, then."

Halfway up the slope, they found a good place to leave their horses, so they left them there and climbed the rest of the way on foot. Upon reaching the top, they made their way cautiously to the rim of the ravine. A thin column of smoke rose lazily from the floor of the defile. It would have been undetectable had it not been for the occasional spark that floated up with it. Inching up even closer, Duke and Johnny

266

reached a rocky ledge where they could see the camp some seventy-five feet below. It had all the appearance of a sleeping camp. The fire was slowly dying out with two sleeping forms on either side. "Too damn peaceful," Duke muttered as he strained to make out more detail on the two forms wrapped in their blankets. Always wary, he looked over at Johnny and asked a wordless question. *Is it them, or just their blankets rolled up to make it look like them?* Guessing Duke's silent question, Johnny simply shrugged in reply. So they waited, watching for some movement from the sleeping forms, any little twitch that would confirm that there was a live body under the blanket.

Still suspicious, Duke pulled back from the edge a couple of feet and took a long look around behind him to make sure no one was sneaking up behind them. Moving back up beside Johnny, he spoke softly. "See either one of 'em move a muscle?" Johnny shook his head without taking his eyes off the camp below them. "I don't know," Duke continued. "I got a funny feelin' about this." No sooner were the words out than the ravine erupted in gunfire.

Startled by the sudden explosion of rifle fire, Duke and Johnny both flattened themselves on the ground, hugging it for dear life, until realizing there were no shots coming their way. Knowing then what had happened, Duke swore, "Damn those bastards! I told them not to shoot until I did!" He got up on his knees then to better see into the camp. Jake and Blackie had decided not to wait any longer, and had opened up with their rifles, sending shot after shot into and around the two blanketed forms. The thunderous volley succeeded in stirring the cattle up and they began milling around in a frantic circle. Boxed in by the cliff at one end of the ravine, they moved toward the lower end of the camp, only to be stopped by the sagebrush fence. There was no sign of any activity in the camp. With the number of holes in both blankets, there was little doubt that, if they were not decoys, both men were dead.

When the rifle fire finally ended, all was quiet again, with no evidence of return fire from anywhere around them. Duke got to his feet and called out across the cliff, "Jake! Let's go down there and make sure they're dead!" He paused a moment. "You hear me?"

"Yeah, we heard you," Jake yelled back. "We're goin'." He and Blackie emerged from behind a sage thicket and started working their way down the side of the ravine.

Johnny got up and started to do the same, but Duke caught him by the arm. "Let's just wait a bit, and let them get down there first." Understanding then, Johnny smiled and nodded. There was still the possibility that an ambush was awaiting them at the bottom of that ravine, and since Jake and Blackie had decided to act on their own, they deserved to be the ones who got caught in the trap — if there was one.

There was no hesitation on the part of Blackie and Jake. Eager to see what spoils they might find on the bodies and in the saddlebags of their victims, they hurried down the steep side of the ravine while Duke and Johnny descended slowly and cautiously. Upon reaching the floor of the ravine, Blackie ran toward the two horses tied beyond the smoldering fire. "I'm claimin' that bay that one feller was ridin'," he yelled out to Jake. He got as far as the campfire before the rifle shot staggered him, causing him to drop to his knees. A second shot knocked him over on his side, dead.

Jake, his brain still somewhat clouded by the effects of too much alcohol, hesitated for a split second as he realized what was happening. Having seen the muzzle flash in the darkness on the other side of the ravine, he turned around to run back to the protection of the steep slope, only to find himself facing the business end of Shorty's rifle. He had time for only one short cry of protest before Shorty cut him down.

"I knew it!" Duke exclaimed, still only a little way down the side of the ravine. He immediately scrambled back toward the top. Johnny, a few feet below him, raised his rifle and fired toward the last muzzle flash he had seen, seconds before Duke could warn him not to. "Don't shoot, damn it! You'll show 'em where we are!" Johnny held his fire then, but it was already too late. A shot from over near the horses found him as he attempted to scale the slope after Duke.

"I'm shot!" Johnny cried out as he fell face forward, grasping the rough ground beneath him in an effort not to slide down the slope. "Duke!"

Duke was not inclined to waste time at that moment. He pulled himself over the edge of the ravine before hesitating to answer his wounded partner. "How bad?" he called back. "Can you walk?"

"I don't think so," Johnny gasped. "I can't feel my legs."

There was no decision to be made as far as Duke was concerned. "I'm sorry, partner, there ain't nothin' I can do to help you. There ain't no sense in me stayin' around to get shot, too." With those final words to a man who had ridden with him for several years, Duke was off, the angry curses from the abandoned comrade fading in the darkness behind him as he hurried to his horse.

Behind the fleeing man, Carson called out to warn Shorty not to shoot, "Shorty! I'm comin' out. You all right?"

"Yeah," Shorty came back. "I'm comin' out." They emerged from the holes they had dug in the sides of the ravine. "One of 'em got away. I think you got the other'n up on the slope."

The main one that Carson was interested in stopping was not one of the two lying dead on the floor of the ravine, so either Duke or Johnny was the man near the top of the ravine. He was disappointed, but not really surprised, that the ambush had not worked to trap all four of the outlaws. He should have guessed that Duke was wary enough not to rush into a trap without checking it out thoroughly. A wry smile crossed his lips when he speculated that Duke had sent the other two in to test it. *I wouldn't be surprised to find that the one lying at the top of the hill is Johnny Briggs,* he thought. There were some men who just seemed to be natural survivors. Duke Slayton appeared to be one of them.

"I reckon we need to find out if that one up the hill is dead before we go after the other one," Carson said.

Judging by the tone of his voice, it was plain to Shorty that Carson was anxious to get after the one now making his escape, so he volunteered to climb up to check on the one still on the slope. "You go after him," he said. "I'll make sure the other'n's dead."

"Right," Carson said at once, and started toward his horse, then paused to warn Shorty. "You'd best be careful, Shorty. He might not be dead, and a shot from a wounded man is just as bad as one from one who ain't."

"Don't you worry," Shorty replied with a chuckle. "I ain't about to let anythin' happen to your ol' woodcuttin' partner."

Carson guided the bay carefully past the makeshift corral he and Shorty had laid across the mouth of the ravine. He could hear sounds of Duke's horse as it came sliding down the hillside, but he was not willing to risk breaking his horse's leg on the rough, uneven surface. So he held him back until he was out of the ravine. By then, Duke had a good head start, so Carson pushed the bay into a full gallop, hoping to close the distance rapidly. He could not see the man he was chasing. There were not even any little dust clouds kicked up by the galloping horse on the grass-covered prairie, so he held the bay to a straight course to the river. It figured that Duke, or Johnny, would first run to Tuttle's range, and then once across the river, he would try to lose him — or wait in ambush for him.

By the time he reached the river, his horse was just about spent from running full out for so long, but there was no sign of the man he pursued. Finding it hard to believe that his horse had been outrun so badly, he entered the water, only to recoil halfway across when he saw a horse standing at the water's edge on the other side. In reflex action, he jerked the Winchester from the saddle scabbard, prepared to shoot, until he realized there was no rider. When he continued across, he walked the bay up to the other horse and discovered it to be the roan that Duke had been riding the day before. The horse was thoroughly spent from the race across the prairie, and he realized then the reason his horse was so badly beaten in his attempt to close the distance. Duke, or Johnny — he still didn't know which one he was chasing — had fled with both horses, and switched to the fresher one here at the river. It might not account for a great difference in the condition of the horses, but Carson knew it was enough to gain an edge.

He felt helpless to do anything about the problem at this point. The bay had given his all when Carson asked for it. To push the horse farther could result in severe damage to its wind. Forgetting his anger for a moment, and thinking rationally, he had to question the wisdom of continuing to follow Duke deeper into Bar-T range. He had no notion as to the layout of the ranch headquarters, or how many men would come to the defense of one of their own. *Ain't worth the risk,* he told himself, *especially when my horse is too tired to run.* He turned around and crossed back over, leading the abandoned horse.

When he got back to the ravine, he called out to Shorty, identifying himself. When Shorty acknowledged, Carson walked back up to their camp, leading the horses. "What about the one up on the hill?" he asked.

"Dead," Shorty answered.

"Long black hair, wearin' a Montana Peak hat and a buckskin coat?"

"No, it was the other one," Shorty said.

So it was Duke who managed to get away, Carson thought. "Figures," he commented.

Duke always got away.

"I see you picked up a spare horse," Shorty said.

"Yeah, Duke ran this one out and switched over to Johnny's. I expect there's two more horses somewhere on the other side of this ravine — if they ain't run off somewhere."

Shorty chuckled. "Wasn't a bad night's work, was it? Got some of our cattle back and picked up three horses, saddles and all."

"I reckon," Carson replied.

They had to think that there was no longer a threat from Duke Slayton on this night, but both men were still too much in a state of readiness to think about trying to sleep the few hours of darkness that remained. They decided instead to rekindle the fire and make some coffee. After finding the gunmen's two horses, they figured to drive the recovered cattle out early the next morning, since there was no water or grass in the ravine.

CHAPTER 10

Lon Tuttle, owner of the Bar-T Ranch, walked down to the cook shack where his men were eating breakfast. He wasted no time with "good mornings" as he went straight to Duke Slayton, who was seated at the head of the long table. "I heard you came in by yourself before daybreak. What happened to the three men who were with you?"

"I was comin' to see you after breakfast," Duke replied respectfully. "I didn't wanna disturb you too early."

"Where's Blackie and Jake and Johnny?" Tuttle insisted impatiently.

"Well . . ." Duke hesitated, aware of the sudden silence that fell over the table as all ears were tuned to his explanation. "We ran into some trouble."

"Some trouble?" Tuttle demanded.

"Yes, sir, we ran into an ambush when we went after some cows they was tryin' to drive back on M/C range. We never had a chance. They set up an ambush and killed everyone but me, and I was lucky to get away. There wasn't much else I could do. There was too many of 'em."

"How many were there?" Tuttle asked, at once concerned that Mathew Cain might be sending large gangs of rustlers to cut out part of his herd.

"I couldn't count all of 'em," Duke lied. "It was too damn dark in that little box canyon, probably ten or twelve guns. They was led by Carson Ryan. That much I know for sure."

"You mean John Carson, that new hand that Cain hired?"

"That ain't his name," Duke replied, realizing an opportunity to take the heat off himself for the failed mission. "His real name's Carson Ryan, and he's wanted in Wyomin' for cattle rustlin' and murder — and one of the men he murdered was a U.S. deputy marshal that was takin' him to prison."

Duke's accusation captured Tuttle's interest immediately, and the possibility of a full-scale range war loomed in his mind. Mathew Cain ran a lot more cattle than he, and consequently had a few more men on his payroll. Tuttle didn't care for his odds in a war with the M/C, especially if Cain had brought in a hired gun. Tuttle had been operating under the impression that Cain had so many cows that he wouldn't miss a few that wandered over to the Bar-T. Duke Slayton had been the chief influence for this policy. Now, thanks to Slayton's botching of last night's incident, Cain knew about the brand switching. "Damn!" he swore when considering the likely results of a war with Cain. Maybe, he thought, it might be a good idea to ride over and talk to Cain and convince him that he had no knowledge of the rustling. He could lay the blame on Duke. "You sure about this John Carson, or Carson, what'd you say his name is?"

"Ryan," Duke replied. "Yes, sir, I'm sure. He rode with me for a short spell."

Tuttle could see what steps he had to take to hopefully settle with Mathew Cain, and the quicker the better with roundup coming up soon. "I reckon the best thing for you now is to pack up your stuff and leave the Bar-T," he said.

Duke was taken aback. He hadn't foreseen that possibility. "What the hell?" he demanded. "You firin' me?"

"That's right," Tuttle replied. "And you ain't got nobody to blame but yourself. I want you off my ranch."

"Why, you sorry son of a bitch!" Duke exploded. "I'm the best hope you've got of fightin' that bunch." His outburst caused a sudden tightening of the tension around the table. Tuttle's foreman, Tom Castor, got up from the bench to stand by his boss. Duke took note of the gesture, but fumed on. "I almost got shot doin' your dirty work, and this is the thanks I get?" There was no sign of yielding in the two stern faces confronting him. After a lengthy pause filled with silence, Duke finally gave in. "Well, by God, if that's the way you want it, then I'll go. I didn't cotton much to workin' for this yellow-dog crew of yours, anyway." He pushed back from the table, knocking over the short stool he had been sitting on, and got to his feet. "Good luck with your war with the M/C without me," he said sarcastically, then stormed out of the cook shack.

Tuttle looked at his foreman and calmly said, "See that he gets outta here without doin' any damage, Tom."

"Yes, sir," Tom replied, and followed Duke out the door. He was more than happy to see Slayton go. He didn't like the man to begin with, and he had harbored some concerns that Duke might be after his job.

Back in the cook shack, Tuttle addressed his men. "I know we've been a little loose when it came to whose cow was whose, but we ain't travelin' that trail no more. I blame myself for listenin' to that man and his three partners, but I aim to be a better neighbor from now on." His statement was met with nods of approval from the men seated around the table, most of them glad to see the last of Duke Slayton.

Lucas Cain called to his older brother back inside the barn, "Justin, riders comin' over the ridge."

Justin took his time walking out to the front of the barn. "Who is it?" he asked.

"Don't know," Lucas replied. "I can't tell yet. There's two of 'em, but it don't look like any of our folks."

They waited a few minutes until the riders descended the ridge and pulled a little closer. "That looks like Lon Tuttle," Justin said, "and Tom Castor." He waited a minute longer to be sure. "Run up to the house and tell Pa he's got company." After Lucas hurried away, Justin muttered, "I wonder what the hell they want."

"Justin," Lon Tuttle acknowledged as he and his foreman pulled up to the barn.

Justin returned the greeting in kind, then waited while the two men stepped down. "What brings you and Tom over?"

"I need to talk to your pa," Tuttle answered. He handed his reins to Tom, who led the horses over and tied them to one of the corral posts.

"He's up at the house," Justin said. "I sent Lucas ahead to tell him you're here. I reckon we can walk up." It was an awkward visit for Justin, since they had expected more trouble from the Bar-T after John Carson and Shorty drove eighteen head of cattle back from Bar-T range, especially since the altercation had resulted in three men getting shot.

They were only halfway across the yard when Mathew Cain appeared on the front porch, with Lucas close behind him. "Well, well, Lon Tuttle," the patriarch of the M/C remarked, truly surprised to see his neighbor. "To what do we owe the pleasure of this visit?"

"How do, Mathew?" Tuttle responded, not at all comfortable in the role of peacemaker. "I expect it's past time to talk about a few things that's happened between our two spreads that mighta caused some misunderstandin'."

"Oh?" Cain replied, knowing full well what Tuttle was referring to. "What kinda things is that?"

"You know what I'm talkin' about," Tuttle

responded. "There ain't no sense in beatin' around the bush about it. There's been some swappin' of brands and downright cattle rustlin', and I came over here to own up to my boys doin' most of it. But what I'm here to tell you is that I just found out about it." He gestured toward Tom Castor. "Neither me nor my foreman knew that some of the men I'd hired to help with roundup were reworkin' the brands on some of your cattle. So I've come to see you today to let you know I fired the ones doin' the stealin'. I'm an honest man, and I won't stand for outlaws on my payroll, so I sent 'em packin'. Tom here tells me that those men I fired musta tried to steal some M/C cattle a couple of nights ago and run up against that gunman you hired. I want you to know that wasn't any of my doin'. Like I said, I fired those men."

Cain listened patiently, although thinking all he was hearing was a pack of lies, thinking there was no reason for any of his men to change the brands unless they were being paid to do it. But the reference to his *gunman* caught his attention. "What the hell are you talkin' about, Tuttle? What gunman?"

"That young feller, that outlaw," Tuttle replied, and turned to Castor. "What's his name, Tom?"

"John Carson," his foreman replied.

"Yeah," Tuttle continued, "John Carson. That's the one. He killed three of those men I just kicked off my ranch."

"John Carson?" Cain exclaimed. He and Justin exchanged astonished glances. "John's sure as hell not a gunman. He's handy with a rifle, all right, but he's just a ranch hand like all the rest of my men — and a damn good man with cattle." He gave Tuttle a stern look. "I don't hire any gunmen on my ranch."

Looking fully contrite, Tuttle shook his head slowly. "That's the main reason I came over here today. I figured it was the right thing to do to make sure you hadn't been lied to, just like I was. I have it on good authority that this feller John Carson's name is really Carson Ryan, and he's wanted in Wyomin' for murder and cattle rustlin'." He paused then to witness the effect his statement had on Cain and his sons.

"Somebody told you wrong, mister," Justin interrupted. "John Carson ain't no outlaw. He didn't shoot all three of your men, anyway. Shorty Wheeler shot one of 'em, and he sure as hell ain't no outlaw. And the only reason anybody got shot was that those four jumped John and Shorty. They were just defendin' themselves, and they were on M/C range. You need to get your facts straight before you go around spreadin' stories about honest men. Hell, you're the one hirin' outlaws."

Still striving to maintain his peaceful countenance, Tuttle responded, "I figured you'd think that. So I figured it best to come over here and talk it over face-to-face. I got rid of my dishonest hands as soon as I found out about 'em. And it's plain to see now that you don't know who you hired, either. One of the men I fired told me he used to ride with Carson Ryan, and they were both charged with cattle rustlin' and murder. Not only that, but your boy John Carson killed a U.S. deputy marshal and escaped on his way to prison." He could no longer hold on to his countenance of innocence, and gave in to a smug look of contentment when he witnessed the profound effect his statement had upon both Cain and his sons.

Stunned for a few moments, Mathew Cain recovered then. "Well, is there anything else you came here to talk about?" He strained to keep any emotion from disturbing his somber expression.

"No, I guess not," Tuttle replied. "I just thought it the neighborly thing to do, in case you didn't know what kind of man you had workin' for you. I'm hopin' we can work together on the roundup comin' up."

"I expect it'd be in both our best interests if we do," Cain replied stiffly. He turned to direct his younger son then. "Lucas, run, fetch the gentlemen's horses. They've got a long ride back to the Bar-T. I suspect they're anxious to get started." With no doubt that they had been rudely dismissed, Tuttle and his foreman turned and walked toward the corral where the horses were tied. When they had gone, Cain turned to Justin and said, "Go get John Carson. Tell him I wanna see him."

"Him and Shorty are still ridin' the north section," Justin said, "up near the Musselshell. It might take me a spell to find 'em."

"Pack you somethin' to eat and go find 'em," Mathew said. "I wanna hear what he has to say about this." It was hard for him to think such a fine-looking young man like John Carson could be the man Tuttle had described, and he wondered how he could have been such a bad judge of character. More than likely it was a case of mistaken identity because of the similarity of their names. He hoped so, anyway. He walked into the house then to see Millie coming from the front bedroom where, unbeknownst to him, she had been sitting at the side of the window, listening to the conversation in the front yard.

"I knew it," Millie muttered. "I knew it."

Lizzie looked up from the potatoes she was peeling when the young girl walked into the kitchen. "What?" Lizzie asked in her heavy German accent. "What you knew?"

"Nothing," Millie replied. "I was just thinking to myself." She paused for a moment, perplexed. Then seeing the half-empty bucket on the sideboard, she announced, "I'm going to go get some water." She met Nancy coming in the back door, and had to step quickly to the side to keep from hitting her with the bucket.

"What's the matter with her?" Nancy asked. "She almost hit me with that bucket."

Lizzie shrugged, not really concerned. "Who knows? She don't say."

Justin did not find Carson and Shorty until the next day. About midday, he spotted them beside a wide creek on the eastern boundary of the M/C range. He was spotted at almost the same time by the two men sitting by a small fire eating jerky and drinking coffee while their horses rested. "Look comin' yonder," Shorty said. "Looks like Justin."

Carson, whose back was turned, looked back over his shoulder in the direction Shorty pointed. "It is Justin," he confirmed. "He might like a little coffee. Any left in that pot?"

"A cup or two," Shorty answered. "Wonder what he's doin' out here."

They got to their feet to greet their boss as Justin reined his horse to a stop before them and dismounted. "I couldn't find you yesterday," he said, "so I figured you might be down this way."

"What was you lookin' for us for?" Shorty asked, joking. "Lookin' to find out if we was just settin' on our behinds drinkin' coffee?"

Justin's stoic features relaxed for an instant with the hint of a smile to acknowledge Shorty's effort to joke. Just as quickly, it reverted to an expression of gravity. "I was comin' to get John," he told them, looking directly at his new ranch hand. "My pa wants to talk to you right away, so we'd best cut straight across and get on back to the house."

"What's he wanna talk to me about?" Carson asked.

"I reckon you'll find that out as soon as we get back," was all Justin offered.

"Am I in trouble?" Carson asked, trying to think of anything he could have done to get in hot water with his boss. Justin was always of a serious demeanor, but he seemed even more tight-lipped than usual.

"Well, you ain't done nothin' to get yourself in trouble with me and my pa," Justin replied. "But Pa wants to talk to you."

Astonished by Justin's attitude, Shorty wondered what Carson could possibly have done that didn't involve him as well. Yet Mathew Cain only wanted to talk to Carson and not the two of them. "Well, I reckon we'll be ridin' back," he commented. "There's coffee left in the pot. How 'bout a cup, Justin?"

"Thanks just the same," he replied, "but we'd best get started back."

"The reason we stopped to eat was that the horses needed a rest," Carson informed him. "We ran 'em pretty hard a little while back when we rounded up some strays and drove 'em back toward the main herd. I think we oughta give 'em a little more time before we head back." He wasn't sure of the urgency of Justin's mission, but he didn't intend to overwork the bay gelding if it wasn't absolutely necessary.

"So you might as well have a cup of coffee," Shorty suggested.

Justin considered that for a moment before replying, "I reckon it can wait that long. I might as well let my horse drink."

"You got any idea what he's talkin' about?" Shorty asked while Justin led his horse to water.

"Nope," Carson answered.

"There ain't much left in this pot," Justin commented as he filled his cup. He refused the offer of a piece of jerky from Shorty and sat down to drink the strong black brew, while making an effort to ignore the awkward silence that his visit had created. He would rather have questioned Carson immediately about Lon Tuttle's accusations, but his father had been specific in his instructions. He couldn't help wondering about Carson's reactions. If he told him what Tuttle had claimed, would he deny it, or would he run? And what difference would it make if he did? As long as he posed no threat to him or his father, there was no harm done. Finally Justin could hold his curiosity in check no longer. "Do you know a man named Duke Slayton?"

Carson became immediately wary, and hesitated before answering, "I know him. That's the man Shorty and me had the gunfight with." He was concerned now, wondering what this was leading up to.

"I know that," Justin said. "But did you know him before you and Shorty had the fight with him and the others?"

Carson felt the blood in his veins suddenly go cold. He didn't like the line of questioning. His first inclination was to simply say no, but he glanced at Shorty's blank stare of curiosity and remembered that he had already told him he had known Duke Slayton before. He had to answer something. Still, he hesitated, asking a question instead. "Is this what Mr. Cain wants to talk to me about?"

"Yeah," Justin replied, "that and some other things."

"Well," Carson said, hoping he could satisfy Justin with as little information as he had given Shorty before, "I met up with Duke Slayton in Wyomin' Territory, but it wasn't for long. I didn't want any part of him and the crowd he rode with. That's the long and short of it."

Having already opened the subject, Justin was eager to proceed. "What about Slayton's claim that your name ain't John Carson, that it's really Carson Ryan, and you're wanted in Wyomin' for murder and cattle rustlin'?"

There was nothing Carson could say. The awful truth was exposed like an open knife wound, laid open for them to see. Duke Slayton had fixed him up good. He looked from Justin's probing stare to Shorty's openmouthed astonishment, both men anxious to hear his explanation. He took his time in deciding how he was going to answer the question, finally deciding that he would tell the simple truth. "Slayton's right. My name was Carson Ryan. It's John Carson now, and I reckon that's the way I'll keep it, since Carson Ryan is wanted in Wyomin'." He went on to tell them that he had hired on with Slayton as a drover, unaware that the herd he was helping to drive had been stolen and a couple of men killed in the process. He told them about his capture by the army, his conviction as a murderer, the killing of deputy marshal Luther Moody by Red Shirt, and his escape. "That's the whole story," he said when finished, "except for one thing." He looked Justin straight in the eye. "I ain't guilty of any of the damn charges, but nobody wanted to hear my side of it. And I don't reckon you do, either."

For a long moment, both Justin and Shorty were struck speechless. Finally Justin spoke. "I don't know. . . . I mean . . . Son of a bitch. . . ." That was all he could manage for the moment, which was more than

Shorty could muster.

Of the two, Shorty might have been rocked the hardest, for he had felt a close friendship building with his woodchopping partner. He could not picture Carson in the role he was accused of, even after witnessing his cool efficiency during the trap they had set for Slayton and the other three. Like Justin, he had difficulty finding the right words. "I swear, John . . . ," he said before his voice trailed off again. Then he stated, "I believe you."

"I 'preciate it, Shorty," Carson said softly. Then he turned again to Justin. "What do you intend to do about it?"

"I don't know," Justin replied. "I ain't no lawman. There's nothin' I'm supposed to do about it, and I don't plan on sendin' word to the U.S. marshal if that's what you're askin' me. I'm askin' you to ride back with me and talk to Pa. I think he oughta hear your side of the story. I don't see how you can stay on with us if you're wanted by the law. Let's see what Pa says. He'll know what's best to do."

"All right," Carson said. "I'll ride back with you. I'll need to pick up my packhorse and my possibles if I have to move on, anyway. I reckon I owe it to your pa, since he was kind enough to hire me on." With the decision made, they smothered the fire after the horses were deemed rested enough, and started back to the M/C, a somber three riders with a shortage of words and an abundance of thoughts.

Lucas Cain alerted his father as soon as the three riders appeared at the top of the ridge east of the ranch house, and the old man walked out on the porch to await them. He stood there, watching, until they were opposite the barn; then he went down the steps and walked across the yard to meet them. Lucas followed several yards behind him. Inside the house, Millie returned to her post by the window in the front bedroom, hoping to catch a word here and there, enough to figure out what was being said.

The three riders pulled up before the old man and dismounted. Cain told Lucas to take the horses to the barn and tie them to the corral. Disappointed, because he very much wanted to hear what was said to the alleged gunman, Lucas did as he was told. "I appreciate you comin' to talk to me," Cain said to Carson. From the concerned look on the faces of all three men, he speculated that Carson knew why he sent for him. "I'm hopin' you can straighten out some things I've been told about you."

"Yes, sir, I can," Carson replied. "Most of what you've heard is true, but not all of it. I'm wanted by the U.S. marshal service. I reckon that's the thing I can't deny." He went on to tell his side of the story. When he had finished, he said, "That's the God's honest truth. I ain't ever murdered anybody, and I ain't ever stole anybody's cattle, but I sure as hell escaped when I had the chance, and I reckon I'd do it again. It was just dumb luck what happened to me. I should have gone back to Texas with Mr. Patterson after we sold that herd at Ogallala, but I wanted to see Montana."

It was a difficult confession for Mathew Cain to hear. The young man seemed so sincere he wanted to believe him, but he didn't see many choices open to him. Knowing what he had just been told, he couldn't keep him on, in effect harboring a felon. And there were the other men to consider. What effect might that have on them if they found out they were working alongside a convicted murderer and an escaped prisoner? And what kind of example would it set for his children? In good conscience, he could not bring himself to turn him over to the federal marshals, either. The man had brought his daughter and son-in-law through perilous hostile territory to reach Big Timber, risking his own life to do so. That being true, he still could not keep him on as if it would all go away in time. Finally he gave Carson his decision. "Son, I got no way of knowin' if you're tellin' the truth or not. I kinda feel like you are, but from what you've confessed to, I can't keep you on here at my ranch. I hope you understand that. I couldn't explain it to the womenfolk, or to the men who work for me. And I ain't got the heart to turn you in to the law, so I'll just ask you to pack up your things and go your own way. And I wish you luck, wherever you end up. I'd advise you not to hang around too close to Big Timber, because there might be a reward on you, and some of those bastards over on the Bar-T might wanna try for it."

"I 'preciate what you're sayin'," Carson said. "I understand the spot I've put you in, and I wouldn't expect no different. I'll get my stuff and get off your land right away."

"There ain't no need to be in that big a hurry, is there, Pa?" Justin spoke up. "No reason he can't rest up, get somethin' to eat, and ride out in the mornin'?"

"Justin's right," Mathew said. "Give yourself time to get ready and leave tomorrow after breakfast." He started to turn around to go back to the house but hesitated to add, "And don't tell none of the men where you might be thinkin' about goin'. If the law shows up here lookin' for you, I don't wanna know where to tell 'em you went."

"Yes, sir, I 'preciate it," Carson said once again as Cain suddenly offered his hand. Surprised, Carson accepted it and the two men shook hands before the old man turned and returned to the house, leaving the three to tend to their horses.

By the time Shorty and Carson pulled the saddles off their horses and let them out with the others, there wasn't much left of the day. Carson used the time to inventory his possibles in speculation of the days ahead and the winter rapidly coming on. He decided that he needed a lot more supplies in preparation for heading off to the mountains to the west of the M/C range. His latest situation had come upon him so suddenly that he had no plans beyond working cattle for Mathew Cain. He had no prospects beyond possibly the chance of a job with another cattle ranch farther west, maybe closer to Helena. He had no money, so he needed to find a place to trade some of the gear he had accumulated from the encounters along the way from the Black

Hills — several good rifles, an extra saddle, a couple of extra handguns, and a few other things that he didn't need. Justin made him an offer to buy the saddle. It was a more than fair offer and Carson was convinced that it was probably nothing less than an act of charity. But Justin insisted that he had had an eye on the saddle from the first, so Carson acquired a few dollars to use for other supplies.

Shorty stayed close by while Carson prepared to leave, and Carson was convinced that the stocky little man was truly sorry to see him go. "Maybe Mr. Cain would rehire you when this mess has a chance to blow over," he told Carson. But Carson told him that this business with the law wasn't something that would ever blow over, so he didn't expect to be back this way again. "Well, what in the hell are you gonna do?" Shorty asked. "Where are you headin' when you leave here? I know Mr. Cain told you not to tell anybody where you're goin', but hell, I ain't gonna tell nobody. Winter ain't far away."

Carson could see that his friend was genuinely worried about him, but he was not concerned about the coming weather. He was confident in his ability to adapt to whatever the conditions happened to be.

"Don't worry 'bout me," he assured him. "If an Injun can live off the land, then I reckon I can, too. I'll find me a hole somewhere up in those mountains, just like a bear in his cave. When spring gets here, I'll be comin' out with the flowers."

"I oughta go with you," Shorty said, halfway serious.

His comment caused Carson to laugh. "Hell, I'll have my hands full keepin' myself alive. You'd best stay here and take care of the rest of the boys."

Supper that night saw the usual bantering that went on around the long table with the exception of Shorty and Justin, who appeared to be especially quiet. Roundup was set to begin in one week's time, so there was a lot of talk about enjoying the food here in the bunkhouse while they could. "We'll be eatin' some more of that swill Mule calls chuck," Pruett Little blurted, taunting the slight man with the ever-forlorn face. "We'll all be a few pounds lighter if he gives us a case of the gallopin' shits, like he did on the spring roundup."

"That warn't none of my fault," Mule replied in self-defense. "That meat had turned when they brought it to my cook pot. Besides, didn't nobody get the runs but you and Slim, and that's because you ate twice as much as ever'body else."

"Well, I'm tellin' you this," Pruett went on, "if you mess up my grub one more time I'm gonna stuff your scrawny ass in that big stew pot of yours."

"I'll put somethin' extra in your supper," Mule came back. "Might put a little spirit in your step."

Pruett decided to turn his annoying japing on the new man then. "Why don't you let ol' John try his hand at the cookin', Justin? He might be as good at cookin' as he is at choppin' wood."

Accustomed to Pruett's horseplay, but not in the mood to indulge, Justin responded with a simple statement. "Mule will be drivin' the chuck wagon, same as always."

"Well, that sure does seem like a shame," Pruett said. "I bet ol' John can cook, but hell, maybe he'll show us all how to round up cattle, like they do in Texas." With no desire to participate in Pruett's game of needling, Carson made no comment, content to eat his supper and get to his bed, anticipating a long day's ride ahead of him. Still, Pruett wasn't through entertaining himself. "Hey, Justin, let John work with me. I ain't too old to learn new tricks."

Justin was becoming weary of Pruett's mouth, so he made one simple statement.

"John ain't gonna ride with nobody on the roundup. He's leavin' M/C in the mornin'. So eat your supper and let him be." His statement caused a sudden lull in the noisy banter as all eyes turned to focus on Carson.

"Leavin'?" Pruett reacted. "You mean he quit?" He turned to Carson. "You quit?"

"You could say that," Carson replied.

"Well, I'll be . . . ," Pruett said. "Couldn't stick it out a week! How 'bout that, boys? Couldn't stick it out a week. That's just like them Texans, ain't it?"

"Why don't you shut that big mouth of yours, Pruett?" Shorty said. "And let us eat in peace."

Suspecting something more than Justin was telling, and that Shorty was in on it, Pruett was not to be silenced. "Somethin's goin' on here." He looked from Justin to Carson, then back to Shorty. "You might as well tell all of us. What did he do? Steal somethin'? Botherin' the women?" He was delighted with the possibility that Carson had been caught doing something and was getting fired for it. He turned his badgering on Carson then. "How 'bout it, Texan? You get caught behind the outhouse peekin' at Millie?"

Finally Carson realized that Justin was not

going to put a stop to the noisy bully. He had enough of Pruett's mouth for one night, so he broke his silence. "Like Shorty told you, Pruett, shut your damn mouth. What I do and why I'm leavin' is my business, so keep your nose out of it."

All talking stopped, and a total silence descended upon the table. It lasted until broken by Pruett. "Whoa, now," he said, his voice low and threatening. "Lookee here, boys, our woodchoppin' Texas rifleman says it ain't none of our business." He waited for a response, but there was none, so he continued. "Well, I say it is our business. Anythin' that goes on here at the M/C is our business. Ain't that right, Justin?"

Forced to intercede, Justin answered him, "No, it ain't, Pruett. It's his personal business, so leave him be, or I'll fire you, too."

"Aha!" Pruett exclaimed. "So he was fired! I thought so!" When he saw Justin's dander start to get up, he quickly backed down. "All right, all right. I ain't sayin' nothin' more. I'll let him be, just like you said." A triumphant sneer spread across his wide face as he turned to Carson and nodded slowly, as if to promise more to come later.

Carson ignored him and concentrated on finishing the fine meal that Lizzie had prepared, feigning oblivion to the eyes upon

301

him. *What the hell is it about me that attracts every bully around?* he thought. *I'm not going to give him the satisfaction of showing how strong he is.*

After supper, he returned to the barn to make sure the saddle Justin had bought from him was clean and in good shape. It was a good saddle. Deputy Marshal Luther Moody must have paid a pretty penny for it, for it was hand-worked and decorated, and Justin had paid a fair price for it, a reasonable deal for both buyer and seller. Satisfied that everything was in order, he left the tack room, almost bumping into Millie as he came out the door. She was holding a single egg in her hand, and quickly stepped back to avoid a collision.

"For goodness' sake!" she exclaimed. "Like a bull coming out the gate."

"I'm sorry, Millie. I didn't expect to see you down here in the barn. I reckon I'd better watch where I'm goin'."

She quickly tried to explain her presence there, for she usually gathered the eggs in the mornings. "I was checking the hay in the last stall. Some of the chickens have been nesting there, and I forgot to check on it this morning." She held up the egg as proof. "One egg, so I did miss one this morning." She made no move to leave, forcing him to move aside to get past. As he started toward the front door of the barn, she called after him, "So it turns out I was right about you from the beginning."

He turned then to face her. "And what might that be?"

"A gunman," she replied, "running from the law."

"Looks that way, doesn't it?" he replied, seeing no reason to deny it.

"I tried to tell them," she said, seeming reluctant to let it go. "But you had everybody convinced that you were a top hand with cattle."

Her tone was beginning to get to him. "I am a top hand with cattle," he said.

"But you're handier with a rifle, right?"

Fully irritated by the apparent dressing-down he was receiving from the precocious young woman, he responded curtly, "Look, miss, I don't know what I did to get on the wrong side of you, but I ain't gonna be here to bother you come mornin', so I'll say good night to you, and hope you have pleasant dreams." He turned away again and headed for the door. She stopped him once again.

"I want to hear you say it," she blurted.

"Say what?" he responded, without turning around.

"Tell me you didn't kill that deputy, or

those men you stole the cattle from. I wonder if you can own up to what you did."

He turned to face her again, looking her straight in the eye. Evidently Justin or Lucas had told her the reason he was forced to leave. "In the first place, I didn't steal no cattle, and I sure as hell didn't shoot Luther Moody." He continued to glare at her for a few moments more. "And yes, ma'am, I can own up to everythin' I've ever done." With that, he turned again and headed for the barn door.

She called out one final time, this time to warn him, "Pruett Little is loafing around by the corner of the corral. You'd best be cautious."

Her warning surprised him. He was astonished that she would bother to tell him, even though she might suspect some ill intent on Pruett's part. He would puzzle over it later. For now he would turn his thoughts toward the possibility that Pruett was planning to exact a measure of revenge for his remarks at the supper table. He had hoped to avoid a confrontation, but he had to round the corner of the corral on his way back to the bunkhouse, unless he sneaked out the back of the barn. And he had no intention of doing that. Thanks to Millie's forewarning, however, he could prepare for trouble if

Pruett had any such ideas in mind. Spotting a coil of rope hanging on a nail driven in a center post, he grabbed it as he went past on his way outside.

Just as Millie had said, Pruett was perched on the top rail at the corner of the corral, smoking a cigarette. He didn't say anything until Carson passed in front of him. Carson nodded, but said nothing. He had taken a couple of steps past the corner when Pruett called after him, "Hey, Texas, where you goin' with that rope?" When Carson turned to face him, he flipped the half-finished cigarette to bounce off Carson's chest. "I heard all you Texans have a mile-wide yellow streak down your backs." He came down from the rail to position himself squarely in front of Carson. "How 'bout pickin' up that cigarette for me? I just rolled it and I'm runnin' a little short of rollin' papers."

"I'm not in a mood to put up with you, Pruett. I've got things I need to do right now. If you're so damn determined to show me how strong you are, go over yonder and pull that little tree up by the roots. If that's too much for you, go pull up some of those weeds growin' along the fence there, and I'll tell all the boys back in the bunkhouse how strong you are. Just leave me the hell alone."

A malicious smile slowly formed on the bully's face. Carson's reaction was what he had expected. It told him that he was reluctant to stand up to him. "I saw Millie go in the back of the barn," he said. "What was you two up to in there? I think Millie would rather be saddle-broke by a real man, instead of a yellow-dog Texan, don't you? Now pick up my cigarette like I told you."

"You ain't gonna let it alone, are you?" Carson replied.

Pruett chuckled, delighted, anticipating the pleasure he planned to enjoy. "Nope. You're gonna have to take a whippin' for tryin' to steal my gal."

"All right, here's your damn cigarette," Carson said, and reached down to pick it up. He blew on the smoldering tobacco to revive a glow, then held it out for Pruett to take. When he was within a step of him, he flipped it at Pruett's face, almost striking the larger man in the eye. Pruett recoiled frantically as the harmless missile bounced off his cheek. Carson didn't wait for him to recover, delivering a stinging blow across his face with the coiled rope. Pruett backed away, but Carson stayed with him step for step, using the rope like a club, raining blow after stinging blow upon his head, and leaving raw red stripes about his neck, ears, and face. The attack was so sudden and devastating that Pruett was kept off balance, and he tried to charge his assailant, only to suffer more blows as he tried in vain to grab hold of the flailing rope. In frustration, he finally tried to pull the pistol he was wearing and charged again. With his head down to keep the cruel blows from striking him across his eyes, he was easy for Carson to sidestep, tripping him as he lunged by. Carson backed away warily, quickly fashioning a loop in the rope as Pruett rose to his knees and hesitated a moment to clear his senses. It was a moment too long, for Carson threw his loop, as if roping a steer, before the startled bully knew his intention. Drawing his noose tight as Pruett lunged up to his feet, Carson succeeded in pinning the big man's arms to his sides. Before Pruett could get the rope worked up high enough to slip out of it, the quicker man ran around him several times, wrapping him up in a helpless bundle. Raging mad, Pruett tried to pull away from his captor, but Carson looped his end of the rope over a corral post and used it as leverage to pull his two-legged steer up tight against the corral rails. Once he had him flat against the rails, he secured him with the rope, binding him with his arms immobile at his sides and his feet tied to the post. When the task was finished, Carson walked away toward the bunkhouse, never saying another word, followed by a hailstorm of enraged curses and threats.

Standing just inside the open barn door, Millie watched the confrontation just finished with excited yet mixed emotions. The last faint light of the sun was fading away as she backed away and went out the back of the barn to return to the house, still marveling over the way Carson had so efficiently handled Pruett. She could have freed the oversized bully, but she chose not to, thinking it a good lesson for him. She had no room in her mind for thoughts of Pruett Little, anyway. Her brain was mired in a confusion of conflicting feelings about the man who had roped him. In a way, she was glad that the truth had come out about the stranger who had landed on her doorstep. She had been determined that she would have no interest in the young man, and this made it easier to accomplish. What if what he had told her, that he was innocent of the charges against him, was the truth of it? Would it make a difference in the way she regarded him? Nancy and Frank thought the sun rose and set on the man they had met on the trail. Were they mistaken? *Why am I even thinking about it?* she thought. She was convinced that the man had never been born whom she would consider worthy of her approval. "I'm glad he's leaving tomorrow," she murmured softly as she went up the kitchen steps.

"Wonder where ol' Pruett is," Mule remarked as he placed a couple of pieces of wood on the fire in the fireplace. "He's usually the first one in his bunk on a chilly night like this'n."

"Well, it ain't likely we'll miss him," Shorty said. It had been quite a while since the supper dishes had been cleaned up, and most of the men were crawling into their bunks. Because of the situation with Carson's sudden termination, the talk in the bunkhouse was a little more subdued than usual, Shorty being the only one who knew the entire story behind the young man's departure.

"You reckon we oughta see if ol' Pruett's fell through the hole in the outhouse or somethin'?" Clem Hastings wondered aloud. Of all the men on the M/C, Clem was the only one who never seemed to mind working with Pruett.

"Nah," Shorty answered him. "Pruett

don't ever use the outhouse."

Already in his bunk, with his blanket pulled up over his shoulders, Carson was concerned only with minding his own business and avoiding questions from the other hands, so he made it obvious that he was intent upon going to sleep. After about half an hour more, all conversation died away and the bunkhouse was settled in for the night. No one was curious enough about Pruett's absence to look into the possible reason for it. When an additional half an hour passed, everyone was awakened, however, startled by the sudden explosion of Pruett's irate entrance into the room.

"Where's that son of a bitch?" he roared, and went straight to Carson's bunk. His outburst of rage caused everyone to sit up immediately, all except Carson, who seemingly ignored him. Pruett planted himself to stand menacingly at the foot of Carson's bunk. "Get up outta that bunk," he commanded. "It's time for you to get a little lesson, and I'm the teacher, so get up."

"Go to hell," Carson responded, without moving.

"What the hell's got into you, Pruett?" Shorty asked. "Why don't you leave him alone and go to bed? We gotta get up early in the mornin'."

"You shut your mouth, Shorty," Pruett told him. "This ain't none of your business."

"What did he ever do to you?" Mule asked.

Lucas Cain, who had followed Pruett in the door, answered for him. "He tied him to the corral post," Lucas volunteered. "If Pa hadn't made me go back to the smokehouse to get the bacon I was supposed to bring Lizzie for breakfast, I reckon he mighta stayed tied to that post all night." The boy had followed Pruett to the bunkhouse after he untied him. He figured it was going to be a show he wouldn't want to miss.

"Well, I'll be . . ." Mule started to speak when he noticed the welts around Pruett's face when the flickering light from the fireplace played upon it. "Looks like you got a whuppin' to boot."

"Not as bad as the whuppin' I'm fixin' to give him," Pruett promised. Back to the man still lying in his bunk, he ordered, "I told you to get up from there."

"You'd best leave me alone," Carson replied, "and just forget about it."

Pruett was not to be denied his revenge. He reached down and pulled the blanket off Carson, only to find himself staring at the muzzle of Carson's Colt .44. "Whoa!"

he blurted involuntarily, and backed away, almost stumbling over his own feet. With the pistol still aimed at Pruett, Carson sat up and pulled the hammer back. The click of the cocking weapon seemed to shatter the silence of the moment before. Pruett backed away in panic, falling over one of the empty bunks in the process.

Deadly calm, Carson shifted his feet over on the floor and stood up, all the while holding the .44 on Pruett. He moved around the empty bunk to stand directly over him. "What am I gonna do with you?" he pondered aloud. "Am I gonna have to shoot you to have any peace?"

Never taking his eyes off the pistol covering him, Pruett rolled over and got up on his hands and knees. "All right," he muttered reluctantly, "it's over. I ain't gonna cause no more trouble. Just let me get to my feet and I'm ready to turn in."

No one in the bunkhouse believed him, especially Carson, but he said, "Go ahead, then." He stepped back to give him room and released the hammer on his .44. Pruett pushed himself up on one knee, then paused there for a few moments, waiting for his opportunity. When Carson lowered his pistol to hang casually by his thigh, Pruett made his move. He lunged to his feet, lowered his head, and charged like a runaway train. Expecting such a move, Carson stepped deftly aside, avoiding the mass of angry muscle and sinew, and administered a solid blow against Pruett's temple with the barrel of his Colt. He took another step back as the huge man crashed to the bunkhouse floor, where he lay motionless for a couple of minutes. Carson hoped that the bully had had enough, but that was not to be the end of it. The massive man began to stir eventually, and when his head cleared enough, he got to his feet, looking around him, trying to locate Carson, who was standing right in front of him. He emitted one great roar and launched himself in Carson's direction. Carson had hoped it would not come to this, but unable to think of anything else to get the peace he desired, he raised his pistol and fired.

The bullet caught Pruett in the leg, causing him to crash to the floor once more, finally stopped as he lay there moaning and holding his leg. "You shot me, you bastard!" Pruett cried out in pain.

"I reckon I did," Carson replied calmly. "You damn fool, if you'da just let it alone, I wouldn't have had to shoot you." He turned then and returned to his bunk, but instead of climbing back in bed, he put the pistol back in its holster and pulled on his pants and shirt. He was just pulling his boots on when Mathew Cain, Justin, and Frank rushed in the door, having heard the gunshot.

"What was that shot?" Mathew demanded.

Carson answered as he stood up to start packing his belongings in his war bag, "That was me sayin' good-bye," he said without emotion.

"What the hell . . . ?" Justin exclaimed when he saw Pruett lying on the floor holding his leg, with Clem trying to help him up. He turned back to Carson then, looking for an explanation, but Carson offered none. He just continued with his packing.

"Looks to me like Pruett picked the wrong man to ride herd on," Mathew Cain remarked after he had taken in the scene. He had pretty much had a hunch that John Carson was not the kind of man to be bullied. "How bad is he hurt, Clem?"

"Well, he's got shot in the leg," Clem replied. "Coulda been a lot worse if John's aim hadda been a little higher."

"I got an idea that John's aim was right on the money," Mathew said. He turned to Shorty then. "What happened here, Shorty?"

Shorty told him that Carson had tried to avoid fighting Pruett, but Pruett kept after him. "John warned him to leave him alone, but Pruett tried to jump him anyway, so he shot him in the leg to put a stop to it."

"I figured somethin' like that musta happened," Cain said. "Mule, take a look at that wound and see if you can fix him up." He bent over Pruett then, who was grimacing with the pain in his thigh. "Don't look like he hit you in a serious place. Mule's gonna take care of it. You might be hobblin' around for a few days, but you'll be all right." With Pruett taken care of, he turned his attention toward Carson. "What are you aimin' to do?"

Carson picked up his sack and his rifle. "I reckon I'll head out tonight, instead of waitin' till mornin'," he said.

"I think that's a good idea, son," Cain said. "Justin and I'll help you saddle up."

"Me, too," Frank volunteered. "I'll help." More than anyone else, he knew that he probably owed Carson his and Nancy's life.

They walked out of the bunkhouse, leaving Mule to doctor Pruett's wound. Several of the other men left their bunks to help catch Carson's horses, and Mathew sent Lucas to the smokehouse to get a side of bacon for Carson to take with him. Carson was somewhat mystified by the going-away party. By the time the bay was saddled, and Luther Moody's blue roan was loaded, everyone at the house was aware of the unscheduled departure. Nancy and Millie walked down to the barn in their robes to see Carson off.

When everything was packed, he slid his Winchester in the saddle scabbard and prepared to step up in the saddle. There were a few wishes of "good luck" from the men, and a hard handshake from Shorty. Frank stepped up then and offered his hand, and Nancy gave him a hug and thanked him for all he had done for them. Millie remained in the background, watching Carson's reactions to the farewells, and wondering why she was troubled by the high regard Nancy seemed to have for one she decided was a no-good drifter. She told herself that she wouldn't give John Carson, or whatever his name was, another thought after this night.

The good-byes over, he stepped up on the bay and rode straight out to the north, a bright moon behind his right shoulder, and a chilly wind on his face. Although disappointed that things had not worked out for him on the M/C, he was not discouraged, for he was confident that he was on the path

he was destined to ride and he would deal
with wherever it led.

CHAPTER 11

Carson decided to put more than a few miles behind him before making a camp. His only goal at this time was to simply find a place to get a peaceful night's sleep without having to worry about Pruett Little recovering enough to pay him another visit. With a full moon rising higher now to light the prairie before him, he felt no risk of crippling his horses, even though the route he had chosen took him over some rough terrain with the Crazy Mountains only a few miles to the east of him. His planned course of travel would take him north of the steep, rugged peaks of the mountains towering ghostlike above the moonlit prairie. He recalled Shorty telling him of the sharp ridges and peaks and the howling winds that whipped around them, inspiring the name given the range by the Indians. Tomorrow, he told himself, he would reach the northern tip of the range and then he would turn to the west toward Helena. There were no lingering feelings of regret, for he decided that his failure to stay on at the M/C was balanced by the opportunity to explore the mountains to the west, his initial reason for leaving Bob Patterson at Ogallala.

He estimated he had ridden about ten miles, and was still on M/C range, when he came upon a healthy stream coming out of the mountains to his left. It looked to be as good a campsite as any he was likely to find, so he guided his horses to a grassy bank bordered by pines and clumps of laurel. Here he made his camp. After his horses were taken care of, he built a small fire for warmth, since he had already eaten supper back in the bunkhouse. He spread his blanket over a bed of pine needles and settled in for the night, unconcerned for any further problems to interrupt his sleep. He didn't think it likely that Pruett would hobble after him on his bad leg. He drifted off with thoughts of the Rocky Mountains before him and the many possible trails a young man might choose to follow. It was a good feeling, although he had to admit that he would miss the opportunity to see how big Mathew Cain's ranch would grow. He saw the potential for the M/C to become the biggest outfit in the territory. Justin Cain was a capable foreman, and Lucas was already a steady ranch hand. With Frank and Nancy to help out, and of course Millie. The thought of Nancy's younger sister caused him to pause there to consider the strange mannerisms of the girl who acted as if she ran the place. He shook his head then as if to clear away thoughts of Millie. The good Lord had not seen fit to give him the gift of understanding women, but he had really had no need for it — up to now.

A day and a half's ride brought him to another range of mountains he would later learn to call the Big Belt Mountains. The call of the mountains was too much to resist, so he followed a busy stream back up a narrow canyon as far as his horses could comfortably manage and made his camp. He planned to go on with the idea of finding Helena, where he intended to trade his extra weapons for supplies he would need to see him through the coming winter. But the plentiful sign of elk in the lower foothills caused him to remain there for almost a week. It was a good week, and gave him the chance to satisfy his natural curiosity about the country he had always imagined when still a boy. From the tops of the mountains, he discovered that he could see a town of good size in the valley to the west. He figured that it had to be Helena. It could wait, he decided, until he had smoke-dried his fresh-killed elk to pack on his extra horse. There were more mountains farther west, beyond Helena, that he could also see from the mountaintop, waiting for him to explore. He knew then that he would spend no more time in the town of Helena than necessary to complete his business.

He awoke one morning to find a light powdering of snow spread across his camp. It served to remind him that a hard winter might not be far behind, and there were things he needed to be ready for it. So he packed up his camp and rode out of the mountains toward Helena.

He slow-walked his horses down the main street of Helena, a street that roughly followed the gulch and was aptly named Last Chance Gulch. The real boom times of the earlier gold strikes were past, but there was still plenty of mining activity, as witnessed by the busy street, the various businesses and the many saloons. When Carson came to a business that advertised on a big sign in front that it dealt in dry goods and hardware, he pulled over and tied his horses at the rail.

"Howdy." Elmer Green greeted him when he walked in the door. "What can I do for you?" He eyed the young stranger up and down. "You new in town?"

"I reckon I am," Carson replied, and stood there for a few moments, looking around at the merchandise on the counters and the shelves behind them. His gaze fell on a glass-top cabinet with several firearms displayed. Thinking then that he was in the right place, he asked, "Might you be interested in buyin' some fine weapons?"

Elmer shrugged indifferently. "That depends," he replied. "I'm in the business of selling new weapons. I don't do much buying of used guns." He waited for a moment while Carson thought that over, then asked, "What are you trying to sell?"

"I've got a good Spencer cavalry carbine, a Winchester, and a couple of Colt handguns," Carson replied.

"What are you looking to get for them?"

"As much as I can, cash money," Carson said, "or maybe trade for some things I need." He knew he couldn't ask for top price. The carbine was in good shape, but the blacksmith back at the Big Horn had taken the best Colt revolver as payment for shoeing his horses.

"Like I said," Elmer responded, "I don't

do much buying of used guns. I'll take a look at what you've got, though." He followed Carson outside to inspect the weapons. After testing the action on the pistols, he looked the carbine over. "I'm afraid I couldn't give you much for the lot of 'em," he finally said. "Maybe somebody else might give you a better deal, but I guess I could let you have twenty dollars in trade if you want."

Carson was disappointed. He had thought he might get a little more than that, but he decided to accept the offer so he could be done with it. But twenty dollars' worth of goods, combined with the seven dollars he still had, wasn't going to take him very far.

Back inside, Elmer studied the young man as Carson carefully selected the items he needed the most desperately for his camp. "You thinking about doing some placer mining?" he asked, thinking Carson was out here for the same reason most men were.

"No, sir," Carson replied. "I don't know nothin' about huntin' for gold. I ain't ever done anything but work with cattle. I'm hopin' maybe I can sign on with somebody in that business. Right now I'm just lookin' to get by till somethin' comes along."

Elmer continued to study Carson intently before making a suggestion. "If you're hard up for money, young fellow, I know where you can hire on for decent wages. That is, if you don't mind a little hard work."

"Where might that be?" Carson asked.

"Fellow name of Jim Saylor runs a sawmill up at the upper end of the gulch. Jim's a friend of mine and I know for a fact that one of the men that cuts timber and snakes the logs out of the mountains west of town for him just up and quit last week. You're a pretty strong-looking young fellow. You might wanna talk to Jim. It's not like finding gold, but it'll give you some spending money."

Carson's first thought was not one of interest, but the more he thought about it, the more he realized that it would help him get through the winter. Then he almost smiled when he recalled that he could claim his status as a champion woodchopper on the M/C. "What the hell?" he replied. "It wouldn't hurt to talk to your friend. What was his name?"

"Jim Saylor," Elmer said. "Tell him I sent you."

"Much obliged," Carson said.

Rena Saylor came from the mill office carrying the dinner pail that her husband had just emptied in time to hear Jim talking to a tall young man who had just ridden up. "Elmer sent you, huh?" she heard him ask the stranger, so she paused to find out what he was about. "Pannin' for gold didn't turn up much color, I reckon," Jim guessed aloud.

"Might have," Carson replied. "I ain't ever tried pannin' for gold." He paused to speak to the woman standing behind Jim now. "Ma'am." She nodded.

"What have you been doin'?" Jim asked.

"Drivin' cattle, mostly."

Saylor studied him for a few moments more before asking his next question. If what Carson said was true, that he wasn't hoping to find gold, then maybe he wouldn't be off to the next strike right away. "Are you wanted by the law?" He preferred that Carson was not, but he wasn't overly concerned, because back in the mountains where he would be working, he wasn't likely to run into any lawmen.

Carson answered the question without hesitation. "I ain't ever done nothin' against the law," he said, answering truthfully. It seemed to satisfy Saylor.

"You ever work with a team of six mules?" he asked. When Carson confessed that he had not, Saylor went on. "Well, don't matter, I guess. You'll be workin' with Bris Bannerman. He'll be drivin' the logs to the mill, anyway. I reckon you can handle one mule draggin' a log."

"I reckon," Carson said.

"You can leave your packhorse here in my corral if you want to," Saylor suggested.

"All the same to you, I'll keep both my horses with me up in the mountains."

Saylor shrugged. "Up to you," he concluded. "Be back here at the sawmill first thing in the mornin' and we'll ride up to the camp. I've got a load of supplies to take up there."

When Saylor arrived at his sawmill early the following morning, he found Carson waiting for him. "How long have you been here?" he asked.

"Since sunup," Carson replied. "You said first thing." His reply was enough to please Saylor. Maybe the young man really was accustomed to hard work.

It was a long half day's ride to the mountains west of town to Saylor's camp at the base of the hills. An old army squad tent was set up beside the corral, but there was no one about. Noticing two of the mules were missing, Saylor commented, "Bris is most likely up the mountain, snakin' logs down. I expect he'll show up directly." By the time Carson took his horses to the small creek nearby and hobbled them to graze, they heard Bris coming down the mountain, driving a two-horse team and dragging a huge log.

"Ho, Jim," Bris called out upon seeing them. "What brings you out here this mornin'?" He didn't stop for an answer, but gave the stranger standing beside his boss a good looking-over as he continued by them to deposit the log next to a pile near the corral. Saylor and Carson walked over to watch as Bris unhitched the mules and left them to stand while he talked to his boss.

"I thought you might oughta be runnin' short of bacon and beans," Saylor said. "This here's John Carson. He's gonna be takin' Pete's place."

"Is that a fact?" Bris responded, looking Carson up and down with a skeptical eye. "That's gonna take some doin'. Pete was a helluva worker." He glanced at Saylor and commented, "He's a big feller, ain't he?" Looking Carson directly in the eye then, he asked, "Reckon you can stand up to the work, boy?"

"If I can't, I reckon you'll fire me," Carson answered as he studied the man he would be working with. At this point, he wasn't sure how long that would be, but he anticipated it would be at least until spring. He could already guess what kind of man Bris was — short and wiry, it was hard to tell how old the man was, but a full set of whiskers was more gray than brown, and Carson couldn't help wondering if he might have been of average height had he not been so bowlegged. His speech was gruff in manner, but Carson noted a twinkle in the little man's eye that betrayed a more congenial nature.

Bris laughed at Carson's response to his question. "I reckon so," he agreed. "That's fair enough, ain't it, Jim?" He turned his attention back to Saylor then. With expecting eyes, he asked, "You didn't happen to bring anythin' with you, did you, Jim?"

"In my saddlebag," Saylor replied.

"Good man," Bris said, his scruffy beard spread with a smile.

Saylor turned to Carson then. "Well, I've got to get back to town before dark, so I'll leave you two to sort it out between you." He went to his saddlebag to get the bottle of whiskey he brought and handed it to Bris. "Bris can show you all you need to know, 'cause he knows what has to be done." When the supplies were unloaded and put away in the tent, he stepped up on the sorrel and bade them good-bye.

"Thanks for the bottle," Bris said. "And tell Rena I still love her, and one of these days I'll be comin' for her."

"I'll tell her," Saylor called back over his shoulder. Carson would learn later that Rena was Jim Saylor's wife, and this promise was a ritual practiced almost every time Saylor visited the lumber camp. In the spirit of the joke, Rena usually cooked Bris a fine meal whenever he brought a load of logs into town.

Carson and Bris got along right from the first day of their work together. The work was hard for just two men, but Carson found that the physical labor was something he needed at this time in his life. Wanted by the federal marshals, he decided it was a good time to be out of sight up in the mountains. The days were spent wielding an ax, trimming the limbs off the pine logs after riding one end of a crosscut saw, then snaking the logs down the mountain to be loaded on a log train that Bris had built for the purpose. Bris was easy to camp with. He insisted on doing all the cooking, and Carson appreciated the fact that he was a fair hand at it — a lot better than Bad Eye had been. That thought caused him to wonder if Bad Eye had escaped the pursuit of the lawmen. Other thoughts of his days with Duke Slayton's gang of outlaws were recurring less and less as winter moved into the hills.

On the days when Bris took a load of logs into the sawmill, he hitched all six mules to the heavy log train, leaving Carson with free time. He could have hitched his horses up to the logs, but he felt that was not a proper job for a cow pony, at least not *his* cow pony. Besides, he felt the time was better spent hunting for something to eat besides salt pork. His talent with a rifle was greatly appreciated by his gnarly little partner, because Bris openly admitted he wasn't much a shot. He was surprised, however, that Carson seemed to have no interest in riding into town with him. He never pried into Carson's history, but after spending the long winter months working so closely with the young man, he decided for himself that Carson had a reason for shunning the town. He figured it was Carson's business, and not his. All he was concerned with was the man's work ethic, and he decided he'd never had a partner who worked as hard and as steady as Carson.

A Montana winter in the wild will change most men, and Carson was no exception. The physical change was more evident to

Bris than it was to him, however. By spring-time, Carson seemed to have gained strength as well as size, thanks to his heavy laboring that added tough muscle to his shoulders and arms. It was hard for Bris to believe he was looking at the same man Jim Saylor had introduced at the end of summer. As for Carson, he was aware of the feeling that he was fit, but he didn't suspect that he had changed that much.

When the snow began melting on the mountaintops, Carson figured it was time to move on, and he told Jim Saylor of his intention. It was at a time when Bris wanted to move the camp, since they had cleared most of the trees that the two-man team could reasonably get to. So they packed up the tent and moved their camp several miles farther along the mountain range. Carson agreed to stay on to help Bris and Jim through the summer, or at least until Jim could find a replacement for him. One year turned into two, with Carson still content to remain, although he began to catch himself wondering what it was like beyond the mountains they were cutting timber in. But thoughts of a different nature also began to enter his idle moments. He found himself wondering if the crew at the M/C came through the hard winter without losing too many cattle — and if Frank and Nancy were glad they had made the hazardous journey from the Black Hills — and Millie, although he couldn't explain why he thought of her at all. And without realizing it, he was missing working with the cattle. The day finally arrived when he changed his mind and accepted Bris's invitation to ride into town with him.

"Well, I'll be . . . ," Bris marveled. "What changed your mind?"

"I don't know," Carson said. "I just ain't been in a long time. I reckon I just wanna see if the town's grown any since I saw it last. Besides, I've got a birthday sometime this month and I think I oughta have myself a drink to celebrate it, maybe two drinks, since I forgot it last year." He paused to make sure of the month. "This is August, ain't it? At least I think that's what Jim said when he brought those last supplies."

"I believe he did," Bris replied, "but I ain't got no notion what day it is."

"Doesn't matter," Carson said, "as long as it's the right month."

So Bris hitched up the mules and they set out for town, Bris sitting on top of the load of pine logs, driving the team, with Carson riding alongside. Reluctant to leave the black horse back in their wilderness camp unprotected, Carson tied it on behind the logs. Impatient with the pace set by the team of mules, he often loped along ahead of Bris, working some of the rust from his horse, acquired after many days of doing nothing more than grazing on the lush meadow grass of the high plains. He realized at once that he had accumulated some rust himself, and realized how much he missed his days in the saddle. It caused some serious thinking about returning somehow to the business of raising cattle. These were thoughts he had to keep to himself, because talk of such plans tended to make Bris melancholy.

It was after dark by the time they unloaded the logs at Saylor's sawmill and went home with Jim to enjoy one of Rena's fine suppers. It was a strange sensation for Carson to be in a house after so long a time camping in the pine-covered hills. And it was hard to disagree with Bris's claim that Rena Saylor was the best cook in Montana Territory. It was a pleasant evening, and Carson would have been content to bed down for the night and call his birthday celebration complete, but Bris insisted that wouldn't do. "John here deserves to go get a drink on his birthday," he said.

"There's no need to go down to a saloon,"

Saylor offered. "I've got a bottle right here."

"That wouldn't be the proper thing to do," Bris was quick to remark. "I mean, drinkin' in front of Rena. That don't show her no respect at all."

Overhearing the conversation, Rena spoke up. "It won't bother me. I don't care if you all get drunk."

Bris was insistent. "John's a young single man. He ain't been in a saloon in a coon's age. He might wanna kick up his heels a little."

It was fairly evident to Carson and Jim that Bris was the one who wanted to visit a saloon. They exchanged knowing smiles and Carson remarked facetiously, "Yeah, that's right. I might wanna kick up my heels." It brought a smile of satisfaction to Bris's whiskered face.

Rena paused a moment on her way to the kitchen with an armload of dirty dishes. "I don't know who you men think you're fooling. Go on, if you're going, but I better not hear about Jim Saylor kicking up his heels, or I'll be the one doing the kicking tomorrow."

"I'll see that he behaves hisself," Bris volunteered. "And I'll get him home before too late." He couldn't resist teasing the patient woman. "If you decide to kick him outta the house, remember that I still love you, so you've got an ace in the hole."

This brought a laugh from both Jim and Carson, and Jim said, "Come on, Ace. Let's go get that drink. I've got to go to work in the morning."

Hands on hips and assuming a mock expression of disgust, Rena watched the men file out the door. She didn't begrudge Bris his desire to ogle the whores who frequented some of the drinking establishments in town. The old man led a lonely existence. She was confident in her husband's ability to behave himself. Watching the last one out the door, the one who literally filled the doorway, she realized that she did not really know John Carson. Tonight was only the second time she had even seen him since Jim first hired him. The transformation of the quiet young man into the formidable, emotionless mystery that she saw on this occasion was difficult to believe. Had she not known for a fact, she might have refused to believe it was the same man.

Of the many saloons in Helena, there was no question as to which establishment Bris wanted to visit. Sullivan's Saloon was his favorite watering hole and the one he visited on every trip to town. Sullivan's was not one of the fanciest bars in town, but there were always a few painted ladies who worked the customers for drinks and whatever else they were interested in. And they were not above showering a little attention on stubby little gray-haired men like Bris.

"Howdy, Bris," Bill Sullivan greeted them when they walked up to the bar. "You bring in a load of logs?"

"Yeah, as a matter of fact," Bris replied. "We need us a drink of whiskey." While Sullivan reached for three shot glasses, Bris remarked to his two companions, "Man's got a helluva memory. I ain't been in here but once or twice before."

Jim grinned at Carson. "Yeah, everybody talks about what a memory Sullivan's got." He picked up his glass. "Let's sit down at that table over there. We might want another drink." Bris and Carson followed him over to a table near the center of the barroom. Two men sitting at a table next to theirs looked up when they sat down. "Harvey," Jim greeted one of them.

"Howdy, Jim," Harvey returned. "You been busy at the sawmill?"

"Not as busy as I'd like to be," Jim replied. He didn't bother to introduce Carson and Bris. It was all the same to Carson, and Bris was already eyeing a rather tired-looking woman two tables over. Catching his eye, she got up from the table and left the two prospectors who had seemed more interested in getting drunk even after she had invested fifteen minutes of her time.

"Hey, darlin'," she said to Bris, who was grinning from ear to ear. "My name's Annie. You lookin' for a little companionship?"

Bris just continued grinning for a long moment before answering, "No, honey. I'm just a looker, I ain't a doer. My pickle ain't good for nothin' no more but passin' a little water now and again, but I'll give you a quarter for a little peek at your merchandise."

"Huh," she snorted, disappointed. "Ain't you the big spender? For twenty-five cents you can take a look at my foot." When his response was nothing more than a continuation of his happy smile, she nodded toward Carson. "What about him?"

"I don't know," Bris answered. "Why don't you ask him?" He had a feeling he already knew what Carson's answer might be, but he was content to delay the woman's departure. He didn't have the opportunity to be this close to a woman as a rule.

"What about it, stud?" Annie asked Carson, who had been listening to the conversation between Saylor and Harvey Johnson, the postmaster.

Distracted momentarily when the woman jabbed him with her finger to get his attention, Carson said, "Reckon not, ma'am, but it's awful temptin'." It was far from tempting, but he didn't want to hurt her feelings. Disgusted, she abruptly got up and returned to the table with the two prospectors where there was still hope as long as they continued to drink. His attention went immediately back to the conversation between Saylor and Johnson.

Noticing Carson's rapt attention, Harvey paused to say howdy to him. "Don't believe I've ever seen you in town before," he said. "My name's Harvey Johnson. I'm the postmaster here in town. You a friend of Jim's?"

Saylor answered for him. "This is John Carson. He's been working with Bris, cuttin' timber. Been working for me for over two years. He just doesn't get into town much."

Carson shook Harvey's offered hand. "Couldn't help hearin' what you were tellin' Jim a minute ago," he remarked, "somethin' about a range war."

"I reckon you could call it that," Harvey replied. "From what I heard, there were some folks killed." He paused to think. "Carson," he repeated, "something familiar about that name." Then he remembered. "I

338

know what it is. I got a wanted notice for a fellow named Carson — only that was his first name — Carson Ryan, if I remember correctly. It's been up with the other notices for a long time." He chuckled then. "He's wanted for murdering a U.S. deputy marshal. I don't reckon that was you, was it?"

The postmaster was obviously making a joke, but it caused the blood to chill in Carson's veins. He attempted a weak chuckle in response. "Well, I know I ain't ever shot a deputy," he said. "Where was the range war you were talkin' about?"

"Oh, it wasn't around here," Harvey replied. "It was on the other side of the Big Belt Mountains, on farther east somewhere around the Crazy Mountains is where I make it to be. It's a wonder there ain't more killing in that country, 'cause there isn't much in the way of law on the open range."

Carson's brain was already frantically working over a variety of situations that he truly hoped had nothing to do with the friends he had left in that area. Harvey's next comment almost stunned him.

"Fellow name of Cain was one of the ones got killed, is what I heard," Harvey said. "Owns a big spread south of the Musselshell."

"Mathew Cain?" Carson blurted, unable

to accept it as fact.

"Mighta been. In fact, I think that was the fellow's name," Harvey said. Noticing the obvious impact his comment had made on Jim's friend, he asked, "You know him?"

Aware then that both Bris and Jim were watching him, waiting for his reply, Carson nodded slowly before uttering a simple statement. "I know him." It was obvious that Jim and Bris wanted more, but that was all Carson cared to impart at that particular moment. His mind was racing. There was more to think about than Mathew Cain alone. Who else might have been killed? What about Justin, and Frank and Nancy, Shorty . . . Millie? He thought about Lon Tuttle. Had a full-blown war broken out between the two ranch owners? He knew that he had to have answers for those and many other questions. And even though his time at the M/C had been brief, he felt a deep obligation to help the people there. He looked up to find Bris studying him intently. The grizzled little man sensed that he was about to lose his partner. His concern spread rapidly to fill Jim Saylor's eyes as well, and both men waited silently for Carson to speak. "I've got to go," he stated simply. "I owe them."

He had never been a man to take obligations lightly, so he deeply regretted leaving Jim and Bris on such short notice. But in all fairness, he reminded himself, he had told them in the beginning that he might leave after the first spring. That fact did not help the feeling of guilt he was left with. Jim had provided a job for him when his prospects were slim, and Bris had proven to be a good man to work with, so it was hard to tell them he wasn't going back to the camp in the mountains. Jim made it easy for him, however, which Carson greatly appreciated. "I know you've gotta do what you've gotta do," he told him after they left the saloon. "It ain't none of my business what you were doin' before you came to Helena, but I think I know you well enough to know that whatever you feel is right is what you'll do. So I wish you good luck. If you get back this way, come and see me." He paid him all the wages he had earned and hadn't collected.

Bris surprised him. He had really expected him to be extremely disappointed that he was leaving so suddenly, but if that was in fact the case, the little man concealed it well. He seemed almost cheerful in his parting comments. "Well, John, I reckon you turned out to be a pretty good worker. If you hadn't, I'da run you off after the first week," he said with a laugh. "Next one Jim sends me to break in, I ain't gonna let him come to town a'tall." He stuck out his hand. "Don't go gettin' into no trouble."

As a precaution, he had left nothing he really needed back in the lumber camp, so he felt it unnecessary to return. It would be easier to part company right away, as far as he was concerned, so he said his farewells that night. And when morning came, he was already gone.

CHAPTER 12

Millie Cain stood with her sister and brother-in-law beside the graves of her father and elder brother, her face a mask of vengeful determination, her eyes dry of tears, as she watched Mule and Shorty filling in the graves. She only glanced at her sister for a moment, when Nancy began to sob anew, her gaze turned then toward her younger brother when Lucas grabbed a shovel and began helping to cover the bodies. *All that's left of the men of the Cain family,* she thought, a terrible burden to place upon the shoulders of one so young. At least Frank was there. His was not the strength of her father and Justin, but he could be depended upon to stand and fight, unlike those who had deserted Mathew Cain when he most needed their support. *I wish I had been there,* she thought as she went over the accounting of it in her mind.

Thinking of that fatal day, she knew that

there had been no way to convince her father to let Justin and the men handle it. It was not in Mathew Cain's nature to sit safely by the fire when outlaws threatened his range. He had insisted upon leading the party that rode after the rustlers who made off with around five hundred M/C cattle. He and Justin, along with four of the men, headed straight for the Musselshell River, knowing full well they would find the missing portion of the herd on the old Bar-T range. It had been over a year since Lon Tuttle had been found hanging by the neck in his barn. The man who supposedly found him was Tuttle's foreman, Tom Castor, who surmised that his boss had taken his own life. Mysteriously, a man Tuttle had supposedly fired returned to help Castor run the ranch. Shorty said the man's name was Duke Slayton, and he brought men with him, one who wore an eye patch. A few weeks later, reports reached them that Castor had been killed when he came off a bucking horse and broke his neck. *An awful lot of bad luck,* she had thought with some suspicion.

She gazed at Lucas as he worked steadily with the shovel, hoping the labor would keep his tears from flowing. Unconsciously, she let her hand drop to rest on the handle of the .44 Colt she now wore constantly. She, unlike her sister, Nancy, was prepared to go to war — and there was no doubt in her mind that this was a war. This demon, Duke Slayton, had succeeded in taking over Lon Tuttle's spread, and was surely planning the same for the M/C. There was no choice but to fight for what her father had built. She was sending Lucas to Big Timber to telegraph the governor of the territory and the federal marshal just as soon as the funeral was over, but she knew help from them would be too long in coming. Still, it was the right thing to do, to notify the law, and it would also remove Lucas from danger. She knew that he would have been a help in defending their home, but if he should fall to the same fate as his father and brother, it would be the end of the Cain line of males.

Duke Slayton would come. She was certain of that, for there seemed to be too few to stop him from pillaging the M/C, just as he had taken the Bar-T. And he had to feel secure in the knowledge that he had already eliminated the strength of the M/C. *Well, it's not going to be such an easy time of it,* she promised herself. She looked at the men standing respectfully around the graves, and felt confident that the defense of her home was not going to be like the ambush that took her father and Justin. She recreated the scene in her mind, as Shorty had related it. Duke Slayton had been waiting for them, knowing Mathew Cain would come after his cattle. The ambush had been well planned, with riflemen hidden in the rocks on both sides of a wide ravine. When the shooting started, every gun seemed to have been aimed at her father and Justin. They fell immediately. Shorty said there must have been half a dozen bullet holes in each one of them. He took cover in a narrow gully and yelled for Pruett Little to find a place to shoot from on the other side, but Pruett and the other two took off, leaving Shorty, Mule, and Clem to fend for themselves. "The last I saw of that coward was his big ass flattened on his horse's neck, flyin' out the mouth of that ravine," Shorty had said. "The good Lord was lookin' out for me on that day. I don't know why, 'cause I ain't ever done nothin' to catch His eye. I know them bastards up on the sides of that ravine knew it was gonna cost 'em to root the three of us outta that gully. I guess they figured we wasn't worth the risk. We got the horses in there with us and waited till dark. Then we got Justin and Mr. Cain across their saddles and rode outta there."

When the graves were filled, Millie thanked Mule, Clem, and Shorty for their loyalty and they humbly responded. "It'll be getting dark pretty soon," she said. "So, Lucas, you'd best saddle up and get started."

"I don't know, Millie," Lucas protested. "I think I'll do more good if I stay here. It ain't gonna do no good waitin' for the law to do anything."

"You need to go," Millie said. "It's important to let the law know what's been going on here. I'd send Lizzie's boy, but he's too young."

"Millie's right, Lucas," Shorty told him, knowing why she didn't want him there. "It's important to let them know." Lucas went reluctantly to the barn to saddle up.

Next she turned to Frank. "Shorty and I think we need to get ready for a visit, and more than likely it'll be tonight. I don't know why they've waited this long. We figure it won't be like an Indian raid. We're not going to worry about them trying to run the horses off, or stealing cattle. They're coming to get rid of us first. Then they won't have to worry about the rest. What do you think? Is that about the way you figure it?" She didn't really care what his thoughts were at this point, for she relied more on Shorty's, but she asked his opinion for his

347

and Nancy's sake. He replied that he agreed. It was what he was thinking best to do.

The question now was where to put their strength. Should they basically defend the house or the barn, or both? Millie was reluctant to lose either. And how many would come against them? Shorty said as best he could determine there were at least eight or ten firing from the sides of that ravine. When she asked for opinions, Mule was the first to respond. "There's a lot of blind spots in the barn," he pointed out. "Might be easy for somebody to sneak in without us seein' 'em."

"Mule's right," Clem said. "We might need at least four good shooters, one on each corner."

"Well, you three are the best shots," Millie said. "Maybe you should be in the barn. If we put one more with you, that doesn't leave much but Frank to defend the house."

At that point, Lizzie spoke up. "You give me gun. By God, they not gonna take my kitchen. I'll give dem a load of buckshot."

Her comment caused Nancy to speak as well. "I know how to use a gun. Frank and I can defend the house with Lizzie." Her statement was followed by one from Lizzie's young son, Karl, who pointed out that he was a good shot with his .22 Remington when it came to rabbits and squirrels. In number, they could therefore have four in the barn and four in the house, but they finally decided to send Karl to the barn, and Millie would post herself in the house. Shorty suggested that he and Clem should ride out to the north ridge to keep a lookout until Lizzie called them in to eat. Then they would go to their respective posts and wait for whatever might come during the night.

The night passed peacefully, with no visits from the gang of outlaws who had taken over the Bar-T, and when morning broke, it was to find eight weary souls to greet the light of day. Millie went down to the barn to tell Shorty and the others that Lizzie would soon have some breakfast for them. "I sure thought that bunch of bushwhackers would come sneakin' around here last night," Shorty said. "Reckon maybe they ain't plannin' on hittin' us after all? Maybe they figure it ain't worth the risk of gettin' shot at."

"I don't know," Millie said, equally surprised. "Maybe they want us to think they're not coming after us, and they'll hit us when we aren't prepared."

"Maybe so," Mule commented. "That's why I think we'd best keep waitin' for 'em. And I don't think it'll be much longer, because they've got to think about the army or the law comin' down on 'em if they wait too long." They were all agreed then, and took turns getting a few hours of sleep during the day. Just as before, when darkness fell, everyone went to their assigned posts to wait out the night.

Duke Slayton had been busy during the time since Lon Tuttle had ordered him off his ranch. Never one to limit his ambitions, he saw a quick and easy way to acquire the biggest herd in Montana Territory. With the scarcity of law in the territory, he saw no reason why he couldn't take cattle from the M/C and move them with Bar-T stock up to Canada where he would establish his ranch, free from U.S. marshals. It made sense to him, enough to encourage him to return to Wyoming to recruit a gang of outlaws to follow him. One of the first he encountered was Bad Eye, who was lying low in an old hideout of theirs near the Rattlesnake Mountains. Bad Eye wasn't the only felon on the run from the law at the hideout. Sid Perkins and his brother, Roy, were there as well, having been flushed out of Oklahoma Indian Territory by a posse of deputies from Fort Smith. Soon he picked up a couple more recruits who, like the

Perkins brothers, were without prospects. In time, he had enlisted a sizable gang of men and considered himself ready to make his assault on the two ranches he had targeted, so he led his pack of assassins north to Montana.

Castor was easy. Duke didn't have to spend much time convincing Tuttle's foreman that he had a lot more to gain if Tuttle was out of the picture. Duke was especially pleased with himself for thinking up Tuttle's death as a suicide so word of a murder wouldn't spread through the territory. Once Tuttle was gone, Duke moved his men in, and after that, it was only logical to eliminate Castor. Duke wasn't interested in sharing command of his dynasty, and Castor was under the impression that this was their original agreement. With Carson Ryan out of the picture, and everything in place at last, the moment he had been waiting for was at hand. He was ready to wipe out all traces of Mathew Cain and his family.

Sid Perkins dropped to a knee beside Duke on the dark ridge to the east of the ranch house. "There's some of 'em in the barn," Sid said. "Looks like they mighta split up."

"I ain't surprised," Duke said. "They knew I'd be comin' after 'em."

"Why don't we just let 'em hole up in there, and we go after the cattle?" Sid asked. "If they try to stop us, we'll catch 'em comin' outta the house." He was not opposed to wholesale murder, but he didn't quite see the sense in putting the house and barn under siege.

Duke quickly set him straight. "Because I want ever' last one of 'em dead," he said. "Don't leave nobody to tell about it."

Sid shrugged. "You're the boss," he said. "Whaddaya wanna do?"

Feeling much like a general directing his troops, Duke issued the order for attack. "Go to the other side of the barn and tell Bad Eye I said to get his boys down there and root 'em outta there. Take them kerosene lanterns and throw 'em in the hayloft. Burn the bastards out into the open. Then we'll take care of the house." He wanted the barn taken care of in order to surround the house without having to worry about someone shooting at them from the barn.

"I don't know . . . ," Bad Eye responded when Sid relayed Duke's orders. Like Sid and some of the others, Bad Eye didn't understand Duke's obsession with destroying the M/C. He was more interested in stealing the cattle and horses and skedaddling across the line into Canada. "Well, hell, if that's what he wants to do, we'll try it," he finally said.

Inside the darkened barn, near the front door, Clem Hastings squinted in an effort to see better. Then he issued a whispered shout. "There's somebody movin' in them cottonwoods by the creek."

"Where?" Shorty asked, coming over from the opposite corner.

"Yonder," Clem said, and pointed.

Shorty saw them then. There were now two figures moving stealthily from the shadows of the trees. Both men raised their rifles to train on the two shadows, but held their fire. "What the hell are they totin'?" Shorty asked. "Lanterns?" It was obvious then what their intentions were. "They're thinkin' 'bout burnin' us out, but there ain't no way they're gonna get that close. You take the one on the right. I'll take the other'n."

Two rifle shots split the nighttime quiet, and the two lanterns dropped to the ground as the men carrying them crumpled beside them. Without waiting for orders from anyone, the remaining men in the cottonwood grove returned fire, doing little damage beyond ripping chunks of wood from the side of the barn. "Stop your damn shootin'," Bad Eye yelled. "You're just wastin' cartridges." He turned to Sid then. "You and Roy get down there and grab them lanterns. Maybe you can get up to the middle of the barn where they can't get a bead on you."

Sid exchanged glances with his brother, then told Bad Eye, "The hell you say. You want them lanterns, you go get 'em. I don't feel like commitin' suicide tonight."

Bad Eye didn't reply, unable to think of what he should do, but he didn't plan to commit suicide, either. He needed Duke to tell him what to do. "I reckon we'll just wait and see if one of 'em sticks his head out," he finally said.

On the ridge on the other side of the house, Duke waited impatiently, having heard the shooting at the barn. "What happened?" he asked one of the men closest to him. He had hoped to see the barn blazing by then.

"It's hard to see, but it looks like a couple of our boys got shot," the man called back to Duke. "I reckon they were tryin' to sneak down to the barn."

"Go tell Bad Eye that he's gonna have to take his men and charge that barn. If he don't, they're just gonna sit there all night. He's gonna have to charge 'em."

When Bad Eye received his orders from

Slayton, he was not very enthusiastic about them, but he dutifully passed them along to his men in the grove. To a man, they refused the order. Whereas Duke saw himself as a general directing an assault, his mistake was the obvious fact that his *command* was not made up of trained soldiers. And the lot of murderous, horse-thieving miscreants were not inclined to expose themselves to the rifles awaiting them in an all-out charge. In deference to their commander's wishes, however, they threw some more harmless shots into the side of the barn. Desperate to make an effective move on the barn, Bad Eye took a couple of his men and made his way down the creek, using the trees as cover. When they had gone far enough to see the back of the barn, he knelt there for a while, looking for signs of anyone. "If there's more of 'em in there," he said, "they must be up at the front with the others." He waited a while longer, and when there was still no sign of anyone guarding the back of the barn, he decided to chance it. "Come on," he said, and made a run for the back window.

Halfway across the yard, he was hit in the shoulder by a shot from Karl's .22 rifle. With a yelp of pain, he turned immediately and retreated to the protection of the trees.

A Winchester from the back door spoke at almost the same time as the small-caliber rifle, dropping one of the men fleeing with Bad Eye. "Good shot, Karl," Mule said as he ejected his spent cartridge.

Inside the barn, the defenders waited and watched behind breastworks of hay bales, ready to repel any further attacks. Inside the dark house, meanwhile, Millie and the others could only guess what was going on. To make sure everyone remained alert, Millie moved quickly from the front of the house to the kitchen, encouraging everyone. "Anybody sing out if you see anything," she said. "They're bound to try to get to the house."

Unable to see what was occurring on the other side of the barn, Duke became more and more impatient for some sign of success. Minutes later, he was surprised when Bad Eye walked up the ridge behind him, moaning that he had been hit. With no concern for the wound in Bad Eye's shoulder, for it looked to be minor to him, Duke demanded, "Who'd you leave in charge over there? When are they gonna charge that damn barn?"

"I don't reckon they're gonna," Bad Eye replied. "I told 'em to, but they said hell no."

"They just gonna sit there in the trees?" Duke exclaimed.

"Ain't nobody in the trees no more," Bad Eye answered between groans of pain. He motioned behind him as Sid and Roy Perkins moved up to join them.

Enraged, Duke walked back down the back of the ridge to find all of his gang gathered up there, with the exception of three, whose bodies were lying back in the barnyard. "What the hell . . . ?" he blurted. "What are you doin' back here?"

Sid Perkins, self-appointed voice for those gang members who were sent to attack the barn, stepped to the fore and answered him, "We're back here to tell you we didn't agree to go on no damn charge across that open yard."

"Why, you bunch of yellow-belly no-accounts!" Slayton roared back at him. "Who's the one who put this gang together? Who's the one who showed you this place for the takin', just like we took the Bar-T? I am, that's who, and I'm the one givin' the orders!"

"Yeah?" Sid blurted back at him. "Well, your big plan's already got three of us killed, and another'n wounded, while you're set-tin' up here on your ass. You ain't givin' me no orders no more, my brother, neither. We joined you to rustle cattle, and that's what we're goin' after."

Furious now, Duke almost yelled in response. "You and your damn brother get the hell outta here, then. The rest of us got a job to do."

"The rest of us is kinda of the same opinion as Sid," Bad Eye spoke up then. "We all think it's best to pull outta here and go after the cattle."

This was almost too much for Duke to believe. "You, too?" he demanded. "After the years we rode together, you're runnin' out on me, too?"

"I reckon," Bad Eye answered meekly. "My shoulder's gettin' kinda stiff already. I wouldn't be much good in a fight right now. No hard feelin's, though, but I reckon I'll go with the rest of the boys."

"No hard feelin's?" Duke exploded. "Why, you ol' son of a bitch, if I see you again, I'll shoot you. You ain't never been worth a shit, anyway. You weren't even any good drivin' a chuck wagon." He stood at the top of the ridge, his hand resting on the handle of his pistol, hardly able to believe the mutiny of his entire gang as they backed warily down the slope, leaving him to stand alone.

"We're goin' after the herd," Roy Perkins called out. "If you decide you wanna help us, you're welcome to collect an equal share. That's fair enough, ain't it, boys?" The question was met with a scattered chorus of affirmative grunts.

"That's mighty generous of you," Duke replied sarcastically. "Just get the hell outta my sight." *You ain't seen the last of me,* he promised himself. *There will be a reckoning, if I have to do it one by one,* he thought. When the last of the deserters had ridden off into the night, he turned again to stare at the house below in the valley. He had attached all his frustrations and failures to that house and the people who lived there, but the person from whom he sought vengeance was not there. There was a need deep inside him to even the score with Carson Ryan. And if Carson wasn't there, then he could still hurt him by showing him his friends could be made to pay for him. *They think I can't reach them there,* he thought. *I killed the old man and his son, and I can strike anyone else in that house.*

Back in the house, as well as in the barn, no one really knew what was going on. There had been no more gunfire, and the raiders who had been in the cottonwood grove appeared to have gone. Leary of the possibility of a trap, no one in either building was willing to declare the siege called off. After waiting for almost an hour with no sound of rustlers, Shorty finally took the risk of running to the house to see if they knew what was going on. "Don't nobody shoot," he called when he ran toward the front door. "It's me, Shorty." Millie opened the door for him.

She greeted him with the statement, "We think they've pulled back. I don't think they're up on the ridge anymore." She gave him a warm grin. "I think you and the boys showed them they'd come to the wrong place."

"You may be right," he said, "but I ain't gonna be sure till I have a look-see for myself." He told them that he was going to go out the back door, slip around behind the smokehouse, and climb up the ridge from that side. When both sisters showed concern for his plan, he assured them that he was going to be careful. "I ain't lookin' to get shot," he told them.

He held the back door ajar and peered out in the dark, toward the smokehouse, then back along the path to the outhouse. There was nothing moving, so he slid quietly out, telling Millie to latch the door behind him. Moving cautiously past the smokehouse, he paused to make sure no one had slipped inside. Satisfied, he trotted across to the foot of the ridge and climbed up the backside. Even in the dark, it was easy to find the place where they had been. A quarter moon provided only a faint light, but he could see that there was no longer anyone there. He stood looking down at the house, halfway wondering if his silhouette against the night sky might provide a tempting target for a sniper. When there was no shot, he decided they had really withdrawn, so he scrambled down the slope to tell the others.

"Thank goodness," Nancy sighed when Shorty came back with the news.

"I reckon they decided it wasn't worth gettin' shot," Shorty said. "Now we gotta see what we can do to keep 'em from drivin' off all our cattle."

Millie shifted her gun belt to relieve the pressure from the heavy weapon on her slender hips. "Well, I'm glad they're gone," she remarked. "I'm going to the outhouse before they decide to come back."

Nancy giggled. "Don't be too long, because I'll be right behind you." It seemed to her that she hadn't even felt the urge until Millie's remark. But now that the severe tension of the terrifying hours just past began to ease, it seemed that her normal bodily functions were operating again. There was still danger, but at least the threat to murder them might have been reduced.

Equally relieved, although she had handled the tension more effectively than her sister, Millie stepped outside the outhouse. *I thought I was going to burst,* she thought as she straightened her gun belt over her skirt again. She took a moment to look at the house, and then she gazed down toward the barn where Mule, Clem, and Karl waited for Shorty to return. It would still be a couple of hours before daybreak, and she wondered if her father and Justin were watching over them all. She was thankful then for Shorty and Frank, and Mule and Clem. They would fight to keep what her father had built. *And I'll fight with them,* she thought. Then she smiled to herself as she thought, *Now I'd better get back before Nancy bursts.* Suddenly her world exploded around her as a large hand covered her mouth at the same time a powerful arm pinned her arms helplessly to her sides. She was lifted off her feet and carried back behind the outhouse, her struggling easily overcome by the monster who had assaulted her.

"Now, ain't I the lucky one?" Duke Slayton taunted, his mouth thrust against her

362

ear. "But you ain't so lucky, are you, missy? I'm gonna have my satisfaction for what you folks have cost me, and I can't think of nobody I'd rather take it out on." He tightened his arm around her, almost squeezing the breath from her lungs.

Terrified, Millie felt her mind reeling with the panic that had captured her brain. At first she struggled to free herself from the powerful arms that held her, but she now realized that her efforts were useless. She was helpless to stop the terrible fate that was to come. Drained of strength, she seemed to go into shock, like a doomed antelope in the jaws of a mountain lion, as she was dragged farther back into the trees by the creek.

Robbed of the wholesale destruction he had planned for the entire family and crew of the M/C, he was now set upon concentrating his vengeance on the girl. His fury was not driven by lust for her, as his passion was for murder, but to defile her first would bring him more satisfaction. "This is gonna hurt like hell," he promised as he forced her to the ground, his face so close to hers that her lungs were filled with his foul breath, one powerful hand around her throat. "By the time I'm through, you'll be ready to die."

Oh, God, please! she prayed. Please, *Shorty, Frank, someone help me!* But she knew they could not hear her prayers. The hand tightened around her throat until she could no longer breathe. Just before she was about to lose consciousness, the hand relaxed enough for her to breathe again. Then suddenly it was gone, and the heavy body was no longer upon her. Confused, she opened her eyes to discover a dark shadow standing before her. It seemed as tall as the trees around her with broad shoulders that seemed to block the faint light of the quarter moon behind it. She was saved, she thought, but was she? For what manner of specter was now standing before her? Still consumed by the terror that had held her seconds before, she could not create rational thought. And then she heard the gentle voice.

"Are you all right?"

A feeling of deliverance swept over her entire being, like the surge of a flooding river. She could still not be sure her mind was not playing tricks on her, but she asked, "John?"

"Yes, ma'am," he answered softly. "Are you all right?"

"Yes, I think so," she said, "but what . . . ?" Confused even more now, she raised herself up on her elbows and found the answer to the question not finished. For there, crumpled at John Carson's feet, was the body of Duke Slayton. She had heard no gunshot, so she didn't understand what had happened. All she was aware of now were the hands that reached down to her, and the arms that lifted her so gently, making it hard to believe what she learned later, that those gentle hands and arms when incited by the fury of that night had broken Duke Slayton's neck. Drained of almost all her strength, she felt her body relax in the haven of his arms as he carried her to the house.

CHAPTER 13

"John Carson!" Shorty blurted in surprise when Carson walked in the back door, carrying Millie in his arms. "Man, am I glad to see you!" He, along with the others who came running into the kitchen when they heard him exclaim, were stopped speechless by the sight of the formidable man as he lowered Millie onto a chair by the table, for he was clearly not the same man they had known.

"Millie!" Nancy cried out in alarm. "What happened?"

"I think she's gonna be all right," Carson said. "Just let her rest a little bit."

Concerned for her sister, Nancy hurried to Millie's side. She glanced up at Carson when he stepped away from the table, and was the first to express what everyone was thinking. "I wasn't sure it was you," she declared, amazed. "You've changed so much."

"Damned if you ain't," Shorty agreed after taking a few moments to realize the transformation that had taken place. "What happened?" he asked then while Nancy and Lizzie comforted an obviously shaken Millie.

He answered with two words. "Duke Slayton." Frank and Shorty both reacted in alarm, but Carson told them there was no danger at the moment. "He's dead."

"Well, by God, that's four of 'em," Shorty announced. "I don't know how many that leaves, but that's four that won't be shootin' at us."

"But what happened to Millie?" Nancy interrupted. There had been no explanation for her sister's obvious state of distress.

"I'll tell you what happened," Millie spoke up then, somewhat recovered from the shock of her near-death experience. "That monster grabbed me when I came out of the outhouse." She went on to tell of her experience as she had lived it, from knowing she was going to die, to sudden deliverance in the form of John Carson.

When she finished, Carson told Shorty that he had come upon the gang of outlaws gathered on the ridge, and worked in close to hear them revolt against Duke Slayton's orders. "He was dead set on rubbin' out everybody here," he said. "But the other fellers didn't like the odds of more of 'em gettin' shot, so they took off and left him up there. I followed 'em down the other side of the ridge to make sure they weren't plannin' on doublin' back on the barn. But they didn't, so I went halfway back up the slope to where there was one horse standin'. I figured that had to be Duke's, so I waited for him to show. When a good bit of time passed and he never showed up, I figured I'd best go look for him. By the time I found him, he'd already grabbed Millie."

"What do we do now?" Frank asked.

"I reckon we'll go to war," Shorty answered him, "if you don't wanna lose all your cattle."

"That's another thing we talked about," Millie said. "Me, Nancy, Lucas, and Frank — we talked it over and decided all of us own the cattle. Since Papa and Justin are gone, we need you, and Mule, and Clem, so we think it's fair if all of us own equal shares in the ranch — Lizzie, too."

Her statement caught Shorty without words for once in his life. When he finally remembered some, he exclaimed, "You mean that?" She nodded and smiled. "That's mighty generous of you folks," he said. "Wait till I tell the fellers in the barn!"

It occurred to him then that they were no doubt wondering why he had never returned. "I'd best go get 'em, anyway, 'cause we've got to decide what we're gonna do to keep our cattle."

Nancy spoke up then to remind them that Lucas had been sent to Big Timber to contact the law. "Should we wait till we hear from them?" she asked. "Maybe they'll send a posse to go after that bunch of murderers."

"By the time a posse got here," Frank answered her, "our cattle would be in Canada."

"Frank's right," Carson said. "We need to stop 'em before they cross the Musselshell. Why don't you get the boys ready to start out at first light in the mornin' and head for the river? Maybe you can catch 'em before they round up a sizable herd and try to cross."

With no better idea of his own, Shorty nodded, then asked, "What about you? You're ridin' with us, ain'tcha?"

"Reckon not," Carson replied. "I don't like the odds. There ain't but four of you against them, so I expect I'll leave now before they get too far ahead. Maybe I can cut the odds down a little better tonight."

Relieved when he understood Carson's

meaning, Shorty nodded and said, "That would sure help some."

"You be careful you don't go get yourself killed," Millie blurted. When she saw the look of surprise in the faces of Nancy and Carson, she flushed slightly, then quickly added, "We need all the guns we can get." She received a disapproving glare from her sister then, so she grimaced and said, "I never thanked you for saving my life. I appreciate it." Nancy's eyes shot up toward the ceiling.

"You're welcome, ma'am," Carson said.

"And quit calling me ma'am," Millie responded. "I'm not your mother, or your aunt."

"Yes, ma'a . . . I mean Millie," he said, confused, wondering how he had happened to make her mad this time. Looking at Shorty then, he said, "I'd best get goin'. I'll see you sometime in the mornin'."

Even in the darkness, he had very little trouble following the tracks of the gang. As he suspected, they made straight for the largest concentration of M/C cattle, and they found them dispersed over a broad valley by a creek some five or six miles north of the M/C ranch house. When he caught sight of the herd, he held back to try to see how the rustlers were going to organize their drive. Watching from a low line of hills, he saw two of the men split from the others and ride out, one to the east to round up a pocket of strays, the other to the west, toward him, to do the same. It appeared that the other rustlers planned to hold the main herd there in the valley until the strays had been brought back. Carson took only a few seconds to decide his plan of attack.

He dismounted and, under the cover of darkness, moved in among a small bunch of cattle that had gathered in a pocket at the mouth of a shallow ravine. There was no feeling of conscience or guilt for what he was about to do. This was war, and these men had killed Mathew Cain and his son. They had made the rules. Now they were to die by them. He stood waiting for them, his rifle ready.

Not quite able to determine what the upright object was in the midst of the group of strays, the rustler continued to approach, until suddenly the object moved and a rifle shot ripped the darkness, leaving an empty saddle. Wasting no time, Carson ran back to his horse and galloped toward the eastern side of the herd.

"What the hell?" Roy Perkins blurted when he heard the shot. "The damn fool will have us in a stampede," he cursed, for he first thought the man had fired his rifle to get the strays moving. The main herd, bedded down before him, were starting to move about, frightened by the shot. There were no more shots after the first one, so he decided to wait to find out the reason for such a stupid act. In about fifteen minutes, he heard another shot, this time from the east of the herd, and he realized what was actually taking place. "Sid!" he yelled to his brother. "We got some trouble! To hell with the strays, let's get this bunch movin!"

"What about the rest of the boys?" Sid yelled back.

"They can hold 'em off while we get this herd movin'," Roy replied, not realizing the two he had sent to chase strays were dead. "They can catch up with us before we get to the river." Pulling his pistol then, he fired a couple of shots into the air to get the cattle started. When Sid and Bad Eye did the same, they soon had a stampede pouring over the dark prairie.

Racing along the flank, Carson managed to overtake the lead steers and turn them away from the river. The rustlers behind the cattle could not guess why they had turned to the east. Intent upon catching up to the lead cows, Sid whipped his horse brutally to gain on them. When he succeeded, he was surprised to find a rider already ahead of him, but in the darkness, he could not tell who it was. "You're turnin' 'em, damn it!" he shouted to the dark horseman.

"I sure as hell am," Carson replied, and leveled his rifle at the approaching rider. Sid came out of the saddle to land hard on the ground when the .44 slug ripped into his chest.

Behind the herd, Roy and Bad Eye heard the shot. "What the hell's goin' on?" Roy demanded. The cattle were continuing to turn in a circle. There were no more shots on either flank, and none behind them. "Where the hell are Mutt and Fred?" he asked, referring to the two men who were supposed to be catching up to them.

Bad Eye stood up in his stirrups and pointed behind them. "Look yonder!" he exclaimed. Roy looked in the direction pointed out to discover two horses with empty saddles following them. "They got us surrounded!"

Not certain what was happening, nor where the rest of the men were, Roy wasn't sure what he should do. Something had gone dreadfully wrong. "We need to get up ahead and see where Sid is," he decided.

"I don't like the look of this," Bad Eye

declared. "I already got a hole in my shoulder. I don't need another'n. Let 'em have their damn cows." He wheeled his horse and kicked it into a hard gallop. His retreat served to incite the others to think about the possibility of more victims, and thinking Bad Eye might be right, they took off in another direction.

"Wait!" Roy shouted, but they were long gone. "Damn you," he cursed, furious over the desertion when he wasn't sure if his brother was in trouble or not. He turned his horse toward the front of the herd, which had been successfully turned back on itself, causing the cattle to mill around and eventually settle down again. At the head of the bawling steers, a dark figure sat his horse, patiently waiting. "Sid?" Roy called out. "Is that you?"

"Yeah," Carson answered.

"What the hell happened?" Roy asked as he approached. He didn't realize his error until there was little more than twenty yards between them. With no time left for questions, he went for his gun, but was not quick enough to draw his weapon before the rifle already aimed at him took his life.

Carson checked to see if Roy Perkins was dead, and then he stood staring down at him for a few minutes. He had never seen the man before, but he had killed him as he would kill a rattlesnake, to prevent him from doing more harm. By his count, four men were dead, and there was no sign of the others. The herd had settled down to mill about peacefully, and it appeared the threat was ended. Suddenly he was very tired, and he remembered that he had not slept since the day before. He took his saddle off the bay and released it to graze, knowing it would not stray far away from him. Then he sat down and reloaded his rifle, content that he had done all he could to avenge the deaths of Mathew and Justin Cain. The decision to be made now was whether to wait for Shorty and the others to show up in the morning or to move on, since he had ended the war by himself. Weary, he leaned back against a low hummock and closed his eyes. He didn't open them again until the sun came up to awaken him.

Bad Eye wasn't sure where he had ended up after almost running his horse to death the night before. But he had made it to sunup with no sign of anyone on his trail. His problem now was the stinging from the bullet hole in his shoulder and the gnawing of an empty stomach as he walked through a grassy ravine, leading his exhausted horse.

He had nothing to eat in his saddlebags, not even the makings for a pot of coffee, or a pot to boil it in, so he felt as if he might expire if he didn't get either a cup of coffee or a drink of whiskey pretty soon. Seeing a double row of sage and small trees ahead, he hoped to find a stream. Halfway down the ravine, he spotted smoke from a camp-fire. At once alert, he proceeded more cautiously lest he walk into an ambush.

Maybe, he thought, *I best back away and take a wide circle around it.* But the hint of a rabbit roasting over the fire caught his nostrils and reminded him that he wanted to eat. He hesitated, undecided for a few moments, until a voice called out, "You comin' on in, or you gonna stand out there smellin' the coffee?"

Startled, Bad Eye started to back away but decided he'd already been spotted, so he might as well find out if the camp was friendly or not. "I'd sure like to have a cup of that coffee, if you've got some to spare," he finally responded.

"Sure, come on in and have some," the man called back. "Maybe you could eat a little somethin', too," he added when Bad Eye led his horse down by the fire. "You look like you been on the run," he said, nodding toward the bloodstains on Bad Eye's shirt.

"Yeah, I ran into a little bad luck a ways back," Bad Eye offered as explanation.

The man grinned at Bad Eye's obvious nervousness. "You ain't got to worry about me," he said, making a quick judgment on a man out in the middle of the prairie, with a bullet hole in his shoulder, walking an exhausted horse, with no sign of anything to make camp with. "I been on the run before, and I've been shot before. So sit down and drink some coffee." When Bad Eye confessed that he didn't even have a cup to drink out of, it caused his host to laugh. "Mister, you're really on the run, ain'tcha?" He couldn't help taking a look back the way Bad Eye had come. "You ain't led the law down on my camp, have you?"

"Nah, it ain't the law I'm runnin' from," Bad Eye answered, "and I'm sure I lost 'em last night." He took the cup offered him, feeling that he had been lucky to chance on an obvious outlaw, like himself, and one who could sympathize with his plight, even though he looked more Indian than white. "Where're you headin'?" he asked.

"I'm lookin' for somebody," Red Shirt replied, "somebody I need to settle a score with, and I ain't had much luck in findin' him. The son of a bitch rode with me for a couple of days before he turned on me and left me with this damn hole in my side." He pulled his shirt up to show an ugly scar. "Damn near killed me, but I'll find him one of these days."

The man looked pretty dangerous. Bad Eye felt sure it was going to be bad news for the man he was after. "You think he's in this part of the country somewhere?"

"That's where he was headin'," Red Shirt replied. "He was ridin' with a man and woman, headin' this way. I got a little unfinished business with them, too." One of them had fired the shot that destroyed part of his lung, leaving him unable to breathe without pain.

It would be an almost impossible co-incidence, but the thought popped into Bad Eye's mind. "Carson Ryan," he blurted, remembering that Duke Slayton had told him of a run-in with Carson on the Mus-selshell.

Red Shirt almost dropped his cup when he heard the name, the muscles in his arms tensed to the point where his veins stood up as if to burst. His face transformed into a mask of black hatred. "You know where he is?" he demanded.

The sudden look of the man frightened

Bad Eye, causing him to stammer in his reply. "I know where he might be, but I didn't lay eyes on him myself." He wondered if the mysterious force that methodically killed the cattle rustlers could have somehow been connected to Carson. He told Red Shirt how to find the M/C, but said that he couldn't go with him. "Once you get to Sweet Grass Creek, you ought'n have any trouble findin' the ranch."

"I 'preciate the information," Red Shirt said, and got to his feet to fetch the coffeepot. "Lemme fill that cup for you."

"Much obliged," Bad Eye said, and tilted his head back to drain the last swallow, never realizing that Red Shirt was still standing directly behind him until he felt a powerful hand grab his hair and the razor-sharp knife as it sliced his throat. He didn't go back to the M/C with Red Shirt, but his scalp made the trip.

The range war between the M/C and the Bar-T was effectively over after the night of the avenger was ended. When Shorty and the others arrived at the site of the battle, there was no longer any enemy to fight. Instead, they found a sleeping warrior in the midst of a large herd of M/C cattle. They could not appreciate the magnitude of his accomplishment until they started rounding up the riderless horses and finding the bodies. When the total tally was complete, there were four bodies, one less than the gang of raiders who had left Duke Slayton behind at the ranch. It served to cast a different light upon the person who was John Carson, and not completely to his liking. He had no wish to be defined as a one-man war party.

Shorty and Mule decided it best to move the cattle to the south range until some arrangement could be worked out to round up the Bar-T cattle, since there was no more Bar-T. There were decisions to be made, one of which was whether to combine the two spreads or keep them as two separate ranches. As Shorty put it, "There's sure as hell gonna be a job for ever'body."

One who was not certain as to whether or not he would be a part of the newly formed partnership of cattle owners was John Carson. There was still the matter of a wanted poster with the name Carson Ryan on it, and he could not see any possibility of proving his innocence. Frank and Nancy begged him to stay on. They tried to convince him that no one of the few who knew his real name would ever tell the authorities, should they ever arrive at the M/C. "Doggone it,"

Nancy pleaded, "we need you — Frank needs you, Lucas needs you — they can't run it without your help." Shorty, Clem, Mule, they all supported her argument. Only Millie kept her thoughts on the matter to herself, keeping her distance from the boy who had morphed into a man. All were unaware of the danger lurking along the ridge that lay north of the house that Mathew Cain had built in the form of a half-breed Lakota outlaw who watched the house, waiting for an opportunity to seek his revenge. He was patient, for he had searched for a long time to find Carson Ryan, and he would not jeopardize his chance of success by acting in haste.

Red Shirt's patience finally paid off. Early one morning, the crew of men came out of the bunkhouse and saddled the horses, all except Carson. The men mounted up and headed out toward the east range. Red Shirt remained in his lookout position on the lower end of the ridge until Carson finally came from the bunkhouse and walked toward the barn. Red Shirt's heart began to beat rapidly. At last his chance had come when there were none of the other men to help Carson. He quickly descended the ridge, circled the smokehouse, and approached the barn.

Carson pulled his saddle off the rail in the tack room. His mind was not on the chore he had assigned himself that morning. Rather it was on the moment the day before, when Millie had come to the barn to check the chickens' nests for eggs, and he had turned around quickly to catch her staring at him. He had caught her eye on other occasions, and just as she did on those occasions, she had turned immediately away. This was what he was thinking of on this morning when he heard a tiny squeak from the back barn door. Determined he was going to face her down this time, he walked out of the tack room only to be confronted by the business end of a .44 Winchester in the hands of what appeared to be a ghost.

"You've changed, Carson," Red Shirt gloated triumphantly, knowing Carson was helpless to make a move. "It took me a helluva long time to find you. You've caused me a lot of pain and trouble. This time, I ain't gonna throw my rifle aside, so say your prayers. I got a new scalp lance since I saw you. I'm gonna tie your scalp right at the top of it."

"You'd better take damn good aim," Carson said, " 'cause I'm gonna be on you before you get off the second shot."

Red Shirt grinned in evil anticipation. "I will," he said, and raised his rifle.

The shot reverberated loudly in the confines of the barn, but Carson felt nothing as he steeled himself for the impact of the bullet. Astonished, he saw the grimace on Red Shirt's face as the half-breed staggered against the side of a stall. He tried to lift his rifle again, but was stopped cold by a second shot that slammed the side of his head. "Damn you! Damn you!" Nancy Thompson screamed. "This time you'll stay dead!" To be sure, she shot the already-still corpse for a third time. She looked at Carson then with eyes wild in panic. "You have to stay alive, John Carson. If you don't, Millie never will get married." Her knees started to fail her then and she would have fainted had not Carson rushed to catch her. The revolver she held dropped to the floor of the barn.

The sound of gunfire brought Frank and Lucas running from the house with guns at the ready. They were met by Carson coming from the barn with Nancy in his arms. "I think she's all right," Carson quickly assured Frank. "After what she just did, I ain't surprised she fainted. She sure as hell saved my life." He placed Nancy in the outstretched arms of her husband, and told them what had caused her distress.

Before he was finished, Millie came running and promptly told Frank to take Nancy to the porch. Then she sent Lucas to the pump to wet a cloth and bring it to her. "I'll be right there to help you with her," she told Frank. Then to reassure him, she said, "She'll be all right. I was supposed to be the one gathering the eggs, but she said she'd do it this morning, even though she was feeling poorly."

"Is she sick?" a worried husband asked. "She didn't say she felt ill."

Millie met his question with the look of one who is impatient with the naïveté all men seemed to exhibit when it came to their wives. "Most women have these little spells when they're carrying a child," she said.

"What!" a startled husband blurted, causing Carson to quickly grab his elbow when he showed signs of fainting himself.

"Better let me take her back," Carson said, and took Nancy from Frank's arms. He carried her to the porch and lowered her onto a chair. Frank sat down in a chair beside her. Leaving them in the care of Millie, he went back to the barn to dispose of Red Shirt's body. He couldn't help hurrying to make sure the body didn't vanish again, as it had done the first time they thought they had killed him. Finding Red Shirt where he had last seen him, he grabbed him by the heels and dragged him out the back of the barn. When Lucas came to help, he told the boy to hitch up the wagon. "I don't wanna bury this piece of shit close to the house," he told him. "He might turn the soil sour." Riding to the other side of the east ridge, he had plenty of time to think about the incident just finished, and he thought back on Nancy's words in the middle of her execution of the hated half-breed. He was not sure what he thought he heard was, in fact, what she had actually said. *Maybe when she's feeling better, I'll ask her,* he thought.

Frank Thompson, on a rare visit to Big Timber, stopped in the post office to post a letter. While there, he commented to the postmaster, "I don't see that wanted notice for that fellow Carson Ryan up on your board anymore."

"No," the postmaster replied, "I got a notice to take it down. I guess they caught him."

This was good news to Frank. He could hardly wait to get back to the ranch to tell everyone about it. The fact of the matter was the U.S. marshal in Omaha received a letter from Robert B. Grimes, a civilian doctor located at Fort Laramie. In that letter, Dr. Grimes requested that the marshal should get in touch with Robert T. Patterson, who was now a congressman for the state of Texas. The purpose was to verify Carson Ryan's employment as a drover for Mr. Patterson in Ogallala on the date Ryan was accused of murder and rustling a herd seventy miles away. Mr. Patterson verified that Carson Ryan was in fact with him in Ogallala at that time.

Almost a month had passed since young Lucas Cain had ridden to Big Timber to telegraph the territorial governor for help before that help showed up in the form of U.S. Deputy Marshal Marvin Bell. He was met at the front door by Millie. She walked out on the porch to talk to him. "Well, Mr. Bell," she commented, "when we sent for help, we were hoping for a detachment of cavalry to fight a gang of murdering cattle rustlers. I guess it's lucky for you that we had enough men to drive the gang away ourselves. It would have been a helluva job for one deputy to take on."

"Yes, ma'am," Bell replied respectfully. "Sometimes we don't get the whole story, so I was sent up here to find out. You're sayin' you drove the rustlers off, and there ain't no more problem here?"

"That's right," Millie said. "All the cattle have been recovered, and everything's back to normal."

"No range war, then?"

She chuckled. "No, no range war. Is that what they told you?"

"Like I said, sometimes we get the wrong information." He was obviously relieved to find out that his visit was going to be brief. "And what is your name, ma'am?"

"I'm Millie Cain," she answered.

He was distracted for a moment when he saw Carson ride up to the barn and dismount. "Is that one of the hands?"

"Oh, that's my husband, John," she quickly replied. *You picked a helluva time to come riding up to the barn,* she thought. "He must have forgotten something."

"Well, sorry to have bothered you, Mrs. Cain. I think I'll go down and talk to your husband." He turned to descend the front steps.

"I'll go with you," she replied at once, and immediately followed him down the steps, fearful now that she might have gotten them in trouble by trying to distract the deputy.

As soon as they reached the barn door, she called out, "John, there's a deputy marshal here to talk about the wire we sent for help."

This was not news that Carson wanted to hear. He had been thankful that there had been no response from the governor. He walked out to meet them, still holding the bush ax he had come to get. "You wanna talk about the cattle rustlin'?" he asked.

"Yes, sir," Bell replied, "although your wife has pretty much told me there ain't anything to investigate."

"My wife?" Carson responded without thinking.

Millie quickly spoke up. "Yes, me. I know you tell me to let you do the talking, but I just told Mr. Bell here what happened, that's all." She turned to the deputy. "John thinks it's not ladylike for me to talk to the authorities."

Carson realized then what she was doing. "I suppose I am a little protective when it comes to the little lady."

"Well, I don't see anything wrong with that," Bell said with a chuckle. "I reckon there's nothin' more for me to do here."

"It was pretty cut-and-dried," Carson said. "We were able to drive 'em off." He glanced at Millie, who frowned when a new thought evidently just then popped into her head. He was not prepared for her next comment.

"I thought you were here to investigate the death of Red Shirt," she said.

"Red Shirt!" Bell exclaimed. "Red Shirt, the half-breed outlaw? Whaddaya mean, his death?" Her remark had triggered a definite interest on the part of the lawman, but Carson could only think that she had betrayed him.

"That's the one," Millie replied smugly. "I know the word was out that he had tried to attack our family, but we killed him. I can show you where he's buried. It hasn't been that long. You might wanna dig him up to make sure it's him."

What are you doing? Carson thought while trying to keep a calm face. He tried to catch Millie's eye, but she purposefully avoided it.

The visit to the M/C suddenly took on new importance to Marvin Bell. Red Shirt had long been wanted all over the territory, but no one had been successful in tracking him down. And if what the girl claimed was true, it would definitely be a feather in his cap. "Yes, ma'am," he replied. "I surely would like to verify it. Can I borrow a shovel?"

"Of course," Millie replied. "John, why don't you get a couple of shovels and help Mr. Bell dig Red Shirt up?" Carson had little choice but to comply. When he went into the tack room to get the shovels, Millie said to the deputy, "I'll be right back." She hurried then to the barn door where Carson had left his horse, and drew the Winchester from the saddle scabbard. Back to the waiting deputy just as Carson returned with the shovels, she handed the rifle to Bell. "This is the rifle we found with him. John naturally didn't bury it with him."

Bell took the Winchester and examined it carefully. "Well, I'll be damned," he muttered softly when he turned it over to discover the letters *L. Moody* carved on one side of the butt. "Well, I'll be . . . ," he started to repeat. "I'm gonna need to take this with me as evidence," he said. "Now let's go take a look at that body."

A close look at the decomposing body convinced the deputy that it was in fact the notorious outlaw Red Shirt, and there was little doubt that he had killed Deputy Marshal Luther Moody to have had the rifle in his possession. He looked up at Carson and smiled. "This was sure enough a worthwhile trip. I wanna thank you both for your help, Mr. and Mrs. Cain." He didn't linger after the grave was filled back in. So anxious was he to return to Helena with his news that he refused an invitation to stay for supper.

They stood watching for a minute or two as the deputy rode off toward the north. Then Carson could hold his tongue no longer. "Mr. and Mrs. Cain?"

"He just made the assumption since I told him my name was Millie Cain," she replied. "I didn't think it was a good idea to tell him your name was Carson."

"I reckon you're right," he said. "I'll tell you the truth, though. For a while there, I thought you were fixin' to get rid of me for good." He shook his head and repeated, "Mr. and Mrs. Cain."

"Well, we've got chores to do," she finally announced. "We can't stand here working our jaws all day." She spun on her heel and headed for the house, but stopped and turned back to him. "I guess my name will be Millie Cain till the day I die if somebody doesn't get busy and start courting me." She turned again and continued on her way.

"You don't mean —" he started.

Without turning her head, she called back, "Well, I'm not going to ask you."

ABOUT THE AUTHOR

Charles G. West lives in Ocala, Florida. His fascination with and respect for the pioneers who braved the wild frontier of the great American West inspire him to devote his full time to writing historical novels.

The employees of Thorndike Press hope you have enjoyed this Large Print book. All our Thorndike, Wheeler, and Kennebec Large Print titles are designed for easy reading, and all our books are made to last. Other Thorndike Press Large Print books are available at your library, through selected bookstores, or directly from us.

For information about titles, please call:
  (800) 223-1244

or visit our Web site at:
  http://gale.cengage.com/thorndike

To share your comments, please write:
  Publisher
  Thorndike Press
  10 Water St., Suite 310
  Waterville, ME 04901